Serpents of Sky and Flame

Merciless Dragons Book One

Rebecca F. Kenney

This book is a work of fiction. Names, characters, places, and incidents are the product of the author's imagination or are used fictitiously. Any resemblance to actual events, locales, or persons, living or dead, is coincidental.

Copyright © 2024 by Rebecca F. Kenney

All rights reserved. In accordance with the U.S. Copyright Act of 1976, the scanning, uploading, and electronic sharing of any part of this book without the permission of the publisher is unlawful piracy and theft of the author's intellectual property. If you would like to use material from the book (other than for review purposes), prior written permission must be obtained by contacting the publisher at rfkenney@gmail.com. Thank you for your support of the author's rights.

First Edition: April 2024

Kenney, Rebecca F.
SERPENTS OF SKY AND FLAME / by Rebecca F. Kenney—First edition.
Cover art by Ann Fleur

PLAYLIST

ROGUE—Poets of the Fall
HOLD MY HEART—Lindsey Stirling, ZZ Ward
SO MUCH (FOR) STARDUST—Fall Out Boy
TROUBLEMAKER—Olly Murs, Flo Rida
THE FIGHT WITHIN—Memphis May Fire
FIRE!—Alan Walker
BLOOM—Aidan Bissett
FIRST FLIGHT—Henry Jackman
LOSE CONTROL—Teddy Swims
DIRTY THOUGHTS—Chloe Adams
FLAMES—R3HAB, ZAYN, Jungleboi
WHAT'S LEFT OF ME—Nick Lachey
SHH…DON'T SAY IT—Fletcher
TITAN—Scott Buckley
PAST LIFE—Trevor Daniel, Selena Gomez
DRAGONWING—Two Steps from Hell
COME AND GET IT FROM ME—Sun Heat
FORCE OF NATURE—Bea Miller
CRUEL SUMMER—Taylor Swift
DARK SIDE—EHLE

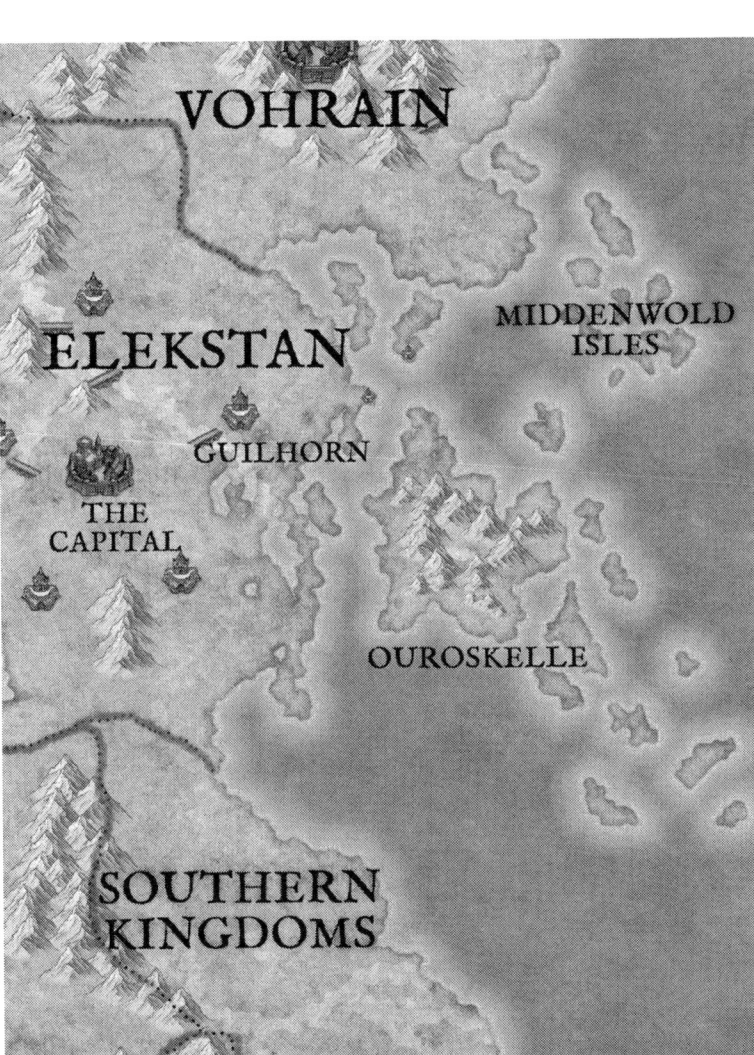

Reading Guidance

Death, gore, war
Perceived threat of rape (due to a misunderstanding)
Light consensual non-consent play with a safe word
Brief suicidal thoughts
Breeding, pregnancy
Brief thoughts of dragon devouring human
(light vore-ish thoughts but not really)

PRONUNCIATION GUIDE

Kyreagan: kai-REE-gahn, ("Ky" rhymes with "sky")
Serylla: seh-RILL-ah
Ouroskelle: oo-ruh-SKEL
Varex: VAIR-ex
Vylar: rhymes with Skylar
Vohrain: Vore-AIN
Ardun: ar-DOON
Ianeth: YAH-neth
Ashvelon: ASH-vell-on

1

KYREAGAN

Rain spits against my wings as I bank to the left and spew a controlled line of liquid fire from my jaws, lighting up a section of the city wall. Soldiers drop their weapons and writhe, tiny four-limbed creatures flailing in the glow, crumpling quickly onto the stone.

My fire is a mercy. Hotter than the flame humans typically wield, it brings death in mere seconds. When I'm precise with it, I can explode stones into ash.

For the survivors, the ones forced to surrender to the King of Vohrain, death will come much more slowly.

A heavy beat of wings on my right draws my attention. Mordessa glides beside me, her golden wings spanning wider than mine.

"One more battle, maybe two. And then home," she says in Dragonish.

"Home, with the Middenwold Isles as our reward," I reply.

"We will have all the food we need for mating season and the resulting brood of hatchlings." She slow-blinks her golden lashes in my direction.

I search within myself for the answering warmth I'm supposed to feel—the surge of joy, of harmony. The most I can summon for my Promised is a feeling of friendship, of pleasant loyalty. It is enough.

It will have to be enough.

A gust of wind passes over both of us—a speeding black shape with white patches on her wings. My sister Vylar, aiming lines of searing light at the remaining guards along the city wall.

"Stop ogling each other and get back to work, you two," she advises.

I dive lower, avoiding an acid bomb launched from a nearby airship.

We must finish this battle, here at Guilhorn, and then suffer through one more to take the capital city and force the Queen of Elekstan to surrender. We expected her to yield weeks ago, but her pride proved more formidable than any of us anticipated. She has sent droves of her people for us to slaughter. By now, she must have barely anyone left, and almost no supplies or weapons. What kind of ruler destroys her own nation in this way?

Our Vohrainian allies have suffered losses, and my clan has endured the deaths of two dragons. But we have slaughtered the Elekstan troops by the hundreds.

Just a little longer, and then we win. A little longer, and my bone-oath to my father will be fulfilled. No more war or killing. No more watching the humans dance like charred insects in Mordessa's lightning or turn to smoke beneath Vylar's intense rays.

The female dragons have been most intent on winning this war. They know what's at stake—the survival of our race. A primal urgency has spurred them through each battle and carried them to a place beyond guilt, where necessity and fear blend into savagery. I've watched it happen, and longed for the day when we're all home again and the dread of extinction no longer drives them.

Vylar mounts higher in the sky, calling orders in Dragonish. She is the chief liaison with the army of Vohrain, and knows what moves we're supposed to make. I've been in the war meetings too, but even though I am the firstborn of the Bone-King, my sister has a better head for battle, so she has taken the lead in this campaign.

A large red-and-black dragon bursts out of the smoke ahead. Grimmaw, mother of the Bone-King—my grandmother. One of the oldest in our clan, and still a formidable warrior despite the occasional aches in her tail and wings. My father took a bone-oath from her, too, before he died... but I have never asked her what promise lives in the piece of his spine that she wears around her neck.

"Guilhorn has fallen," she says, hovering near Mordessa and me. "The highest tower of the fortress bears a black flag."

"The sign of dishonor and a dark day." I dip my head, relief flooding my body. "It's over then. Perhaps the Queen will finally yield and we can avoid an all-out battle against the capital."

"Perhaps—" begins Grimmaw, but before she can continue, a spasm runs through her body. Her jaws gape for a moment, as if she's trying to speak.

Then she falls. Wings lax, neck limp, tail inert... she falls.

I plunge after her, but a great golden shape catches my eye. At first I think Mordessa is diving to help me catch Grimmaw—and then I realize she is also plummeting to earth, unconscious.

Grimmaw smashes into a building and rolls into the street in a shower of bricks. Humans run screaming from the scene, but several are crushed immediately as Mordessa's golden body thunders to the ground. One of her wings demolishes three rickety buildings, sends them toppling aside one after the other.

I land between my grandmother and my Promised. With a roar I warn the humans to stay back, and they scatter.

As I turn to Grimmaw, I see the thing I most feared—a smoky serpent gliding from her open jaws. It writhes into the sky and vanishes before I can cry out.

I whirl to Mordessa in time to see her spirit leave as well, a serpentine wisp of golden mist. It climbs high before evanescing into the roaring chaos of burning buildings and smoking towers that once was the prosperous city of Guilhorn.

From the canopy of the night sky, I see more dragons falling, one after another, scales flashing, necks and tails limp, wings at strange angles. The sound of each impact reverberates through the city. A deafening *boom* for each heavy body. The tumbling roar of destroyed buildings, the quake of the earth at the concussive force of death.

"Kyreagan!" cries my brother Varex, his voice taut with grief and terror. Varex, Vylar, and I were all born in the same hatching season—a rarity among dragons. "Kyreagan, what is happening?"

A cataclysm. The end of the world. My voice will not work, my mind cannot form thoughts...

"Kyreagan!" It's Ashvelon, one of our section leaders, a dark gray dragon gifted with frost-fire. "My Prince, we can't stay here on the ground. Come. We must fly."

At his urging, and with the prodding of my brother's spiked wingtip, I muster the energy to climb a nearby building and take off from its roof before it crumbles beneath my weight. Human structures, like their bodies, are flimsy and fragile.

Ashvelon, Varex, and I rise together in a triangle formation. As we gain altitude, I spot the tallest tower in the city—the one Grimmaw mentioned, the one that bears the flag of surrender.

Skewered on that flagpole, its metal spike wet with her blood, is my sister. Vylar's body drapes the steep cone-shaped roof of the tower, black wings spread against the red shingles. The white patches on her wings shine like reflected moonlight.

Varex and I roar at the same time, red fire spewing from my mouth and black void magic from his. The void orb Varex emitted flies straight toward the nearby airship, sucks in the entire vessel, and implodes on itself.

"It's the females," says Ashvelon. "Can you feel it?"

But neither Varex nor I have been through our first mating season yet. We do not have the same link to the females of our race that the older males do.

"We *can't* feel it," I snarl at him. "Speak! What is happening? Is some magic targeting the females in this battle? Should we tell the rest of the clan to withdraw?"

Ashvelon's blue eyes are wide, stricken. "It's too late. They're already dead."

I can feel more fire building in my belly. Fire and panic. "Every female warrior, dead?"

"Not just the warriors." Ashvelon's wings beat slowly, devastation threading his tone. "All of them. Every female dragon, of every age, everywhere."

"The fuck?" chokes out Varex.

Every female dragon, of every age, everywhere.

I sweep my wings, great pulses against the air, pushing me higher, higher. The rest of the dragons follow me up, away from the burning, defeated city.

We're half the number we were. I scan all of them quickly, my eyes raking through the gloom, finding the jaw spikes and elbow spurs on each dragon. They're all male.

Ashvelon is right.

I turn to an elder dragon with more jaw spikes than any of us. "Did you sense it? Is it true? Are they all—"

"Yes, my Prince." He's weeping, great tears rolling along his scales and dripping from his snout. It's rare to see another male cry. Among dragons, tears are reserved for the greatest of grief.

Every female of our race, dead. And with mating season just one week away...

This was never part of the plan. Vohrain never indicated that their enemies were capable of such devastating magic. If we'd known, my father would never have agreed to the alliance. This is wrong, this cannot be happening, this is a nightmare, the end of the world—

"Kyreagan." Varex brushes his wingtip against mine. "What do we do?"

My anger is slow to spark, but when ignited, it burns hot and furious. I can feel it now, churning in my chest, flaming along every nerve.

"We will determine who is responsible for this," I announce to the other dragons, my growl echoing through the sky. "And we will take from them what was taken from us."

2

SERYLLA

"I made these pastries myself. Would you like one?" I lift the puffed confection, dusted with sugar, and hold it out to the warrior sitting on the bed.

He's been staring down at his bandaged fingers, but he looks up at me, his eyes burning like coals in a face seamed with ash. "Thank you, Princess. With all due respect, I'm not feeling up to munching on pastries."

"Maybe later? A sweet treat always cheers me up when I'm feeling down." I pluck a delicate linen napkin from the basket my maid is carrying and lay it on the bed beside him. I set the pastry in the very center of the napkin, turning it slightly so its sugared surface is displayed to the best advantage.

The warrior scoffs a laugh, or tries to—but he chokes suddenly and coughs, sending a splatter of dark blood over my hand. Flecks of blood dot the pastry.

For a moment we all freeze—my maid, the warrior, and me with my bloodstained hand.

My bodyguards each take a step forward.

Like a finger punching through pastry crust, my glossy surface crumples. I feel it happening—the bright, encouraging smile fading from my lips, the frantically cheerful veneer melting from my eyes.

"I'm sorry, Your Highness," croaks the warrior.

"It's my fault," I say tightly. "This was a stupid idea. Here, you should rest." I knock the pastry off the bed, pull back the blanket, and arrange the pillows so he can recline against them. "That's an order from your princess."

The soldier leans back against the pillows and swings his feet up into the bed. I can't help noticing how filthy his feet are. "Norril, bring me that wash basin."

My bodyguard obeys immediately, setting the basin beside the warrior's bed. My gaze latches on the thick cloth lining the basket of pastries. Just what I need. I pull it free, tumbling the sweets into chaos. After dampening the cloth in the basin, I begin wiping dirt from the warrior's feet.

"The sweets were my mother's idea," I tell him quietly as I work. "I'm a decent cook, and she thought it would be good for morale if I pranced through the soldiers' hospital in my finest dress. A pretty face and some baked goods. I should have known better."

"Not a bad idea," he wheezes. "Many of the wounded will be glad of the sweets... and the pretty face."

"But you're hurt worse than the physician realized, aren't you?" I turn to my bodyguards again. "Norril, get a doctor immediately—or better yet, a healer."

"I can try, Princess," Norril answers. "But my cousin says healers are in short supply these days. Most of them are needed in the burn wards."

His tone chills my heart. I haven't walked through the burn wards, but I've seen the men and women who emerge from them, permanently scarred despite the medicine of doctors or the magic of healers. The scars aren't just from fire, either. There are frost burns from ice dragons, acid burns from dragons who spit venom, void burns from dragons who vomit dark energy. And those with void burns are the lucky ones. They say that if someone is struck full-on with an orb of void magic, they are sucked into its center and disappear for good.

The dragons joined the fight just six weeks ago, and they are the reason we're losing the war with Vohrain. The moment the Vohrainian king made an alliance with those beasts, we were defeated. My mother was just too stubborn to admit it. She and the Supreme Sorcerer claim they're working on a secret weapon, a way to turn the tide of the war in Elekstan's favor. But we just keep dying instead.

I say *we* keep dying, but it's *they*. Our strongest citizens, fed to the machine of war, crushed between its gears like this warrior on the bed, whose breath rattles in his chest as if Death is tapping cold fingers along his rib bones.

"Both of you go look for a doctor, a healer—whoever you can find," I command my guards. "Don't come back unless you bring one with you. Hurry!"

"But, Your Highness, our duty is protecting you," Norril protests. "One of the nurses can—"

"Look around, Norril. There are two nurses in this ward, both occupied with other patients. I'll be fine. I won't move from this spot, I promise. Now go!"

My bodyguards hurry away, driven to greater speed by a spasm of coughing from the injured warrior. I rinse the filthy cloth, squeeze it out, and hand it to him so he can wipe his bloody palm.

Throughout the seventeen months of this wretched war, I've felt helpless a number of times, but never so much as now.

I glance over my shoulder at my maid, Parma. She's salt-white and looks as if she might pass out any second.

"Parma, go and hand out the pastries to anyone who might want one," I tell her. "I'll stay with him."

She nods and hurries off down the aisle between the beds of the wounded.

I turn back to the warrior just as he begins coughing again. Instinctively I reach for his hand, and he grips mine with grateful desperation.

"I wish I knew what to do," I whisper. "How to help you."

He doesn't answer. He's struggling to breathe.

Hurry, Norril. Hurry, please hurry.

If only I had magic. If only I could touch this man's chest and spread healing energy through his body, calm his blood vessels, relax his muscles, staunch the inner wounds, ease his spasming lungs.

"Hold on," I tell him. "Hold on. Help is coming."

But he's stiff, his eyes wide, his body arched and straining for air. His fingers crush mine with frenzied strength.

"Help!" I shout. "We need a nurse here!"

But the two nurses I saw in this ward moments ago must have left to fetch something. There's no one but me and Parma and the injured soldiers. The woman in the nearest bed seems to be unconscious, and none of the others respond to my call. Perhaps death has become commonplace to them, or perhaps they are too weary and anguished to help anyone else.

The warrior's grip on my hand slackens. When I look over at him, he has relaxed against the pillows. His mouth goes loose and his eyes turn glassy, unseeing. Blood trails from the corner of his lips.

Dead.

At the sound of running footsteps, I whirl around, hoping for some miracle that could save him—but the runner is a girl dressed in the garb of a royal messenger. I recognize her; she's one of my mother's favorites, several years younger than me, maybe sixteen or so.

"Princess!" she gasps. "I was sent to tell you this quietly, before everyone finds out—the war is over."

My stomach drops, even though I knew this was coming. "We lost."

"Yes. The dragons and the Vohrainians took Guilhorn last night and they're on their way here. The Royal Guard will make a last stand in the capital, but—"

"There's no hope of victory." I inhale slowly, trying to cope with the warrior's death, my kingdom's fall, and the uncertainty of my future all in one breath. I can feel every nerve in my body tightening.

"Your mother wants you to leave the city and make for the southern border," says the messenger.

"It's too late. She must know that." I frown, confused. "The time to flee would have been last month, or last week. If we go now, the dragons will catch us long before we get to the border. Besides, the Vohrainian king promised that if Mother surrenders, he won't kill us. We'll be exiled to some distant outpost under guard, but we don't have to run."

The messenger bites her lip anxiously and lowers her voice. "I don't think that deal is on the table anymore, Princess. You see, the Supreme Sorcerer is dead. He died performing one last great spell."

"Oh shit," I breathe. "What did he do?"

"I'm not sure. The Queen didn't say, exactly. But I overheard a report of dragons falling from the sky by the dozens. About half the dragon army, slaughtered within moments."

"Fuck," I whisper. "They'll be furious."

The messenger nods. "By your leave, my lady—I'm going home to my parents. Whatever happens, I'd like to be with them."

"Of course." I grasp her arm reassuringly, before I remember how bloody and grimy my fingers are. My hand drops, and we both stare at the marks I left on her white sleeve.

"I wish you would run, Your Highness." Tears glimmer in the girl's eyes. "The dragons are a vengeful race. They'll kill you for what the Supreme Sorcerer did."

"How long until they reach the capital?"

But as the question leaves my lips, I hear the distant, droning windup of the dragon alarm. It grows in volume until its hideous blare fills the room, the city, the entire sky. One of the airships floating over the capital has spotted dragons in the distance. Dragons coming to kill us with fire and void, with lightning and ice.

Parma screams, drops her basket, and runs toward me. "We have to go, Princess!"

"Go where?" I laugh helplessly. "They're going to kill me either way, and I'll be damned if I die hiding in a hole or fleeing in a panic. You go, Parma. Both of you, go!"

"But, Your Highness—" the messenger girl protests.

I don't try to argue with her. I've been seized with an idea—inspired by the death of the Supreme Sorcerer, I suppose. He perished, yes, but he managed to take dozens of those winged motherfuckers with him. If I could take down at least *one* before I'm incinerated, I think I could die happy.

I bend and place a single, swift kiss on the forehead of the dead warrior. Ignoring the sobs and pleas of the messenger and the maid, I race through the recovery ward and burst out the rear doors, into the gloomy afternoon. It rained this morning, but the masses of dark, blue-gray clouds have shifted since then, and light glances through them in beams of misty peach and translucent gold.

The makeshift hospital wards stand along the northeast border of the city, so our soldiers can be brought within the shelter of the walls and treated quickly. I grasp my fluffy pink skirts in both hands and run across the stretch of cobblestones toward the outer wall. The blare of the dragon alarm fades, its duty fulfilled. Soldiers hurry this way and that, shouting instructions or repeating orders. One of them calls out to me, but I don't respond.

The stone stairs leading up to the parapet are incredibly narrow, still slick from the morning's rain. I struggle up them, teetering and nearly tumbling off the edge. By the time I reach the top, I'm breathing hard, and the back of my neck is sweating despite the cool afternoon breeze.

My brain designed music during the climb—a synchronous glory of trumpets and strings, an anthem to this city's final stand. I wish I had an orchestra here to play it proudly for all to hear. But I've never found the courage to share my music with anyone.

The top of the wall bears a variegated pattern, older stones cemented against newer ones to repair deep breaches. Decades ago, parts of the city were struck by the lightning of the Mordvorren, a sentient, magical super-storm that moves across the ocean in unpredictable patterns. Sometimes it will squat over an island or a city for days, bombarding everything below with caustic lightning and earth-shaking thunder. Magic functions strangely under the Mordvorren's shadow. When the storm is done flooding streets and demolishing homes, it moves on to its next target.

Lucky for us, the Mordvorren has not come this far inland in a very long time. A mercy of the Maker, perhaps. Or maybe the storm simply recognizes that we're doing a fabulous job of destroying ourselves.

I bend over, gripping my thighs as I take a moment to catch my breath. No one notices me. Every warrior lining the top of the wall is focused outward and upward, scanning the horizon and the clouds for dragons. On gray days like this, I've heard that the dragons like to fly above the clouds and then drop in for a surprise attack.

So far, the capital has been spared from such incursions. The five cities surrounding the royal seat are all heavily armed with catapults, enormous crossbows, cannon-studded airships, and other countermeasures specifically designed to stave off dragons. But two of those strongholds have fallen in the last month, and with the conquest of Guilhorn last night, we are left vulnerable. If the servants' whispers are accurate, my mother has been sending our remaining weapons and technology to fortify other cities. I'm not sure we have much left to defend ourselves.

But I do know there's a big crossbow at the top of the tower nearest me. Captain Ritcheld let me fire it once, when I was visiting the guards along the wall to boost their morale—Mother's idea, of course.

"Nothing inspires a man more than the sight of the pretty princess he's sworn to protect," she said.

To be fair, my presence did seem to cheer the guards, no matter what their gender. For me, the highlight of that day was cranking the lever to prepare the giant crossbow, rotating it into position, and launching an immense iron arrow into the sky.

Of course, I wasn't firing at anything in particular then. Today, if I get my hands on one of those great machines, accuracy will matter. I can't wield a sword or throw a knife, but I'm a decent shot with a regular handheld crossbow. Too bad that skill isn't so helpful when the crossbow is the size of my four-poster bed and the arrow is as big as me.

I tuck my skirts up as best I can and climb the ladder to the tower. Two guards stand there, flanking the huge crossbow on its rotating mount.

At the scuff of my slippers on the stone, one of the men turns around. "Your Highness!" He and his companion bow hastily.

"No need for that." I tug a ribbon from my wrist and use it to bundle my yellow hair into a knot so it's off my neck. "How close is the enemy?"

"The ground troops from Vohrain are not yet in sight. Usually the dragons remain with the Vohrainian army, but today they have flown far ahead. They're coming straight for us. You should take shelter, my lady." The first man points to the horizon, where I can make out black winged shapes against the dramatic dark gray and gold of the sky.

At this distance, the dragons still look so small. So harmless. It's hard to believe they're responsible for the past weeks of terror and pain among my people.

"I'll fetch the Captain, Princess," says the second man. "We can spare a few guards to escort you to safety."

"But there is no safety, not anymore," I counter. "Please don't tell the Captain. I want to stay up here."

The soldiers glance at each other, unsure. "But your esteemed mother, the Queen—"

"I don't care what my mother says. I don't want to huddle in some closet, only to be dragged out and publicly executed. If I must die, I'd rather be up here with you, fighting for my city and my kingdom. Please allow me that dignity."

With another glance at each other, they relent. "As our Princess wishes."

"Good." I step up behind the crossbow and grasp the handles, tilting it up toward the sky. I bend my knees as the Captain showed me, lining up the sights with the tip of the iron arrow. "Be ready to reload after my first shot. I intend to take down at least half a dozen of these overgrown bats."

The first guard clears his throat nervously. "We've got three arrows, Your Highness."

"Only three?" I lean back from the sights and glance down at the stone recess where the ammunition is typically stored. "We'll have to get more."

"There aren't any more. We were ordered to send everything to Guilhorn two days ago. Three arrows per tower—that's all we have left."

"Then I should let one of you take the shot." I swallow hard and step back. "I've only fired this weapon once."

"That's once more than either of us."

"Wait—you've never fired it before?"

Both guards shake their heads.

I frown, peering more closely at them. The helmets and the armor make them look older, but now that I'm paying attention, I think they're both younger than I am. Seventeen or eighteen, I'd wager.

My mother is manning the walls with boys, and sending girls to carry urgent, private messages. She has poured lives into this war like water into a sieve, until our kingdom has nothing but children left.

Hatred for her, for the dragons, and for Vohrain seethes hot in my chest. I feel suddenly, violently protective of these boys, even though at age twenty-three, I'm not much older.

"What are your names?" I ask.

"Listor," says one.

"Verros," answers the other.

"And I'm Serylla. That's what you'll call me if we're going to fight together, not 'Your Highness,' and not 'Princess.' Now, what other weapons do we have?"

"A hand cannon, a longbow, a dozen arrows, a spear, and our swords." Listor winces apologetically. "We're just a secondary tower. The towers by the gate and at the corners of the wall have more supplies, more men."

"Almost everyone has been pulled back to the castle, to defend the Queen," adds Verros.

"So the rest of the city must fend for itself?"

"I would never speak ill of the Captain or the Queen, or the generals…"

"Maybe someone should have spoken ill of them before things got to this point." Maybe *I* should have. I want to scream, and sob, and beat my fists against my mother's chest, and maybe punch Captain Ritcheld in the face, but I can't do any of that, so I shake out my frilly skirts, tug up the low neckline of my gown, and renew my hold on the grips of the great crossbow. "I'll need your help to reload after I fire. God, they're getting close. Do they always fly this fast?"

"I'm not sure, Your Highn—Serylla."

"They're angry," I murmur. I can almost sense the dragons' rage in the sharp outlines of their pointed wings, the angles of their necks and tails, the streamlined intensity of their bodies as they streak toward my city like arrows of doom.

As a bank of smoky blue cloud shifts, streams of golden light shine through, illuminating the rooftops of the city's outlying neighborhoods, the homes and businesses of those who aren't wealthy enough to live within the walls. The light also gleams on faraway fields of grain and corn, distant pastures and belts of thick forest. It shines through the dragons' wings, turning them fiery and translucent. A quick count tells me there are at least thirty dragons headed our way—perhaps more.

At the head of the oncoming swarm is a sleek black dragon with muscular, scaly legs, a wicked-looking muzzle, two long horns, and a spine decorated with hideous spikes, each of which is probably longer than my body, though it's hard to tell at this distance. I've never seen a dragon this close—except a hatchling once, when I was seven. It was part of a circus that came to entertain us at court. The hatchling dragon had its wings and muzzle banded with iron, and I cried so hard at the sight that my mother had to send the performers away.

I'm older now, and I understand now that the most harmless, adorable-looking creatures can grow up to be winged ravagers devoid of pity—like the one headed straight for the tower on which I stand.

I'm not sure why the black dragon is aiming for this particular tower, unless my pink gown, fluttering in the brisk spring breeze, is acting like a beacon, a taunt, a cry for attention.

The dragon flings up his great long neck and bellows to the sky—a call of rage and command. Immediately the dragons behind him split off from the group, circling wide to approach the city from different directions.

But he doesn't change course. He aims straight for me.

"Shit," quavers Verros. "He's going to crash right into us."

"Not if I hit him first." I bend my knees, angle the crossbow, and reach for the trigger. It's so huge I'll have to use my whole hand to pull it.

One deep, slow breath in. Another out.

Aim for a spot slightly higher than I intend, to match the dragon's trajectory.

Something booms off to my right—a cannon fired from another tower. The bitter tang of gunpowder smoke fills the air.

My palms are sweating. Shit.

Line up the sights. Make another adjustment.

It's now or never, Serylla. Fucking fire already.

I yank the trigger.

The iron arrow leaps from the coiled spring with a resounding twang that nearly deafens me. I'm on the ground, kicked back by the recoil, my breastbone aching. I forgot to dart aside after firing, like Captain Ritcheld showed me. My ears feel as if they've been stuffed with cotton. The guards' anxious voices are distant, garbled, but there's a loud ringing inside my skull.

"Did I hit it?" My voice sounds muffled. Shaking my head against the disorientation, I scramble to my feet and stagger to the parapet.

A huge dark body roars upward, filling my vision with glossy black belly-scales, dagger-like claws, and a steaming pair of nostrils. Above that long, narrow snout, two baleful yellow eyes blaze into mine.

The dragon's claws curl around the edge of the tower, crumbling stone and mortar. Verros and Listor are screaming. Verros pelts the monumental beast with shots from the handcannon while Listor pokes the belly-scales with his sword.

The dragon's great neck snakes down. His jaws close neatly around Listor's head and upper body, and he flings the guard off the tower like a man plucking a spider from his shirt sleeve and tossing it away.

Listor's dying shriek pierces the haze in my head and becomes the first thing I can hear clearly since I fired the giant crossbow.

The dragon opens his jaws again, lunges toward Verros—

"No!" I scream. "No, no!"

I grab the spear propped against the battlement and I leap forward, right between Verros and that gaping maw. I shove the spear upward, into the roof of the dragon's mouth, as hard as I can. I don't think it goes in very far.

"Your Highness, be careful!" shouts Verros.

"Run!" I shriek at him.

The soldier scrambles down the tower ladder, and I prepare to follow him.

The dragon tosses his head and crunches the spear, snapping it in two. He growls something that sounds like a swear, but I don't speak Dragonish so I can't be sure.

I'm poised at the top of the ladder, my feet on the rungs, my hands gripping the stone parapet on either side. The dragon faces me, his nostrils flaring. Smoke gusts from them as he blows out a breath, proof that he could wither me with one blast of fire.

But he doesn't. Instead he lifts his head, looking past me.

I twist around to follow his gaze and realize, to my shock, that the other dragons aren't really fighting. They're dodging the attacks of the guards, not even bothering to vomit fire or acid onto the soldiers. The cannons of a single airship overhead spatter them with gunfire and acid bombs, but the dragons ignore most of it, heading deeper into the city, plunging down into the streets briefly before rising up again. Every dragon that ascends has something clasped in his claws—a person.

They're taking people. Why? As prisoners? For food? To torture?

A particularly strong gust of wind hits me as I cling there, poised on the ladder. My skirts fly up around my thighs, my hair whips free of its ribbon—and my sweaty hands lose their grip on the stone.

The next second, I'm falling backward, at the worst possible angle—I'll miss the walkway along the top of the wall and crash onto the courtyard far below. I'll be broken, splattered on the cobblestones.

For a heart-stopping moment, I'm in midair, my stomach thrilling with horror, limbs flailing, my own imminent death flashing through my brain—

And then I'm caught up, grasped between huge claws, borne high into the sky in a rushing blur of immense, beating wings.

I don't even have breath to scream.

But the black dragon screams—a shrill cry of triumph, a summons. His wings pound the bright air, carrying him high, high, above my city. I can see the castle where my mother is making her final stand. It looks miniscule, and I'm dangling far above it, held only by the cage of the dragon's claws around my torso and legs.

I do scream then. But my cry is thin and tiny up here, in so much vast air and sunlight. It's like the wail of a rabbit in the grip of a mighty eagle.

"Let me go!" I cry out.

And a deep voice replies, "Very well."

The claws uncurl, and I fall.

I plummet toward the earth, my dress and hair torn by the wind. Tears stream from my eyes. I can't breathe.

The dragon's shadow passes over me, and his claws pluck me neatly from gravity's hold, securing me again.

"Next time you beg for your freedom, be more specific." His voice reverberates through the dark bone of those claws, into my body. It's terrifying, the depth of that voice. The fact that it speaks the Eventongue. The fact that this creature was playing with me like prey.

"You must not know who I am," I manage. I'm not sure it's wise to tell him, but perhaps it will grant me either a quick death or some value as a hostage.

"I know exactly who you are," he replies. "Ridiculous attire, more frivolous than that of other humans—fine gold jewelry dangling from your ears and throat—an overblown sense of your own importance and skills—and that soldier called you 'Highness.' You're the Crown Princess of Elekstan, the Queen's only child. But that title is meaningless from this day forward. From now on, your only title is 'captive,' and your only place is within my nest. Your will, your future, and your body are mine."

3

KYREAGAN

Mordessa.
Grimmaw.
Vylar.
Elegrin.
Eshterel.
Nyreza.
And dozens more.

I repeat the names of the dead as I fly with the other males toward Ouroskelle, the largest in the archipelago of rocky islands that our kind has called home for millennia.

I already know what we'll find. The few males we left behind, mourning over the skeletons of the other females. All of them, gone.

At least the ones who died on Ouroskelle can have their bone ceremonies. But my heart aches for the corpses of the beloved dragons lying in the city of Guilhorn.

My grandmother, my sister, my Promised… all gone.

When my father died, I made a pact with my brother and sister that even though I broke the shell of my egg first, I would not be the new Bone-King. Instead, the three of us would rule together, two princes and a princess. We would check each other, balance each other, and support each other, under the guidance of Grimmaw, whose century of wisdom far surpassed our own.

Now one part of our sibling trinity is gone, and only Varex and I remain.

A low moan issues from my throat at the thought, at the memory of Vylar pierced by that tower. When the sun rose this morning, her body would have disintegrated, turning to ash and whisking away in the wind, leaving only bones behind. We are creatures of sky and flame, and once our fire has died, we return to the air.

I should have stayed to collect bones from Vylar, Mordessa, and Grimmaw. But I was too intent on my plan, too desperate to carry it out before I could convince myself otherwise. I told myself and the other warriors that it was the perfect solution, the ultimate revenge.

I've done the right thing. By stealing the daughters of our enemies, we have sent a message to Elekstan that their Supreme Sorcerer's magical genocide did not go unanswered. My clan has been avenged.

But no frail human females can ever replace the glorious warriors, the strong mothers, and the beautiful partners we lost.

I moan again, louder. Answering moans of sorrow echo from the nearest of the other dragons.

"I realize you're upset," chirps the little human in my claws. "Is it true that my mother's sorcerer did a spell that killed many dragons?"

"He killed all the female dragons, everywhere." I tighten my claws until she squeaks.

"So you're angry." Her voice is strained now, threaded with a note of terror. "You're in pain. I understand that. But eating me isn't going to make you feel better."

"Why would I eat a scrawny little worm like you? Barely a scrap on your bones. You would probably taste disgusting anyway. A coddled little wine-sap with over-perfumed skin and too much hair."

"I'm not a wine-sap, I'm only wearing a *little* perfume, and I have just the right amount of hair."

"Human hair is strange. If it was fur, wool, or hide, it would make more sense, but it sprouts out of the tops of your heads for no reason."

"It sprouts out of other places too," she says stoutly.

"What places?"

"Well, men have beards—I'm sure you've noticed that. And there are… other places… that are none of your damn business, and why am I discussing this with you? Are we headed over the ocean? Oh *fuck* no… Put me down, you big ugly lizard, or I swear—"

"Or what?" I respond. "What will you do? What can a soft little slug like you do to a dragon?"

"I can make your life miserable."

A harsh laugh rumbles in my throat. "I am already miserable."

She's silent for a few blessed moments, and then she says, "I am sorry for what happened. I was not the cause of it, nor did I realize my mother and the Supreme Sorcerer were planning such a horrible thing. If I had any power at all, or any say in the matter, I would have stopped it. I would have stopped this entire war, months ago."

"But you did not."

"Because I couldn't."

"The Crown Princess had no say whatsoever in matters of the kingdom?"

"No."

"That smacks of laziness on your part."

"The *fuck* it does!" She bucks in my grasp. "You know nothing about my relationship with my mother or my country. And I fail to see what kidnapping me or anyone else will achieve for you. My mother will be dead or imprisoned soon, and there's no one to pay a ransom for me, so if you're not going to eat me or kill me, you may as well let me go."

I fly on, my wings beating slowly and steadily. The other dragons keep pace, each soaring some distance away. I wonder if their captives are as talkative as mine. My brother Varex seems to be having trouble keeping hold of his.

This plan of mine was an impulsive one, but I'm convinced it will work. It must.

We're gliding over the sea now. Dark water dappled with white foam surges below, and the sky above is a riot of color. The torn clouds glow amber and rose and gold. I like to think that the heavens themselves are paying tribute to the fallen—

"I'm hungry."

Fucking humans. I ignore the girl's comment and flare my nostrils, drawing in breaths of the salt-tinged evening air. The glory of the sky cannot fail to—

"I'm hungry."

"You'll have to wait."

"But I'm starving. I haven't eaten since breakfast, and that was just a piece of fruit and a tiny wedge of cheese. I was baking all morning and part of the afternoon, making pastries for the wounded soldiers, so I skipped lunch, and I'm so hungry I feel sick. Can't we turn around and go back? Maybe I can find some berries, or pilfer a pie from someone's windowsill—people do that, don't they? Leave their pies on windowsills to cool? I saw a picture like that in a storybook once… do you know what a storybook is? Have you ever read a book? Of course you haven't, because dragons can't read—"

I growl low in my throat and tighten my claws again. The girl gasps with pain, but she keeps talking.

"Listen, I don't know what you plan to do with me but if I die of hunger before you achieve it, that will be a disappointment for both of us. I need food, and I need it now."

"I'll feed you when we reach our destination. Humans don't die of hunger after a few hours without food." I say it confidently, but in truth, I'm not well-versed in the habits and care of humans. I shall have to do some research when we get to Ouroskelle. Perhaps one of the elders can—

"Where are we going? What kind of food do you have there?"

By the bones of my ancestors, am I never to finish a full thought again? "We have meat, berries, and vegetables. And sometimes fish."

"Do you have tea?"

"What the fuck is tea?"

"It's a drink. I'm very fond of it. I drink several cups a day. A light fruit tea with breakfast, something darker and stronger during the morning, cold sweetened tea with lunch, spiced tea with honey for the afternoon, and an herbal blend to promote sleep in the evening. I take that last cup with a little milk."

"But... what *is* it?"

"It's hot water flavored with different kinds of leaves depending on the taste and properties you want."

Hot water... with leaves.

I'm regretting my choice of human. Regretting it deeply. If I could go back and snatch a different one, I would. Why did I have to choose the fluffy pink girl on the tower instead of a decent peasant woman with simple clothing and some common sense?

I glance over at Varex and am astonished to see his woman climbing up his foreleg. She manages to claw her way over his shoulder and swing astride his neck. Did Varex suggest that she ride him, or did she get the idea herself? Her red hair streams behind her as they fly, and even though Varex does a few swerves and dives, she stays firmly lodged on his back.

"I'm thirsty," complains the Princess.

I stifle a groan.

The flight to Ouroskelle has never seemed so long.

4

SERYLLA

It's dark when we land. Thanks to the patches of cloud strewn across the night sky, there's not much starlight or moonlight. The dragons can apparently see in the dark; they don't seem to want or need a light source. As a result, all I can discern of our destination is a heaping, mountainous bulk.

The black dragon soars into a rocky tunnel. Cool wind rushes beneath his wings and across my face. We break out again, into an open space, but only for a second, and then we're weaving between rocky pillars, dark columns flashing by on either side at breathtaking speed, and I'm so sure we'll crash into one of them that I almost scream. He streaks upward, skimming close to the face of a cliff until he reaches the top. He darts into a cave, flying a little way in before he drops me.

I suck in a sharp breath, expecting to tumble painfully onto the rocky floor—but instead I land on a thick mat of soft, feathery grass. At least, that's what it feels like. Everything is deep, inky black, except for the roundish entrance of the cave, which is a lighter, chalky sort of black, a window into the night.

I hear the dragon land, his claws scraping against stone, his wings flapping in the dark. He exhales, and a puff of superheated air illuminates the cave briefly. Rock walls covered in symbols surround me, and I'm lying in a gigantic nest.

When the fiery breath fades, the only light left is the faint shimmer of the dragon's two yellow eyes—not bright enough to illuminate anything, but enough to let me know he's looking at me.

"I will be gone for most of the night," he says. "As a prince of Ouroskelle, I must visit the bereaved and accept bone-tribute from the dead. After that, I will bring you food, and we will speak more of your purpose here. Until then, sleep. Do not leave the nest."

With a rush of wings and incandescent breath, he soars out of the cave.

My bones ache, and I'm sore in every place his claws touched. I'll be covered with bruises in the morning. But the pain isn't what keeps me awake. It's what he said to me, right after he grabbed me.

From now on, your only title is 'captive,' and your only place is within my nest. Your will, your future, and your body are mine.

Once, when I was far too young to be hearing such things, I heard a story about a male dragon, mind-sick and exiled from his clan, who would kidnap human women and rape them until they died of their injuries. I knew, even then, that he was an exception to the rest, not a monster by which to judge the entire race. In fact, until the dragons allied with Vohrain and began killing my people, I had no reason to hate them. They rather fascinated me.

But through the war, I've seen their true nature. Their cruelty. And now I can imagine them enacting vengeance in all sorts of wicked ways.

Which is why, as the dragon was carrying me, I decided on a strategy. I will be the most annoying prisoner that any dragon has ever had. I will pester my captor night and day. I will criticize, demand, whine, and complain until desire for me is the very *last* thought in his head. I will drive him mad until he releases me or kills me.

That way, I'll avoid the anguish of being raped to death by his enormous, serrated dragon-cock.

To be fair, I haven't seen any dragon genitals. The males keep their equipment tucked away and only extrude it for pissing or procreation. But I've heard that dragon cocks are thorny, spiky, toothed monstrosities that come in all shapes and sizes. Female dragons are probably tough inside, designed to handle such rough breeding—but human vaginas would be torn apart instantly.

I'm determined that won't happen to me. But what about all the other women who were taken? I saw them distantly as we flew; I even thought I recognized a couple of them. In saving my own life, I must also think of theirs. After all, their captivity is my mother's fault—my goddamn mother and her Supreme Sorcerer.

I'm not going to be able to sleep at all. Not with these bruises, not with this dress, not with my stomach growling and my thoughts racing and the grass rustling every time I move the tiniest bit. But I may as well try to make myself more comfortable.

I remove my slippers and stockings first. Next I unfasten the stiff crinoline and the bustled overskirt. This was a ridiculous outfit to wear to the hospital wards, but my mother had the maids lay it out for me, and I'm not in the habit of defying her over small things. I've learned that if I want to say "no" to her, I must build up credit first—earn the single "no" with a thousand small instances of "yes."

I'm far more comfortable without the crinoline. I spread my silky overskirt across my resting place, hoping it will make the grass less noisy.

My eyes have barely adjusted to the darkness at all, so I don't dare climb out of the nest and look for an escape route. I suspect there isn't one, anyway—just a sheer cliff dropping straight down from the mouth of the cave.

Once I settle back down, I realize that I have to pee. There's no privy, of course, but that's not a deterrent for me. My plan is to make myself unpleasant to the dragon, so unpleasant I shall be. Since I don't care to lie in my own urine for hours, I crawl to the far side of the nest and pee on the grass. He's a beast with a sensitive nose, no doubt. He's bound to smell it.

I return to my resting place and settle in, thinking of all the ways I can infuriate him. I'll pitch my voice higher than usual, I'll whine incessantly, I'll sing the most repetitive songs I know. And I'll never stop trying to escape. Never.

No matter how firmly I center my thoughts on the plan, they keep creeping back to the fate of my kingdom, my people. My bodyguards, so familiar they seem like brothers. My maids, who tell me the juiciest gossip and whisper things my mother doesn't want me to know. The palace cooks, launderers, repair staff, and groundskeepers who shared their skills and knowledge with me whenever I asked, and seemed so pleased that I noticed and cared about their work. The jolly dukes and handsome lords who never failed to make me laugh on feast days.

It has been so long since we had a feast day. The last one took place on my twenty-third birthday. I discovered later that my mother confiscated an entire village's sugar ration to create the towering cake we enjoyed that night. I didn't know. Didn't realize how dire things had become. After I found out, I felt sick and guilty for eating two slices of that cake. I tried to speak to my mother about it, but she wouldn't see me. Too busy, her steward said.

Twenty-three years, and the queen still treats me like a foundling child instead of her daughter. But I'm hers, no doubt of it. I've been told the story countless times, how she went into labor while she was holding court. She sent the citizens out of the throne room, gave birth to me right there, in front of her servants and guards, and sent me off with a nurse while she rearranged her skirts and resumed hearing cases. "All true," said the court physician when I asked him about the story. "A woman of steel and ice, that one." Then he glanced around nervously, as if he thought his words might have been overheard.

A woman of steel and ice. The phrase clung to my mind after that, and it's how I always think of her. Tall and regal, with thin lips and prominent cheekbones. Eyes that glint like daggers. Black hair shot through with steel-gray streaks. I look like my father, not her. She would never tell me who he was. Probably some peasant or guard she fucked on a whim, without taking precautions. I suppose I'm lucky she decided not to end the pregnancy through magical or herbal means.

I used to wonder if my father ever tried to find me—if she had him killed or imprisoned just to keep him away. I wouldn't put it past her.

Wherever my mother is right now, I doubt she is thinking of me. So I put her out of my mind, resolutely. The tears that slip from my eyes aren't for her, but for the people of the palace, the ones who raised me and loved me when she couldn't be bothered.

5

KYREAGAN

Grief is the absence of rest.

Grief gives no reprieve, no space for a moment's relief. It gnaws at the heart, a steady ache with the occasional sting of teeth.

It is the deepest hour of the night. I have visited many bereaved families already, and the cord around my neck is heavy with bone-tribute. When I reach my cave, I will remove the cord and place it in some dry place until I can carve a hook from which to hang it.

Each bone comes from one of the dragons we lost. Some families gave me a tooth, others a claw, a piece of spine, or a toe bone. The Dragonish symbols for the lost one's name are carved into every tribute. The families choose a few bones to keep for themselves, as well. Some will wear the relics, while others will display them in their caves.

Varex flies at my side as we head toward the next cave. As a prince of equal standing, he could also request bone-tribute, but he has allowed me that honor.

Over the next several weeks, my clan will arrange the remaining bones of the dead upon the plains of the island, creating paths and spirals, designs we can see from the sky. With time, the bones will sink into the earth, and the grass will cover them, and we will heal.

"Mordessa's family is the last one," Varex murmurs.

My Promised had two fathers, Ardun and Ianeth. They paired decades ago and adopted Mordessa after her parents were killed in a rockfall. Ever since, Mordessa has been their cherished daughter, their pride and delight.

"I have no bone of hers to give the fathers." My voice is rough from groaning my grief with the other families. "I made a terrible mistake, Varex. We should have waited at Guilhorn until dawn and gathered bone-tribute from the dead. I was too eager to have our revenge."

"We had to take the capital by surprise," he answers.

"No, we could have waited and attacked with the army. We could have captured the women later, after the city fell."

"The king of Vohrain might not have given the women to us," Varex points out. "Such tribute wasn't part of our deal with him. Our agreement was that we would ensure his victory over Elekstan, and he would give us the Middenwold Isles in exchange."

"At the very least, we should have stayed to ensure that the capital of Elekstan fell before we left for home. We abandoned the final battle."

"Vohrain's victory was certain," Varex assures me. "Our clan won the war for King Rahzien. The contract was completed."

Technically we did fulfill the bargain. But I should have stayed for a final word with the king, face to face, to confirm the victory and to secure our ownership of the islands he promised. Instead, I sent word of my plan to him through one of his commanders, and I did not wait for a reply.

We need those islands. They are rich with pastureland, well-stocked with wild pigs, deer, and goats. Several months ago, a strange disease swept through Ouroskelle and the neighboring isles. It killed several dragons, including my father, and decimated the animals.

Since then, game has been more scarce, barely enough to feed the existing primes and elders, especially with the growing numbers of fenwolves who lurk in the narrow cracks of the mountains, where dragons cannot go. And the voratrice dens take prey, too—more than we can spare. Once we add hatchlings into the mix, we'll be facing starvation. We must have the Middenwold Isles as our new hunting grounds.

We could have taken the Isles by force, or hunted there without permission. But that is not our way. When my father finally succumbed to the plague, he had already forged the bargain with Vohrain, and he made me swear that I would uphold the contract. I gave him my bone-oath, the most sacred promise among our kind. If a bone-oath is broken, the dragon who breaks it loses his fire forever.

And thus, in the Bone-King's name, I have led the slaughter of countless humans.

But the humans will recover quickly. They breed almost daily and spawn many offspring. Our race is not so fortunate.

"You left your woman in your cave?" Varex asks.

I was so deep in my thoughts that his question startles me. "I... yes."

"Some of the other males put their women all together in that old cavern where we used to keep flocks. You know the one—at the base of the Whistling Peak. Rothkuri thought they might be more comfortable on the ground."

"They will be more vulnerable to wolves."

"The fence is still intact. Besides, Gosrik is on guard there."

"And Gosrik is so reliable?" I snort. "Perhaps you should go and check on them."

"I will, after we visit Ardun and Ianeth. And then I must see to my own prize. She is—obstinate."

"Did I see her *riding* you?"

Varex growls. "Yes."

"I believe you and I chose the most troublesome women of the bunch." A dry chuckle escapes me. It feels wrong, like a betrayal. Guilt forms a stone in my throat.

I can see the spiked entrance to Ardun and Ianeth's cave ahead. In a moment I will have to face them. And I will have to face the loss of my Promised.

I'm not ready.

She's there, in my mind, with those glorious yellow wings, each scale like a lustrous coin. Brighter than me, bigger than me, and yet she wanted me, she *loved* me, and I—

Unworthy. The word reverberates in my head, through my bones. I was unworthy of her love. I am unworthy of avenging her, unworthy of carrying this terrible news to her fathers.

My heart booms through my body like the thunderous crash of huge waves against a mountain. The fiery liquid in my gut, the source of my flame, roils and churns until the pressure is unbearable—I feel like I'm going to explode. My lungs tighten, and though I stretch my neck, straining to draw a deep breath, I can't manage it. I think I'm dying. Fire is going to fountain through my throat, terrible and uncontrollable, and after that, my heart will burst. It has never pounded this fast, not even during battle. It can't sustain this speed for long.

I bank sharply aside and land on the rocky surface of a steep mountain slope. I cling there, huffing panicked breaths tinged with orange fire.

Varex lands near me, his amber eyes wide with concern. "Brother."

"A moment," I gasp. "I need a moment."

This is foolishness. This is weakness. I need to calm down, calm down, *calm the fuck down!*

"I'm here," Varex says quietly. "I'm still here. You and I—we are still strong."

I choke out a mouthful of liquid fire. It doesn't ignite and spray forth in a rush of flame like usual—instead it drizzles from my jaws onto the rocks, melting several of them.

"Breathe, Kyreagan," Varex urges. "Slowly. One long breath, all the way in."

"I'm trying."

"You can do this."

His steady voice sinks through my scales, and I manage to release some of my tension. My heart rate slows, and I'm able to suck in one full, deep breath.

Wingbeats shatter the night air above us, and I glance up to see Ashvelon and Fortunix descending. Fortunix did not accompany us to the war on the mainland. He is older than Grimmaw was, approaching his one hundred and twenty-fifth year. If he survives twenty-five more, his life will end just after the next mating season. No dragon lives beyond a hundred and fifty years.

"My Princes," says Ashvelon, landing gracefully on a ledge a little farther up the slope. Fortunix perches beside him and folds his great scarred wings. He lived through a difficult time forty years ago, when the humans of Elekstan thought it amusing to hunt dragons for sport. I suppose that dark history between our races justified the contract with Vohrain in my father's mind. The enemy of our enemy may as well be an ally.

The presence of the two warriors is both a comfort and a challenge. I am their lord, and I must not appear weak, so I fight to gain control of my breathing.

"I am still collecting bone-tribute," I inform them. "Ashvelon, how goes it with your female?"

He exchanges an apprehensive glance with Fortunix. "I was just telling Fortunix that I—I dropped her."

"You what?" exclaims Varex.

"She wriggled out of my grasp. I couldn't catch her, and then she was gone, lost to the sea. It was dark—I couldn't see her anywhere. I failed you, my lord. And I—I killed her." He bows his horned head.

"You haven't failed me," I assure him. "And her loss is of little consequence at such a time. Count it against the losses we have endured, and feel no guilt. I have another task for you, which I trust you will accomplish with greater care. I need you to find the enchantress Thelise, daughter of the Supreme Sorcerer of Elekstan, and bring her to Ouroskelle."

"And perhaps some supplies as well," says Fortunix dryly. "You have transported many human women here, but you have nothing with which to care for them."

"Because I plan to have the enchantress turn them all into female dragons."

"Yes. Ashvelon told me of your plan." Fortunix makes a sound that's almost like a snort. In anyone younger, I would greet such disrespect with a battle challenge, but he is an elder, so I let it pass.

"My plan is based on fact," I tell him. "Rothkuri told me that Hinarax told him that he heard from a Vohrainian soldier that Thelise can transform herds of sheep into rabbits, or chickens into rats. The soldier's cousin witnessed it with his own eyes. A whole species transformed into another. She can do this for us. Ashvelon, see to it that she has all the supplies she needs to perform the spell."

"Ashvelon needs a companion for this mission," says Fortunix. "I will accompany him."

"You will?" Varex sounds surprised. "But you're so ol—" He cuts himself off and coughs. "What I mean is—you didn't join us for the war."

"Because I have done my share of fighting." Fortunix gives him a sharp look. "Not because I am frail and infirm. I'm perfectly capable of flying to the mainland and helping Ashvelon carry supplies. Or perhaps I'll carry the enchantress, since our friend Ash seems to have slippery claws." He nudges Ashvelon with the edge of his wing.

"I would welcome your company," Ashvelon mutters.

"We'll set off at first light, then. Before I leave, princes, would you like me to explain to you the proper care and feeding of human women?"

"Have *you* ever cared for one?" I ask.

"Not exactly, but I have more experience with humans than either of you."

Something in his manner irritates me. Perhaps I'm overtired, my patience thinned with grief, but the last thing I want is to cling to this slope and listen to Fortunix pontificate about the habits of humans.

"We've been allied with humans for several weeks," I say. "I believe we can figure out how to keep them alive. And we all speak the Eventongue more or less fluently, so they can tell us what they need."

"Oh, they'll tell you." Fortunix chuckles. "Humans are nothing if not demanding and entitled. Very well, my Princes. We shall go and prepare for the journey." He heaves himself up and takes to the air, gliding a bit before he manages to rise with several aggressive wingbeats.

Ashvelon is about to take off and follow him, but I say quickly, "Ash… bring back something for tea."

He cocks his head at me, confused. "Something for tea? What does that mean?"

"Fuck if I know. Ask the enchantress what is required."

"As you wish, my Prince." He dips his head to me and takes off.

My brother and I cling there in the dark, unmoving. My night vision is not as good as his, but I can tell by the tension of his jaws and the angle of his neck spikes that he is suffering, too. He did not have a Promised life-mate, but he lost Grimmaw, like

I did. And we both lost Vylar. That loss bites deeper. For twenty-five years, the three of us have been inseparable.

"I remember when Vylar hatched," I say, low. "I had been out of the egg for a day already, and I considered myself an expert on the world around me. But when she came out, she crawled farther, stretched her wings wider, and screeched louder than I did. She was always the smartest of us, and the quickest. Our parents were so excited to witness our hatching. Their first mating did not produce eggs, and they could not believe their luck to have three eggs in the nest after their second season. Once Vylar and I had arrived, we all waited for you to hatch."

"And I was late. As I usually am." Varex's voice is thick with emotion.

"Yes, you were late. Weeks late. Our parents thought you had died in the egg, and they were ready to deliver you to the sea, but Vylar wrapped both her tiny wings around your egg and would not let them take you. She had learned some words by then, and she kept saying, 'Mine. Mine.' So they left you in the nest, and finally you hatched."

Varex makes a choking sound, his shoulders heaving. He throws back his head and lets out a blast of his magic, a huge void orb edged with purple lightning. It's not safe for him to release such a large one here, but I don't chide him. I hang onto the cliff with all my might until the void orb implodes on itself and its sucking pull vanishes. As dragons, our own fire cannot damage us, and we're mostly resistant to each other's powers, but Varex's void magic is the dangerous exception.

"We should go. I'm as ready as I'll ever be." I detach from the cliffside and flare my wings, catching a gust of wind and banking into a glide. Varex follows me toward the cave of Mordessa's family.

By now, Ardun and Ianeth know their daughter is dead. They have heard the mourning from the rest of the clan, and they know something terrible has happened. It is up to me to explain the details, to offer what comfort I can.

The other relatives of those who died at Guilhorn understood why I did not bring back a bone from every fallen dragon. They were disappointed, but they accepted it. I can only hope the fathers of my Promised will understand as well.

We land on the ledge of their cave. Six cube-shaped dyre-stones glow along the floor, illuminating the space. Dyre-stones are found in the deepest caves on the island. Once they are heated with dragon fire, they glow brightly for several hours before they must be reheated. Every family possesses them as a means of illumination, since the quality of our night vision varies from dragon to dragon. On nights of mourning or celebration, the cliffs are dotted with the reddish-gold light of dozens of dyre-stones.

Within the cave, Ianeth and Ardun sit side by side, their shoulders pressed closely together. Both males are seventy-five, primes full of wisdom and strength, but Ardun lost his sight in a terrible encounter with a voratrice. He was lucky to survive, and since then, Ianeth has been his eyes. Neither of them could accompany us to war, but they sent their powerful daughter instead. And now they wait for me to say the words I never thought I would have to speak.

"It is with the greatest sorrow that I must tell you—Mordessa has fallen, and her spirit has ascended." I struggle to keep my voice calm and steady. "She fell in the company of many great dragons, among them my grandmother and my sister."

"How?" croaks Ardun. "You swore that our army was powerful, that the humans did not have the strength to withstand us. You said there was little risk, that their acid bombs were weak, their airships flimsy, and their crossbows inaccurate. What happened?"

My jaws part, but I cannot speak.

Varex moves forward. "When Elekstan's Supreme Sorcerer saw that his nation would be defeated, he cast a curse more terrible than any spell ever performed in this world. He died casting it, and he took with him every female dragon. No one could have known such a thing was possible."

"You believe the Vohrainians, your allies, did not know of such magic?" says Ardun.

"If they had known, I believe they would have warned us," Varex replies. "And they would have been more cautious themselves, lest he turn his spells upon them."

"Killing thousands of humans would have been much more difficult than cursing a few dozen dragons," Ianeth says in his slow, ponderous voice. "But there is no use considering what might have been, only what is. We share your grief for the loss of Grimmaw and Vylar, my Princes."

"And I share your grief for the loss of Mordessa," I reply. Her name feels wrong between my teeth—no longer the name of a living being, only the title of a memory.

"She was glad to be your Promised," Ianeth says. "She spoke of you all the time. She said she was pleased to have found such a love—a love like mine and Ardun's." His sorrowful gaze holds mine. "And you loved her well, I am sure. Have you brought bone-tribute?"

Here is the moment I've been dreading. "We could not wait for dawn on the night of the battle. We had to fly swiftly to the capital city before the forces of Elekstan had time to regroup and prepare for our arrival. The Vohrainian army marched from Guilhorn immediately, and we flew ahead."

"You did not take a bone for us." Ardun's voice trembles. His pale, scarred eyes are void of sight, but they seem to hold even more grief and anger than Ianeth's. "Did you take one for yourself?"

"No."

"You were her Promised." He trembles, and his voice rises. "You did not wait for her dissipation?"

"I saw her spirit go, Ardun, but we had to leave. We had to find some means of vengeance, a way to save our race."

"I heard," he snaps. "I heard that all of you came back with human females. As if such paltry creatures could ever replace those we lost."

"Not replace them, no," I grit out. "But we had to do something. We cannot suffer a mating season without females."

"Ianeth and I have been through mating seasons without females," Ardun retorts.

"Yes, because you were born to thrive together. But most of us need the energy of the mating frenzy, the hope that a new generation brings, the joy of hatching season. It fuels our power, strengthens our bodies, binds us together as a clan. We are already far fewer in number than usual because of the plague and the war. What if another plague comes, or another war? If we wait twenty-five years until the next mating season, there may not be enough of us left to repopulate Ouroskelle."

Without meaning to, I have allowed my voice to grow in volume and depth until it booms through the cave and beyond.

"Brother." Varex touches his nose to my neck. It's a sign of submission, of sympathy, and of warning.

He is right. I must control myself. I came here to mourn with the fathers of my Promised, and instead I am berating them as if they are the enemy. Both dragons sit grim-jawed, proud and silent.

"Forgive me," I say. "I have been absent from home for a long time, and this was not the return I hoped to make. I have allowed my own sorrow and anger to overshadow your loss, and that was not my intention. Forgive the lack of bone-tribute, I beg of you."

"I could have borne it," says Ardun, "knowing that her bones will not grace the green fields under a cloudless sky. But to have *nothing*—" His voice breaks.

"I'm sorry," I manage. "If it helps, remember that I have nothing as well. Nothing from my sister, or Grimmaw. Nothing from any of them."

I leave the cave and burst into the night, fighting my way upward as hard and fast as I can despite a contrary wind. I climb and climb, until my breath comes short and my wings ache and the stars surround me like a glistening forest. It angers me how they sparkle there, pleasantly remote, untouched by the ravages we endure far below, among the cliffs and cities.

Swinging my head from side to side, I spray long arcs of flame through that black sky, through the emptiness. But I cannot burn the stars.

Varex joins me after I've drained my fire to the dregs. He glides below me, a silent presence. At last he says, "That did not go well."

"No. It did not."

"But it's done. And now you must rest."

"How? How does one rest after such a day, and such a night?"

"Judging from what I saw, you've emptied your fire. Your body will be craving rest to replenish it. You should be able to sleep, at least for a while."

"And you?" I gaze down at him.

"I need to speak with the woman I stole," he says. "And then, I will try to rest, too."

We head down, angling in the direction of the east-facing cliff in which my cave is located. His cave is in another mountain, along the same valley.

As we fly, a confession builds inside me, a weight that has been dragging at my heart since Guilhorn. Suddenly I can bear it no longer.

"I did not love Mordessa." The confession hangs in the night air, cold as starlight. "Not like she loved me. Not like her fathers love each other."

"You cared for her," says Varex.

"Not enough. Not like she deserved."

He doesn't answer, and I respect him for not offering false comfort. I don't speak the rest of my thoughts aloud, but I sink their truth into my own heart like a bloodied shard of bone.

If I could not give her the love she deserved, then I am not deserving of love.

6

SERYLLA

Pale light glows through the pink lens of my eyelids. My lashes flutter apart.

Instead of a creamy, gold-fringed, brocade canopy, there's rock above me. Rock etched with a million delicate patterns—interlocked circles, overlapping triangles, curlicues, diamond shapes, and waves.

Instead of cool satin sheets and a sumptuous mattress, I'm lying on my own discarded clothing and a thick mat of compacted, feathery grasses.

Instead of the gentle tones of my maids rousing me and the hiss of steaming hot water running into my marble tub, I'm greeted with a low, repetitive rumble and the distant whisper of the ocean somewhere far away.

Memory hits me like nausea, like a dagger in my brain.

Everything is gone. The war is over. Lost. My mother was defeated, probably imprisoned by now, or dead. The kingdom, ravaged. Everyone I ever knew, everyone I took for granted, gone. My maids, my bodyguards, the cooks and gardeners, the messengers and attendants, the clerks and physicians, the stablemaster and his boys, and the farmers who would bring their carts to the palace and fill our larders with good things. I used to love to greet them and ask about their families. They were always delighted when I remembered details about their loved ones. Sometimes, if they brought their sons or daughters along, I would give the children small gifts just to watch their eyes light up.

One of the people I miss the most is the second cook's adorable little son Taren, whose birth I witnessed two years ago. His mother, Huli, asked if I would be his guardian if anything ever happened to her, and I agreed. I adore babies, in general, but I love that tiny boy with all my heart—I've been his caretaker and playmate more times than I can count. And now I have no idea if he and his family are safe.

Gone. All of it.

Because of the fucking dragons. Because of my mother, because of Vohrain, because of a whole host of reasons, both foolish and rational, that lay behind this war. But right now, all my fury and resentment centers on the great black dragon sleeping on the stone floor. The jagged spikes along his back rise and fall with his slow breath.

They say everything looks better in the morning, but he's just as hulking and terrifying as he was yesterday. His ebony scales glimmer in the light that pools in the mouth of the cave.

On any other day, I might love that tender morning light, and the bits of rosy cloud I can see outside. I might delight in the wheeling of sea birds against the sky, in their raucous cries, in the fresh breeze that buoys them up and pours into the cave, brushing softly against my cheeks. But my pain, fear, and uncertainty are too great to be relieved by a pretty morning.

Maybe it affects me a little, though. Lifts my spirits just enough so that I remember my strategy—to annoy the black dragon until he goes out of his mind. To make his life as wretched as I possibly can. To learn everything about him so I can hurt him with my words, even if I can't damage him with weapons.

He's intelligent and proud, that much is clear. That plays in my favor. Intelligent people are easier to irritate—the small, bothersome bits of life distress them more painfully. And anyone with true pride is exquisitely sensitive to being wrongfully perceived.

Those finer tortures will come later. For now, I'll start with something absurdly simple. Something to test my captor's endurance. It might end in me being thrown off a cliff, but I'll take my chances.

First I pee quietly, on a different part of the nest. The dragon's nostrils twitch, but his breathing doesn't change, and his eyes remain closed.

The nest is gigantic, big enough to fit two dragons of his size with room to spare. Not far beyond it, a rivulet of water spurts out of the rock wall and trickles down, running through a groove in the floor before disappearing into the rocks again. I clamber out of the nest and sniff the water. It smells clean. When I taste it cautiously, it's sweet and fresh, so I gulp it down until my tongue and throat are less parched.

With the immediate necessities taken care of, I walk along the nearest wall of the cave, my fingertips grazing the rows of decorative etchings. *Beautiful*, my heart says quietly, but I stifle the admiration and the line of lyrics that springs into my mind, a melodic homage to the presence of such exquisite art in such a brutal place.

Songs come to me like this, in unguarded moments. Usually a line or two will appear, fully formed, music and words in perfect sync, and then I mentally play with the concept until I flesh it out into something fuller, richer.

But I refuse to create a song about this place. My captor and his murderous clan don't deserve it. So instead I select the most annoying tune I know and I begin to sing it. Loudly. Cheerfully.

*"I once had a wife
Who took my life
And she buried me
Beneath the sea
A sailor caught me in his net
From a boat that he won in a drunken bet
I swallowed his soul
So I could be whole
Then I went to the tavern to barter for ale
And the barmaid begged, "Will you tell me a tale?"
So I said...
I once had a wife
Who took my life
And she buried me
Beneath the sea—"*

At the third line, the dragon's eyes fly open. His long neck rises, lifting his huge triangular head with its elegant, tapered jaws. He blinks thick black lashes over slit-pupiled yellow eyes and shakes himself a little. The ridges above his eyes contract in an expression so similar to a confused frown that I almost laugh. But I keep singing, and he keeps staring, as if he thinks I've gone out of my mind.

I see the precise moment he realizes that it's a circular song, one that never ends, and that I intend to keep singing it indefinitely.

"I've had very little sleep." His deep voice rolls through the cave, rippling over my skin, but I keep singing at the same pace while he talks. "It has been a difficult night. But you're human, so I suppose it's no use to ask for a little consideration."

Consideration? As if he didn't *kidnap* me yesterday. The sheer arrogance. He's lucky I have a nice voice. This could be much worse for him.

The dragon rises to a sitting position, which looks so doglike that I remember another loss—the hounds in the palace's hunting kennels. I used to visit them secretly, even though my mother warned me not to. She said they were savage animals bred to kill. But not one of them ever scratched me with a single tooth.

I sing louder, adding a defiant twang to the words.

The dragon huffs in disgust, and then he sniffs, his gaze sharpening. "Did you—did you piss in my nest?"

"—I swallowed his soul, so I could be whole, then I went to the tavern to barter for ale," I sing sweetly.

"Do you know how long I worked on this nest? Gathering the materials, selecting only the finest pieces to include, compressing the grasses, shaping and weaving the edges—" Instead of rising, the dragon's voice grows deeper, deeper, like building thunder, and his body seems to grow taller, broader, and more terrifying by the second. His shoulders and chest heave with angry breaths, and a haze of orange heat glows in his nostrils.

I want to be defiant, but a tremor enters my voice in spite of my best efforts.

"This nest was for *her*. For our hatchlings." Fire flickers in his mouth as he speaks. "And you pissed all over it."

My voice breaks, shrills into a terrified squeak as he charges me. His broad, scaly cheek strikes my shoulder, a sideswipe that sends me flying into the nest again.

"When hatchlings piss or shit in their nest, we put their faces in the mess so they learn not to soil where they sleep." The dragon lifts his sinewy foreleg and nudges me over with his claws, turning me face down. His claw hooks into the back of my dress, and he drags me toward the spot where I relieved myself this morning.

"I'm not a hatchling," I gasp, desperate. "I'm an adult, a princess."

"Do all princesses piss in their beds?"

"Where else was I supposed to go?"

"Anywhere else."

"You told me to stay in the nest." I cling to those words, sensing they might be my salvation. "You said that, remember? I was obeying you."

He stops moving, and I cringe, my face inches from the wet spot.

"I did say that. You're right... I should have been more specific. I should have remembered your physical needs." His claw slips free from my dress, and I scramble back, away from the piss-soaked grass.

The dragon's scaly jaw tenses. "I apologize for the oversight. I'm not used to having such a weak, helpless life form to care for."

I want to protest that I'm neither weak nor helpless, but the truth is, compared to him, I *am*, much as I hate to admit it.

"Yes, well... you're a terrible kidnapper," I say. "Any captor worth their salt knows that they need to provide their prisoner with food, drink, and a place to relieve themselves. I've had to take care of *two* of those needs on my own. So you're a complete failure at this."

The dragon's yellow eyes widen. "Right. You're still hungry. Shit."

"Yes." I wrap my arms over my stomach. "Is that your plan? To starve me to death?"

"I—no." He wheels away, his immense wings flaring. I barely noticed the wings this morning, they were folded so tightly against his body. "I'll return shortly with sustenance for us both."

He leaps into the wind and soars away from the cave.

I collapse against the straw, drawing a long breath. I succeeded in angering him, that's for certain. And I discovered something important—he planned to share this nest with a female dragon. She died yesterday.

I can use that.

I venture toward the cave entrance, cringing as I approach the cliff's edge. Climbing the steps of the city wall yesterday was frightening, but I was so determined to shoot at dragons, I barely considered the peril. Without that frantic energy, my usual caution about heights has returned. And this height is dizzying beyond belief. If I'd been able to see how high this mountain really was last night, I would have screamed during the whole flight to its peak.

The view is stunning, though. Across the valley from us are more mountains, shorter than this one. Between them I can see flat stretches of grassy land, then more craggy peaks and bluffs, some cloaked with forest. To my left, beyond the mouth of the valley, I glimpse the ocean between tall columns of rock.

White lines march across the windswept meadows of the island. At first I think the lines are marked with shells, but then I realize I'm too far up for mere shells to stand out so clearly. I wonder... could they be... bones? That must be what they are— huge bones, bleached white by sun and sea. Dragon bones.

As I squint down at the valley floor, something small and distant crosses my vision. Then another shape, and a third. Too big to be birds. Those are dragons.

I lean slightly forward, peering down, trying to see if any of the dragons are carrying humans.

The hideous height seizes my mind, tilting everything, skewing my sense of balance, my perception. Frantically I grab for the cave wall, but my bare toes skid off a smooth part of the rock and I lose my footing. I waver on the edge, clawing rock, scrambling for stability.

With a crack of thunderous wings, the black dragon sweeps down from the sky and lands on the ledge, flinging something limp onto the floor of the cave. The gust of wind from his arrival finishes me, and I slip into midair with a shriek.

"Fuck," growls the dragon, and he dives off the edge as well. He sweeps underneath me—a stupid idea, really, because his back is like a forest of lethal blades. Somehow I avoid being skewered. I smack into his shoulder and immediately slide off—there's nothing to grip. My fingers catch on his scales, one of my nails tearing half off with a blazing rip of agony.

I'm falling again, tumbling ass over ankles through the clear, bright morning air.

The dragon roars with frustration and grabs at me, but he doesn't catch me as neatly as he did yesterday—he's weary, clumsy. His claws shear right through my dress and slash it wide open before he manages to grip my body. His wings pound the air, hoisting us both back up to the ledge.

He throws me into the cave. The bruises he gave me yesterday scream at the impact, and I choke out a pained sob.

"Foolish human," he growls. "Do you want to die?"

Yes, whispers a voice inside me. But another voice cries, even louder, *No*.

I'm not sure which is true.

7

KYREAGAN

The human girl lies on her belly, propped on her forearms, her tangled yellow hair tumbling over her shoulder. Her tiny fists are clenched. The bits of gold jewelry at her ears and throat glitter in the sunlight.

I tore her dress when I was trying to save her. One of her slim legs is exposed, all the way up to her hip. The plump, soft mounds on her chest are showing as well. She notices and tugs her ruined garment up to partially cover them.

Those mounds—I believe humans call them breasts. I know that they are teats for suckling young, similar to those of a cow, a pig, or a sheep. Female dragons have no teats like other animals. We feed our hatchlings food that we soften in our own mouths.

The shape of the girl's teats is strangely pleasing to me. But I'm distracted by the marks all over her arms and legs.

"What are those spots?" I ask. "Are you diseased?"

"No," she hisses at me, her eyes blazing. "Those are *bruises*. It's blood pooling beneath the surface of my skin. It means you hurt me."

Dread coils in my belly. "But you have so many of them."

"You hurt me many times yesterday, while you were carrying me so tightly."

Fuck.

I want to apologize. But the words would feel strange, coming from the dragon who incinerated so many of her people, to the princess whose royal sorcerer slaughtered half a species.

"I will be more careful," I tell her. "I need you in good health for the change."

"The change?"

Instead of answering, I nudge the mountain goat carcass with my snout, pushing it closer to her. "I found prey quickly today. Unusual, and fortunate. You may have the first bite."

The girl stares. "Do you know anything at all about humans?"

"Not much," I admit.

"But you fought with the armies of Vohrain. Surely you perceived some of their habits."

"We did not camp with them. We had our own roosts, and only met with their leaders outside the camp, when it was necessary."

She shakes her head. "I can't eat this."

"It's a young goat, fresh and tender." With my claw I slice open the goat's haunch, splitting the hide and revealing the rich, red flesh. My mouth waters at the sight. "Good meat. Take some. We must learn to share meals if you are to live here."

"Live here? Share meals? What the hell are you talking about?" Her voice is strained, her blue eyes wide.

"Our females are dead," I explain. "We need new ones for breeding."

"Fuck," she says faintly. "Then you... you're going to... No, that won't work. I'll die."

Somehow she must have guessed my plan. She's afraid of the transformation into dragon form. "You will not die. It will be over quickly, I promise. Any pain will be minimal."

"So you'll just..." She presses a shaking hand to her forehead. "It won't fit."

What is she talking about? Perhaps she is speaking of the time it will take for the newly-made female dragons to fit in here at Ouroskelle. "It may not be a good fit at first, but we will give you time to adjust."

"How kind of you," says the Princess hoarsely. She rises and walks calmly past me, straight toward the edge of the cliff. "Don't catch me this time."

I understand her meaning an instant before she leaps off the ledge. My wing whips out, curling around her body, herding her back into the cave.

"Is the prospect so abhorrent to you that you would kill yourself?" I exclaim.

"Let me think... um... *yes*," she snaps.

"You'll be one of us, with all the privileges of any dragon," I tell her. "Of course you fear this new future, because you don't understand our ways, but you will learn. You will adapt. Consider this—that your race owes mine reparation for destroying so many of our beloved warriors, mates, daughters, and sisters. We can never replace those we lost, but if we do nothing, there will be no new hatchlings, and dragons will cease to exist."

The Princess is salt-white. She presses both palms over her lower belly. "I'm not carrying your hatchlings."

By the bones, she is obtuse. "Not the hatchlings," I explain patiently. "You will birth our eggs, from which the hatchlings will be born."

Her lack of dragon knowledge is excusable, I suppose. After all, I know precious little about humans. But she should begin educating herself about dragon anatomy, life cycles, and lore prior to her transformation. And since she seems liable to jump off the cliff at the slightest provocation, I suppose I shall have to keep her with me and teach her myself.

"Let this be your first lesson in our ways." I carve a chunk of thick red meat from the goat carcass and hold it out to her on the tip of my claw. "Accept what is given to you with goodwill."

The Princess stares at the meat, then at me.

And then she vomits, on herself and on the floor of my cave.

Dragons occasionally vomit when they're ill. It's a disgusting occurrence, and there's usually far more of it than the tiny puddle the Princess made. Her vomit is mostly bile, since there's nothing in her stomach.

Why is she so difficult to deal with? I've been anxious about the proper care of my first hatchling, but from what I remember of my own upbringing, hatchlings are easy to care for compared to this human. Perhaps I should take Fortunix up on his offer of advice when he returns.

For now, I think it's best that we both leave the cave until the smell abates. I'll ask Rothkuri to remove the soiled parts of the nest and use his water magic to rinse the floor. Half the goat will sate my hunger for now, and I'll give him the remaining half as payment.

And perhaps, while we're out, I can find something that the Princess will deign to eat.

8

SERYLLA

I wanted to appear disgusting to the dragon, and my wish has certainly been granted. I've peed on his nest and vomited all over myself. I'm not sure I can bring myself to be any more disgusting than that.

After I threw up, he hastily devoured part of the goat, the sight of which nearly made me vomit again. I'm not sure why he's so precious about piss and vomit in his living space when he digs into bloody raw flesh with such gusto. Though to be fair, he eats rather neatly for a dragon, and licks every bit of blood off his claws and muzzle afterward.

Following his meal, he picks me up and flies out of the cave, clasping me firmly but gently in his claws. Again, his actions don't match what I expect. It's contradictory that he would be so cautious about bruising me when he plans to breed me by force.

During our conversation, he didn't seem to understand why I was so upset. All his talk of giving me time to adjust to his cock—that it will be over quickly and that the pain will be minimal—it's as if he doesn't see any issues with a giant dragon fucking a tiny woman. He must not grasp the fact that our anatomy is fundamentally incompatible.

Just the thought of him trying to wedge his massive dick inside my hole has me wanting to scream and flail and possibly faint. But I need to control my thoughts, calm down, and keep working on my plan. If only I had something to eat, maybe I'd feel stronger, more focused. I can only hope his next offering of food is less stomach-churning.

We stop at a nearby cave, little more than a recess in the rock, and my captor speaks to a slender blue dragon in Dragonish. I have no idea what they're saying to each other. At the back of the recess sits a plump girl, swathed in a scarlet cloak, her cheeks red and her eyes bright. She doesn't look particularly unhappy to be there, which puzzles me. I want to call out to her, but before I can decide what to say, my captor and I leave again.

The black dragon carries me away from the mountainous cliffs and broad plains of the coast, toward the center of the island, where lies a great hollow valley, perhaps the mouth of some ancient, dormant volcano. Smaller gorges and ravines stretch outward from it like the rays of the sun in a child's drawing. The dragon dives toward a blue lake in the middle of the valley.

"This is where we hunt deer," he says. "They are a delicacy, since we try not to enter the forest too often. It's difficult to move through the trees with our size and our wings. Most of our diet is plant life, goats, sheep, or wild pigs. And fish or eels, for those with the skill to catch them. In the meadows to the south we keep a herd of cattle, supervised and protected by a rotating guard. Those are for feast days."

I perk up at that. "You have cows? I want milk."

The dragon swoops lower, over the grassy bank of the lake, and drops me into some ferns before landing nearby. He gives me a stern look. "You would suckle at the udder of a cow?"

"No! I would milk it, I suppose." I've never milked a cow in my life, although I've wanted to try it. I shouldn't appear too eager to do menial tasks, though. I'm supposed to play the part of a demanding, spoiled brat.

Holding my ruined dress in place, I lift my chin haughtily. "What about the other women your dragons took? Have one of them milk a cow for me. I am a princess, after all."

"So you keep saying." His upper lip curls, revealing the glint of huge fangs. "Bathe, human. You stink of vomit."

"Maybe I like to stink."

"You don't. You smelled delightful yesterday, so I assume that when you have the choice, you prefer to be clean and fragrant. Remove those rags and wash yourself."

Before answering, I survey my surroundings. Thick, soft grass caresses my toes. It's so much greener and richer than the closely trimmed stuff in the palace gardens. I used to run barefoot on that grass whenever I got the chance, though I was usually rebuked by one of my mother's sycophants—I mean, "ladies of the court."

I can run on the grass barefoot as much as I want here. And the air is far sweeter and cleaner than the air of the capital. The glassy surface of the lake reflects the azure sky overhead, and the nearby forest rustles in the breeze, each green leaf quivering as if it's delighted to exist in the broad sunlight and the mountain air.

Clear lake water laps at the pebbled beach, turning the stones shiny and dark. A little further in, the pebbles give way to sandy shallows, perfect for easing the pain of weary feet and bruised limbs.

I feel wretched, soiled, and grimy. And that cool water looks inviting, even though I'm a little nervous about what creatures might wriggle beneath the waters.

"Are there leeches in there? Eels? Snakes?" I ask. "What about other creatures? Is it slimy?"

"It's safe. Now be quiet, and clean yourself."

"I will bathe, but not in front of you."

"Why not?"

"I don't want you to see me naked."

He adjusts his wings, pinning them close to his sides. "Again, why not?"

"Because…" Fuck, I've never had to explain this before. "I don't want you to see my body and desire me."

He snorts. "I can see you right now. There is nothing desirable about you."

"You haven't seen all of me."

"And seeing you unclothed would make a difference?" he says dryly. "You think a few bits of pasty human flesh would send me into a mating frenzy?"

"Well, when you put it like that, I suppose not. But for human males, the sight or even the hint of such things is usually enough to spur sexual desire."

"Dragons do not experience such feelings, except every twenty-five years, during mating season," he replies. "At that time, every dragon past their twenty-fourth year goes into heat for one week, and we couple to produce eggs."

Surprise shocks me out of my discomfort. "You don't have sex at any other time?"

"No."

"What about with spouses or partners?"

"Most of us choose a mate with whom to raise hatchlings and share a life. That partner may or may not be one of the dragons we spawn with during mating season. Choosing one's partner is about mental synergy and character compatibility, not the passion of mating."

"Sounds like a very cerebral process. What about love? Do dragons fall in love?"

He glances away. "Some do."

"So if I undress, you won't be tempted to any kind of sexual aggression. Not until this mating season occurs," I say cautiously. There's hope in that idea. A reprieve. A chance to escape.

"That is correct," says the dragon. "Mating season will begin in about a week, when the Rib Moon shines."

One week. It's better than nothing. At least I don't have to fear a brutal breeding session until then.

"Very well." I tug at the remnants of my soiled dress. It doesn't take much for them to fall away. I stand naked in the sunshine, all except for my lacy underwear.

The dragon eyes me, blinking. So far his inflections and expressions have been human enough for me to interpret them, but I have no idea what he's thinking now.

Slowly I slide the underwear off my legs and stand there, utterly bare before him.

He huffs a hot, glowing breath, still staring. His gaze drops to the area between my legs.

"Have you seen a woman's body before?" I ask quietly.

"No." His voice is lower than ever. "It looks soft and fragile, which is unfortunate. But your teats suit you."

A hot flush rises in my face. "That is the most disgusting compliment I have ever received."

He rumbles in his throat, disgruntled. "It wasn't a compliment. Simply a statement of fact. That you are... proportional. At least I think you are. For a human, that is."

"Go away," I snap. "Stop looking at me."

"I must keep watch, since you seem willing to do yourself harm," he replies. "While you bathe, I will search for berries or roots to feed you."

Turning my back on him, I wade into the cool water of the lake. I can feel his eyes on me as I move deeper, as the water rises up to my knees, my thighs, my ass, my waist. Only when I'm shoulder-deep in the lake do I hear the thump of his ponderous steps and the rustle of bushes as he begins to forage for food.

I don't have any soap, and the water is much colder than I expected, but I manage to clean myself, and I work the tangles out of my hair with my fingers until it's reasonably decent. By the time I emerge from the water, I'm shaking from the cold. My skin is stippled with goosebumps and my legs are trembling.

I step onto the beach, expecting—

Fuck. Was I really expecting a maid to greet me with a warm towel and a soft robe? Such luxuries are a thing of the past. The only substantial scrap of clothing available is the ragged, vomit-stained dress I removed before I went into the lake, and I'm certainly not putting that on again. I could try to wash it, but then I'd have to wait for it to dry.

My underwear is still lying on the beach, but when I pick it up, I notice that the backside is coated with wet sand. So that garment is also out of the question.

I'm alone, stark naked and soaking wet, beside a lake in the center of the dragons' domain. And *where* did the black dragon go? Not that he'd be of much help—I doubt there's a chest of women's clothing tucked away in some cleft of his cave.

Maybe I can find some leaves to wrap around myself.

I pick my way across the pebbles to the grass, and from there I walk into the forest. Huge, ancient trees spread a thick canopy overhead, so the undergrowth is minimal. Not far away, some vines with broad arrow-shaped leaves twist around one of the trunks. I head over and reach for them.

"I wouldn't do that." The dragon's voice vibrates through me, right down to my core.

"Why not?"

"Those vines are poisonous. They are lethal to ingest, and if a dragon so much as licks them, his tongue will break out in huge blisters. I assume they would wreak similar havoc on your delicate human skin."

"I need something to cover up with. And I'm freezing." I whirl and glare at him. "You're the worst captor *ever*. Didn't you say you were a prince? If you can't take care of one little human, how on earth do you rule an entire race of dragons?"

"Very poorly, apparently, since half my clan have perished. Now if you're done insulting me—"

"I'm *not* done." Cold and shaky though I am, my anger spurs me on. "If you're going to kidnap someone, you need to know how to keep them alive, do you understand? You brought me here to bathe, yet you didn't provide any clothing or any way for me to get warm afterward. There's no soap, no towels, no hot water. Your cave is uncomfortable and primitive, not fit for the lowliest peasant, let alone a king of dragons. There's no privy, not so much as a wash basin to clean my hands—no pillows, no sheets, no blankets. I've had no food, I'm cold, I'm wet, and I want a cup of fucking *tea*!"

The dragon recoils a little at my vehemence and huffs out a hot, indignant breath of orange mist.

"Go and get me something to wear!" I scream at him.

He backs out of the woods carefully, his wings pinned so they won't bump into the trees. "I set some food on a rock for you, by the lake."

"Is it more raw, bloody meat? Because I refuse to eat that. We humans cook our food. Maybe you've heard of the concept."

"I'm not an idiot," he replies coldly.

"You're doing a marvelous impression of one."

He bares his teeth at me, eyes narrowing. "I collected berries, nuts, and cresslily stalks."

"Wonderful," I spit. "Now I get to choose between eating berries and stalks that may or may not be poisonous for me, or breaking my teeth on some nuts. That's fucking perfect." Arms crossed, I stalk toward the lake.

I've just passed him when something warm and wet glides across my backside. My skin ignites instantly, shock blending with my craving for heat. I whirl around. "Did you *lick* me?"

The dragon's purple tongue glides over his fangs. "No."

"Liar."

"I was only thinking—if you're cold, I can provide heat."

"I need *clothes*. I can't walk around naked like this all the time."

"Can't you?" He blinks slowly at me. "Your form is not unpleasant. Why conceal it?"

"For privacy and protection. Humans don't have hides or scales. Our clothes provide some defense from the elements as well as concealment for our private parts. You dragons hide *your* private parts, don't you?"

"Yes, but I don't mind showing them, if you want to see—"

"No!" I gasp. "No, I'd rather not."

I turn my back on him and head for the bank of the lake. Off to the left, I spot the flat rock where he placed the food he collected, including an assortment of dark blue fruits as big as my fist, which must seem like berries to him. Not a single one of the fruits is smushed, though a few have punctures through their thin skin, thanks to his claws. I pick one up and nibble cautiously. Once the sweet juice hits my tongue, I sink my teeth in with a moan of relief.

The dragon drapes his immense body on the grass, moves his head nearer to me, and opens his jaws, releasing breath after slow breath of hot air.

Gradually the heat sinks into my body, and within moments I've stopped shivering. I actually feel deliciously warm standing here in my bare skin, with the luscious fruit filling my belly and the sugared juice coating my tongue. The nuts are tasty as well, with frail shells that easily yield the meat within. The stalks the dragon gathered are fibrous, but they have a decent flavor.

"This will do, for now," I tell him. "But you'll have to learn how to feed me properly. And what about the other women? Are they being fed?"

"I'll see to it that they are." The dragon's nostrils flare slightly. "Spare clothing will be arriving soon. Contrary to your low opinion of me, I do have some common sense. Ashvelon and Fortunix will bring supplies when they return with the enchantress."

"The enchantress?"

He doesn't seem to hear my question. "Your scent is much more enticing now." His thick, forked tongue flickers out again. "You are calm and happy, yes?"

"Calm, fed, and warm. Not happy. Not until you let me go."

He sighs, and the intense gust of heat makes me jump back with a yelp.

"My apologies," he rumbles. "But I've explained why I cannot let you go. You are here to participate in mating season."

Despair clutches my heart again. How can someone so intelligent be so very bone-headed? Maybe a visual demonstration is in order. After all, it's not only my life at stake, but the lives of the other women the dragons kidnapped.

"As I told you before, it won't fit." I prop my butt against a rock and arch one leg, my foot planted against the stone. I open my thighs, giving the dragon a full view of my pussy. With my fingers I pull back the lips of my sex. "Human women have three holes. A tiny one at the front for pissing, another at the back for shitting. You see this? The opening in the middle?"

He makes a choked sort of sound, which I take as a *yes*.

"This one is for sex, and for birthing babies. You must understand now that the holes I have are too small to accommodate a dragon's cock. You'll kill me. You'll kill all of us. Besides which, it's wicked to penetrate or breed someone without their consent."

"I never planned to mate with you in *this* form!" he exclaims. "That's why the enchantress is being brought here—to change you and the other human women into dragons. And even then, no one will force you to breed. The males will court you and perform mating dances for you. Then you may select the male you prefer."

Oh.

I'm relieved there won't be any forced breeding of human women by dragons, and yet—being permanently transformed into a dragon is not necessarily a better prospect.

"You can't do this," I tell him. "You can't transform us into a different species against our will."

"It's an unfortunate necessity."

"There's no enchantress who can perform such magic."

"Yes, there is. Thelise, daughter of your mother's Supreme Sorcerer."

"But she was banished from court years ago, for magical malpractice," I protest. "She's talented, but she's careless. Sometimes her spells go very, very wrong."

"We have no other choice," the dragon replies calmly. "She is the most powerful wielder of magic in this region, and I don't have time to find anyone else. Mating season is nearly upon us."

"Every woman you transform will *hate* you," I say vehemently. "None of us will want to mate."

"Ah, but you will. As dragons, you'll experience the mating frenzy like the rest of us. You won't be able to resist. And if you do resist, we will have twenty-five years to court you and charm you before the next mating season." He glances down between my legs again, and I realize that I've been sitting splayed open during the entire conversation. I pull my thighs together, my thoughts racing.

So he doesn't want to eat me or rape me. He wants to transform all of us into dragons and either couple with us during the mating season or court us for twenty-five years. Unacceptable. Which means I need to go back to my original plan of making myself so unpleasant that the thought of having me around for twenty-five years will make *him* vomit.

I pick up another fruit and snap my fingers imperiously at him. "Go ahead, keep breathing on me. I need more heat, dragon."

9

KYREAGAN

I've been reduced to the role of a fireplace for this smooth-skinned little creature with the abundant yellow hair. The longer I crouch here, breathing on her, watching her skin grow pink with warmth, the more I desire to lick her again. I can't be sure if it's a primal desire for prey, or some other urge with which I'm unfamiliar. Either way, I must not indulge the impulse. I might come too close to gobbling her up.

I imagine it for a second. Not tearing her flesh, but swallowing her down whole, feeling the flutter of her limbs thrashing in my stomach. Her, still alive, inside me. Part of me. It's a dark, hideous thought, born from the deepest chasms of my nature, from some ancient, less civilized aspect of my being.

For generations, dragons have striven to rise above our bestial roots. From the egg we are taught both Dragonish and the Eventongue. We are trained to recite oral histories, poetry, and essays. We write long passages in Dragonish on the walls of caves, and translate them aloud into the Eventongue.

I suppose that is why I thought I knew enough about humans to carry out my plan. I've studied their language and their politics for my entire quarter-century. But my studies did not encompass the small details of their everyday lives, things like tea and soap, their eating habits and their hygiene preferences. A significant oversight, it would seem.

My gaze travels the Princess's body, noting each bruise I caused. Their presence disturbs me. I wish I could heal those damaged places immediately.

"I want more of these." The Princess turns to me and holds up a half-eaten berry. "Fetch me more."

I'm momentarily distracted by the triangle of rosy flesh between her legs—two plump lips with a groove between them. She showed me her genitals earlier, out of sheer panic, and I'm interested in seeing them again. They look far more complex than the mating slit a female dragon possesses.

Now that she knows I would never breed her in this form, she seems shy about her parts again. When she notices me staring, she covers that area with her free hand. "Go fetch me what I want," she snaps.

I prowl away, seething at how she commands me—*me*, a prince of dragons. When I return with another berry, she is rinsing out one of her garments in the lake. She puts the garment on, soaking wet. It mostly conceals her rump and her genitals from me.

"Where are the clothes you promised?" she asks.

"They will be here soon. Tomorrow."

"That's not soon enough. I need something now."

"Perhaps one of the other captives has something you can wear," I say. "Or there may be a remnant of a tapestry somewhere, a bit of sailcloth—"

"You expect me, a *princess*, to wear a bit of sailcloth?" Her blue eyes are wide, her manner haughty and furious. "Go and fetch me a gown, dragon. I demand it. I want a gown, right now. Go find one."

"As Your Highness wishes," I snarl. "I will strip one off the back of another captive if I must."

Her expression changes instantly. The shift is so dramatic that I begin to suspect her complaints and demands are not true to her nature. She's putting on an act, though I'm not sure why.

"Don't strip another captive," she exclaims in a softer tone. "There's no need for that. Just—find me something. Perhaps one of the other prisoners has a spare cloak. Or I suppose I could fashion the overskirt of my gown into some kind of temporary clothing. It's back in your cave."

"We'll go fetch it then. Rothkuri should have finished cleaning up your mess by now."

"Rothkuri—that's the blue dragon you spoke to on the way here?"

"Yes." I don't tell her what else Rothkuri said to me… that he licked his captive and she liked it immensely. He said the more he did it, the more agreeable she was to the idea of remaining with him. His story was the reason I licked the Princess's backside earlier. But the act did not seem to have the same effect on her as it did on Rothkuri's girl. Perhaps I licked her in the wrong place.

"I'd rather not be toted around in your claws," says the Princess. "Is there a place on your back where I could safely ride?"

I lower my body to the ground. "You may look and see."

She approaches me, places her bare foot on my foreleg, and hoists herself up to peer at my back.

Tough as they are, my scales are pressure-sensitive, and the light weight of her foot on my leg sends an unexpected shiver through me. She's touching my neck, too, bracing herself, one small hand splayed over my scales.

Somewhere near the root of my tail, I feel a low, pulsing thrill, and my cock nudges at the slit that conceals it.

This isn't what I feel when I need to piss. It's an altogether different sensation.

"I think there's a spot between two of your spikes where I can sit and hold on," says the Princess. "I'll try to climb up."

She's going to sit on me, astride me, with those delicate genitals pressed right against my scales. Another ripple of sensation passes through my body—a richer, heavier thrill, and my cock swells inside its concealment. If it grows much more, it will emerge from the slit on its own. That's an embarrassment I can't afford.

I rise abruptly, and the Princess tumbles off my leg onto the grass. She looks deeply perturbed.

"I'm carrying you in my claws," I tell her.

She crosses her arms over her bare breasts. "No."

"You cannot refuse me. You are not in control here."

"You *stole* me from my city at a moment of crisis," she retorts. "I don't know the fate of my friends, or any of the good people in the palace, or my mother—" Her voice cracks a little. "You owe me the dignity of being transported the way I prefer."

Grief swallows me up, a cataclysmic tidal wave overwhelming any softer emotion. I lunge for the girl, teeth bared, and I loom over her like the menacing monster I am, like a thunderous mountain of rage. Her face goes white, but she does not cringe, not even when I speak to her in my darkest tones, my jaws a mere breath from her face.

"Your kingdom used to hunt my people, years ago," I growl. "For that alone, you deserved the carnage we wrought upon your armies. As if that wasn't enough, your Supreme Sorcerer killed the grandmother I adored, on whom I counted for advice. He killed my precious sister, without whom my brother and I are utterly lost. He stole my Promised, the warrior dragon who would have been my life-mate. She was more beautiful and powerful than a worm like you could ever be. You and yours have not only doomed my entire race, but ruined my happiness forever. I owe you *nothing*. You are nothing."

It's true. She's a mere mouthful for a creature of my size. I could open my jaws now, nip her into them, crunch her between my teeth.

She stares at me, her chest heaving with terror. But then something changes in her face—her eyes grow softer, warmer. Carefully she places her hand on my nose, right between my nostrils.

For a second I'm frozen. Anchored and paralyzed by that gentle hand.

She doesn't apologize for what her people did to mine. She only touches me, as if that's enough.

It is not enough.

I recoil with a snarl and scoop her up in my front claws as I take to the air.

When we return to the cave, two small chunks are missing from the nest, and the stone floor has been freshly washed.

I drop the girl into the nest. "From now on, if you need to relieve yourself, you will do so in this." With a claw, I drag a shallow clay bowl from the back of the cave. "I will dispose of your leavings as needed."

"Where do dragons relieve themselves?" she asks.

"Sometimes off the edge of a cliff. Usually in the ocean or in some private hollow on the ground, where we can bury it." I lie down across the mouth of the cave with my back to her. "Clothe yourself."

The afternoon sun has warmed the rock, and it seeps through my scales into my bones. I can create my own heat, but it feels good to bask in the delicious warmth.

My father used to tell me that different elements or facets of nature fuel each dragon's power. My ability is bright orange fire, so it makes sense that sunning myself would recharge my energy faster than merely resting. Varex, with his void magic, prefers the moonless dark, and will often go on midnight flights.

The sun may be restoring my magic, but it's also making me sleepy. I am wounded at heart and weary in body, and the little rest I got last night wasn't enough, so when I feel my eyes closing, I don't fight it. My form is blocking the cave entrance. If the Princess heads for the cliff again, I will feel it, and I can stop her. Fortunately she seems less self-destructive now that she understands my true purpose. I should have explained it clearly from the beginning.

But as I said, I owe her nothing.

Bathed in the warm sunshine, I drift into sleep.

Until her voice breaks the silence.

"I once had a wife
Who took my life
And she buried me
Beneath the sea—"

Fuck. Her.

She's singing loudly, jauntily. Disturbing my rest on purpose, as a small means of vengeance.

I will not give her the satisfaction of knowing she woke me up. Although the twitch of my pointed ears may have already given me away.

The Princess continues to sing:

"A sailor caught me in his net
From a boat that he won in a drunken bet
I swallowed his soul
So I could be whole—"

What a foolish tale, and what a stupid song. It goes round and round and there is no end to it, *no end*—who would invent such a despicable means of torture?

> *"Then I went to the tavern to barter for ale*
> *And the barmaid begged, "Will you tell me a tale?"*
> *So I said...*
> *I once had a wife*
> *Who took my life—"*

Every time I begin to doze off again, the Princess changes the pitch or the volume of her voice. At last I can't bear it any longer. I spring up and whip around, my tail lashing, my wings arched, and my jaws clenched.

She's sitting in the nest, clad in ragged fragments of pink silk—one tied around her waist, the other wrapped around her chest. Her eyes are wide with mingled terror and excitement, and she's smiling with triumph at eliciting a reaction from me.

By the bones, she's fucking beautiful.

Words leave my throat in a reflexive snarl. "You disgust me."

Her grin takes on a vicious edge. "Says the disgusting beast."

I prowl toward her slowly, as if I'm approaching prey. "You will stop singing that song."

"Make me."

"Such defiance in one so frail and defenseless."

She draws in a shaky breath as I tower over her and glare down into her eyes. The air around us feels thick and taut, charged with a force like lightning. I don't know what I intend to do. I refuse to damage her, but she makes me so angry that I *need* to do something to her. I want her body between my teeth, under my tongue, pressed along my scales. I admire that bright, vivacious courage of hers, and yet I want her to obey me, to submit.

I lower my nose and skim it along her cheek, letting her feel my hot breath.

"You," I murmur. "You need to be a good fucking girl."

She inhales sharply. Doesn't pull away.

My tongue flickers out and traces along the hot, rosy softness of her cheek. This time the thrill is more powerful, rushing through me from horns to tail.

She begins to sing again, softly. "I swallowed his soul, so I could be whole—"

A growl rips from my chest. "Do you want me to kill you?"

"Maybe." Something haunted flickers in her eyes.

"I don't think you do. You're too full of spirit, of life. You reek of vitality, of virility… something…" I inhale her scent, that fragile sweetness.

"I'm not doing this because I want you to kill me… not anymore. But I want you to suffer. You deserve suffering. All dragons do, for what they have done."

"You hunted us."

"Did we hunt you first? Because I've heard that in centuries past, dragons ate humans. We were tasty little snacks for your kind."

"Tasty… little… snacks," I rumble, sweeping my tongue along her throat. "Keep taunting me, Princess. See what happens."

She's breathing hard and fast, but she tilts her chin up. As if she's allowing me access to her throat.

I nuzzle along the column of her neck, painting it with wet swipes of my tongue. I scarcely know what I'm doing, and I don't understand it. Heat pulsates between us, a hectic hunger, a visceral need.

When she speaks, her voice trembles. "You didn't ally with Vohrain merely out of spite for a past wrong. There must have been something else."

At her perceptive comment, I pause. "Yes. We were struck by a new kind of plague this year, and it decimated the prey throughout this archipelago. The other isles have been stripped of anything but the smallest game."

"The plague traveled between islands? That's rather unusual, isn't it?"

"I suppose so." I never really thought about it before, but it is odd, the way the plague spread so quickly. It wasn't transported by dragons—we would arrive on one of the smaller islands, hoping for prey, only to find that the plague had already wiped out most of the game. Almost as if the disease had a mind of its own, and was attempting to starve us on purpose.

"We have enough food on Ouroskelle to survive, barely," I tell her. "But when the next brood of hatchlings arrives, we must have better hunting grounds, or many of us will starve. Hatchlings grow quickly, and they require large amounts of food to sustain that growth. The well-being of the hatchlings must come before that of the primes and elders."

"The primes are the adult dragons?" She eases back, cautiously moving out of reach of my tongue. "How old are you?"

"I will be twenty-five years old three weeks after the Rib Moon."

"And how long do dragons live?"

"The lucky ones live to a hundred and fifty. Any dragon above eighty years is considered an elder." I am hesitant to tell her more, but since she will soon be a dragon, I suppose it is information she should have. "Elders and primes experience the mating frenzy every quarter century without fail, but we are only fertile for two or three of those cycles. Some dragons mate many times each season and never produce a brood, while others produce one or two eggs, not all of which may hatch."

"And how long does it take for a dragon egg to hatch?"

"They are laid about a week after mating, and they may hatch up to seven days after that. Some eggs take a little longer. My brother was three weeks late, but his was a rare case. Usually by that time, we accept that the egg is not viable."

A twinge of pain enters my heart as I remember my conversation with Varex about his hatching. I long to experience the joy of the hatching days with the members of my clan.

The Princess furrows her small brows. "As I understand it, this will be your first mating season."

"Yes." I draw back from her, feeling suddenly guilty. "I was supposed to experience it with Mordessa, but she is gone now."

"She was your intended?"

"My Promised, yes. She would have been my life-mate."

"So you loved her."

Why does that concept seem so important to everyone? Love, love, fucking *love*... there are other bonds, just as vital.

"I felt admiration for her," I say grimly. "She was strong and intelligent. A skilled warrior and huntress. Beautiful and healthy."

The Princess cocks an eyebrow at me. "Is that all?"

"I told you, not all dragons choose a life-mate based on passion."

"Seems unfortunate. I would think a union of both admiration *and* passion would be ideal."

"Well... yes, I suppose so. Not all are fortunate enough to have that." I think of Mordessa's fathers, the intensity of their connection, the hint of jealousy I felt upon seeing it.

"And you plan to turn all of us into female dragons, after which you will..." her mouth twitches at the corner, "perform mating dances for us? What are these dances like?"

"I feel as though you're mocking me."

"Do you?" She blinks innocently.

"The mating dances are sacred, regal performances."

"I'm sure they are. Will you show me one?"

I move farther from her, growling. "I would not perform a mating dance for you if you were the last female on earth. For now, it is my duty to keep you alive and healthy, but I have decided that when your transformation is complete, you will be put with the other females until the mating frenzy, during which some other male will be your partner. Perhaps his patience will be greater than mine. Or perhaps the change into dragon form will alter your insolent disposition into something more palatable."

I pace toward the mouth of the cave. A moment later, a rock bounces off my side. No more than a pebble, really, but it must have cost the Princess quite the effort to hurl it.

Turning back, I see her standing outside the nest, flushed and furious.

"I do not need to be made *palatable* to you," she says. "And you know nothing about my true disposition."

"I only know what you've shown me. Is there any more to you, besides the girl who soils where she sleeps and fusses constantly about soap and clothing and tea?"

She stands there, fists tight. When she doesn't reply, I turn my back on her again and move into the sunlight.

After several long moments, I hear the faint scuff of her bare feet on the rock, approaching me. She sits down cross-legged at my side, where I can see her out of the corner of my eye.

"I like to read," she says quietly. "I like to memorize poems and songs. All kinds of songs, not just the annoying ones. Sometimes I write my own songs, too, but I never sing them for anyone. I enjoy cooking. I like to sew and embroider. And I like ironing. That's a process for smoothing the wrinkles out of clothes. Most people think it's tedious, but I find it soothing, and I don't mind the heat."

I don't understand what "embroider" means, or why wrinkles must be removed from clothing, but I don't ask.

"I've never been a do-nothing princess," she continues. "I've always liked to help the servants with chores, or with their children. Sometimes they would bring their babies to the palace and I would rock them or play with them while their parents worked. The best age is when the babies begin trying to speak. Their eyes are so bright and they make all these soft, eager, cooing sounds, and they look at you with so much joy and hope. I love little ones. Always have. I love animals, too—dogs and horses. My favorite horse is called Fairweather. She will miss me terribly. I hope the Vohrainians don't ride her too hard and break her spirit."

The quiet sorrow in her voice stirs my own pain, but gently, like a breeze ruffling the grass.

"I always thought I might have been better as a housemaid, not a princess," she murmurs. "I like arranging closets and cabinets. Shaking out the rugs on a fine morning. Sweeping while composing songs in my head. Maybe I was meant to be a peasant wife on some thriving farm, surrounded by sweet, rosy-cheeked babies. Maybe I was born into the palace life by mistake. I've always lacked the keen ambition and the ruthless conviction necessary to be a ruler. That's what my mother thought, anyway. It's the reason she would not tell me much about the war, or ask for my opinions on matters of state, or give me any responsibilities beyond the occasional goodwill mission to visit the poor or the sick. She used me like a toy, to distract and pacify the people. And she probably would have arranged a strategic marriage for me in a year or two, if Elekstan managed to survive the war intact."

"She is stubborn, your mother," I say. "During the weeks we battled for Vohrain, I often wondered why she did not surrender. Your kingdom's defeat was inevitable from the moment we allied with your enemies. If she had yielded, we would not have had to kill so many of your soldiers."

"Her stubbornness may be the one thing I inherited from her," the Princess admits. "You said, she *is* stubborn, not *was* stubborn. Do you think she's still alive? The King of Vohrain promised to imprison both of us rather than kill us, but I would like to know for sure if he spared her."

"I will need to meet with him soon. I can ask him then."

"I would be grateful."

The word "grateful" unsettles me, and it seems to disturb her as well. She gets up, muttering a curse under her breath, and stalks back into the depths of my cave.

We don't speak again. I suppose I should hunt, or visit the clan, but for some reason I cannot make myself leave my lair. The thought of facing the other dragons is unbearable. I'd much rather curl up morosely in my nest and not move, speak, or eat for several days.

But as one of the princes of Ouroskelle, I don't have the luxury of such doleful peace. Issirian appears in the cave mouth not long after my conversation with my captive. He dips his head to me, but I can tell by the stiff position of his neck ridges that he's troubled. He eyes the Princess, skulking in the shadows by the nest, and then speaks to me in Dragonish, apparently not wanting her to hear.

"My prisoner keeps demanding a 'hairbrush.' She's very insistent on it. Do you know what she means?"

"Did you ask her?"

"I don't want her to think me foolish and ill-educated in human lore," Issirian admits. "I want her to admire me."

"Very well..." I cast a sidelong glance at my own captive, but I feel a similar reluctance asking her to define the term. "I would guess that a hairbrush is... a brush... for hair."

"Brush?"

"I saw the Vohrainian soldiers stroking their horses with large wooden paddles covered in bristles. They called those 'brushes.'"

"A large paddle covered in bristles." Issirian nods eagerly. "I saw a broken boat paddle on the northwest beach. Must have washed up during a shipwreck. I think I can fashion something out of that. Thank you, my Prince."

After he leaves, I crawl into the nest, only to climb out again so I can properly greet the next arrival—Rorris, an ivory-colored dragon with scarlet wings.

"My Prince." He too speaks in Dragonish. "My woman has been crying ever since I took her to my cave. Can humans perish from crying? I don't know how to make it stop."

"Perish from crying? No, I don't believe that's possible. But since she is losing liquid from her eyes in such quantities, you should make sure she drinks plenty of water."

"Saltwater?" suggests Rorris. "Tears are salty. Perhaps she needs to drink seawater to replenish her body's saltwater supply."

"I think spring water will do the trick. But perhaps you could try saltwater and see how she reacts."

"I will, thank you."

After he leaves, I enjoy nearly an hour's reprieve before Gavenath explodes into my cave, his purple tail lashing anxiously as he exclaims in Dragonish, "My captive is bleeding!"

"Bleeding? Did you injure her? Bite her?"

"No, my Prince."

"Where is the injury?"

"Between her legs. She does not seem concerned, but I can smell the blood. I believe she has placed bandages inside her clothing to staunch it, but from what I can tell, it continues to flow."

"Does she seem to be in pain?"

"She seems angry. No matter what I do, she yells and curses me."

"Make her lie in your nest and rest," I tell him. "Cover her with extra grass to keep her warm, and bring her plenty of berries for sustenance. If the bleeding continues, tell her you need to inspect the wound to ensure it is not fatal."

"And if she won't allow me to inspect it?"

"Then return to me, and I will bring the Princess to your cave. Perhaps your captive will let a fellow human examine her."

Gavenath thanks me and flies away. I don't bother settling down in my nest again. I have a feeling it will be a long day.

10

SERYLLA

I don't know why I said "grateful" when the dragon offered to find out the truth of my mother's fate. I could never be grateful to someone like him, no matter what scraps of news he might deign to bring me. And what was I thinking, letting him nuzzle me and lick my neck? At first I thought he might actually eat me… and then I couldn't think clearly about anything, because his damp, velvety tongue was stroking my skin, and his deep voice was throbbing in my blood, thrumming and thrilling all the way down to my—

God, no. No, no, no.

I did the right thing putting distance between us. I can't allow him to get that close to me again.

The afternoon and evening pass slowly. Dragons stop by the cave several times to converse with my captor in Dragonish. They always lower their heads in deference to him before starting to speak. It seems they are bringing him problems and concerns to solve, which he addresses in a calm, steady tone. Each visitor leaves the cave reassured.

I hate to admit it to myself, but he seems like a decent ruler... except for the widespread slaughter of my people, of course. But as he said, my mother is somewhat to blame for that. Her pride would not allow her to yield, not even when our doom was certain.

The last visitor of the day arrives at sunset. It's Rothkuri, the blue dragon whose captive seemed far more content than I am. A delicious fragrance precedes his arrival, and when he lands, I can't help hurrying forward. He carries a cloth bundle between his jaws, and when he sets it down and scrapes back the fabric with one claw, a hunk of roasted meat tumbles out.

A cry of eagerness breaks from me before I can stop it. The meat is still hot, its juices steaming.

"My Prince, this venison was prepared by some of the women," he says in the Eventongue. "It's for your treasure." He bows his head to me.

Treasure? I like that better than "captive."

"She's not my treasure," growls the black dragon.

I return Rothkuri's bow. "Here's someone who knows how to treat a woman," I say pointedly. "You have my thanks."

The blue dragon's eyes brighten, and he moves forward with sinuous grace. If I didn't know better, I'd say there was a lustful light in his gaze, a suggestive flair in the way his tongue darts between his fangs when he says, "You are most welcome, Your Loveliness. If there's anything I can do to help you feel more comfortable, more welcome—"

"Enough," snarls my captor. "Leave the meat, and see to your own woman."

"Of course, my Prince." With another dip of his head to me, Rothkuri flies away.

I seize the meat at once and take a bite. It's delicious, seasoned with herbs.

"They shouldn't be pampering their women like this," says my captor. "You must all learn to consume your meat raw, as dragons do."

"Why must we learn it *now*? There's plenty of time for that after we become dragons—if we ever do." I take another bite, moaning a little at the flavor of the venison.

The black dragon watches with narrowed eyes. "Next time, I will cook your meat for you, with my fire."

"You think I want meat that's been charred black by your dragon-breath? No, thank you."

"You're very picky."

"Is it picky to want edible food?" I raise my eyebrows at him. "Perhaps you should fly off to the other caves and see how your people are treating their women. Apparently some of them are much better at it than you."

"And some are far worse," he retorts. "I'm leaving to hunt. Don't destroy yourself while I'm out."

"Clearly I'm interested in surviving, at least until I've finished this meal. Go on, and stay out as late as possible. I'll sleep better without your stench befouling the place."

He rears back with an offended snort. "I do not have a stench."

"I'm just saying, one of us bathed today, and one of us didn't. You smell like raw goat and old saddle… and dirt."

He hisses at me, and I hide my grin by taking another bite of roasted venison. With my mouth full, I say, "Before you go, I need a source of light and heat. Fetch me some wood for a fire."

"I have dyre-stones here in the cave. I can heat one of those for you."

"I don't know what a dyre-stone is, but I want a fire. A crackling, popping fire that smells good and is fun to watch. Make me a fire."

"You misunderstand your situation," he replies. "You seem to be laboring under the delusion that I must provide you with everything you want, and obey your every demand. That is not the case at all."

"Fine. The next time I see one of your fellow dragons, I'll make it known how poorly their leader is treating me. Perhaps one of them will adopt me and care for me as I deserve."

"What you deserve," he snarls, "is a dark pit full of stagnant water and blood-beetles, you little irritant. You're such a nuisance, it's no wonder your mother didn't—" He cuts himself off, but it's too late. I can guess what he was about to say.

Fuck. Him.

I opened up to him a little, and he used my confession to wound me. He's beating me at my own game.

I set the meat back on its cloth wrapping, wipe my mouth on the back of my hand, and draw myself up to my full height. "What I deserve is to live my life the way I choose, instead of being subjected to a magical transformation without my consent. If you think forcing the females of another species to become dragons is being a good prince, you're wrong. In fact, I think you're quite possibly the worst ruler your clan has ever had. You involved them in a war, got half of them killed, then ordered the other half to become the kidnappers of helpless women. You have failed them. And because you led your clan to war, the deaths of the female dragons—your Promised, your grandmother, your sister—they're *all your fault.*"

I did it. I hurt him back. I see it in the flare of his eyes, the orange glow of his nostrils. Dragonesque though his features are, I can read them as clearly as I can read my own heart. I know the signs of internal agony.

Regret rushes through me almost immediately. Not because he doesn't deserve the pain, but because I don't want to become the person I'm pretending to be—selfish, demanding, callous and cruel.

Why am I even doing this? It seemed like the ideal strategy at first, but now, with what I know of the situation—is this even the right tactic? What do I truly gain by taunting him, other than a perverse satisfaction?

The black dragon doesn't say a word. A moment later he dives off the ledge and soars away into the darkening sky.

Well... I fucked that up. No way is he bringing me firewood now. I'm alone in the cave, gazing out at mountains clothed in purple shadow.

I could swear I hear music echoing from somewhere far below. Cautiously I crawl to the edge of the cliff and peer down. Sure enough, there are two campfires glowing like fireflies.

The other kidnapped women are celebrating, or at least putting on a brave face during their captivity. I'm sure they don't want to stay here and turn into dragons, so they must have some alternate strategy for getting themselves out of this. Or perhaps the people of my city were worse off than I thought, and escaping right before Vohrain's final invasion felt like salvation to them. I can't be sure, because I can't reach the women, or speak to them.

The dragon's comment about my mother, coupled with the sight of the campfires, wrecks me. I've only cried a little since my capture, but I've been growing more and more brittle inside. Bantering with the dragon distracted me today, but he's gone now, and there's no one to defy or to tease. Nothing to take my mind off my wretchedness.

A desolate thread of music twines through my heart—the sigh of strings, the hollow murmur of pipes, and the distant voice of a woman mourning in clear, wistful notes. Sobs swell in my lungs, pressing outward. I try to hold them in, but that only makes them uglier when they explode out of my throat, horrible and jagged. My whole body convulses while tears trail down my cheeks and drip from my chin. I bow over against the stone floor, weeping.

A heavy, rhythmic sound penetrates my thoughts. Wingbeats.

The black dragon sweeps into the cave before I can pull myself together. I look up at him, my face slicked with tears.

He opens his claws, and a bunch of dry sticks roll onto the floor. He nudges them into a pile with his snout, blows a puff of superheated air to set them alight, then takes off again without a word.

I stare at the flickering fire, dumfounded.

After what I said to him about his loved ones… he brought the firewood anyway.

I scoot toward the fire, collecting my remaining hunk of meat. I nibble at it while the tears dry on my cheeks. I still ache inside, but the sharpest pain has eased, salved by that simple act of kindness.

Slowly, my energy and my courage return. My interest was piqued when the dragon pulled the clay bowl from some inner recess of his lair, so once I've finished my meal, I explore the cave more thoroughly by the flickering light of the fire. In a cleft at the back of the cave, I find several rudimentary clay bowls. One bowl contains multicolored seashells, while three others are overflowing with pieces of expensive-looking jewelry. A small dish contains the teeth of numerous animals—predators, I think. I recognize the fangs of vipers, the triangular teeth of sharks, and the canines of some wolflike creature.

Nearby lies a thick cord woven of grass or seaweed, with bones tied to it. I suspect they are the claws, toe-bones, vertebrae, or teeth of dragons. Each one bears symbols like the ones that decorate the cave. They look like relics—recent ones, I would guess. Perhaps they're from some of the deceased female dragons. The prince did mention something about "collecting bone-tribute from the dead."

On a stone shelf chiseled into the wall sits an enormous tooth etched with symbols, and beside it rests a large ebony claw, with white markings scratched onto its surface. Bits of shiny shells and a few coins are scattered around the tooth and the claw.

I recognize a shrine when I see one. But these losses aren't recent—there's a light coating of dust on the objects. Perhaps these came from his parents. He and his siblings obviously inherited the leadership of this island, so their parents must have died.

My gaze drops to the clay bowls again. I suppose the dragons occasionally need to store things. With their forepaws and talons they could fashion these rudimentary dishes, and with their heated breath, they wouldn't need a kiln to fire the pottery.

The discovery of the relics sobers me, and I return to the nest burdened by the thought of all the deaths caused by the war. I begin to imagine that I hear the rattle of wing-bones and the hiss of spectral dragons, tethered to this world by the mementos their prince has kept. The eerie tune my mind generates to accompany my morbid fantasy doesn't help matters.

When the black dragon returns, I'm actually relieved to see him. The fire is low—thank god he came back before it went out, or I might have perished from fear of ghost-dragons.

He stands on all fours on the opposite side of the fire and flares his wings a bit to catch the residual heat. The hollows beneath his wing joints look rather damp, and his scales are shinier than usual.

"Did you bathe?" I ask.

He gives me the side-eye and shakes himself slightly before prowling over to the nest. He prods at the gaps where the soiled chunks were removed, clearly irritated by the resulting asymmetry. But he gives up his fussing after a few moments and curls up in the nest, his thorny black tail draped over the edge, trailing on the stone.

Apparently we're sharing the nest tonight. Which isn't a problem, since it was built to accommodate two adult dragons and a hatchling or two—but somehow, lying down near him feels too vulnerable. Too intimate. I can't stop thinking about how he licked my cheek, my neck—*be a good fucking girl*—

Oh god.

I hate him, hate hate *hate*.

I shift over in the nest until I'm on the opposite side from him, and I lie down at the very edge, right where the grasses are banked and woven to form the rim. Dragons are like big birds with their nesting habits, but they also resemble lizards, and sometimes the way the prince moves is downright catlike in its fluid grace.

He's watching me with golden eyes. "Are you cold?"

"No." But I am chilly. Despite the spring warmth we enjoyed today, we're high up, on an island, in a cave that's breezy more often than not. I'm wearing a scrap of cloth tied over my breasts and another wrapped around my waist. Not much protection against the elements. I can't help longing for the soft, downy depths of my royal bed back home.

"You are cold," says the dragon firmly. "Come here."

"Why?"

"You can lie against my belly and feel my warmth."

Oh, fuck no. That is not happening.

"I don't think so." My voice sounds high and fake, even to me. "I'm very comfortable right here."

"Princess." His tone deepens, rumbling with command. "Come to me."

"I don't want to lie against you, or be near you at all. At least grant me that choice. You've taken everything else."

Silence. The fire gives a final glimmer and a spark before the last stick crumbles into ash.

The dragon speaks, low and weary. "Do you want me to let you all go? You want me to find women who would agree to become dragons?"

"Yes."

"And how many humans do you think would be willing to go through that transformation, to save our species?"

I grimace in the dark. "I'm sure there are some."

"Precious few, I'd wager. We don't have time to seek out the willing ones, or to persuade the unwilling."

"Can't you wait to mate until the next season?"

"The mating frenzy is a powerful compulsion. We have some control over it, but dragons who do not mate during their heat lose some of their power. Their magic abates, and they become more vulnerable to sickness."

"That's not fair."

"Life rarely is. We are civilized in many ways, yet we remain trapped by the impulse to breed. Even pairings of the same gender mate during the heat, though they do not produce eggs."

I lie still, pondering. "What of those who prefer not to choose a gender? I had a friend in the palace who did not like to limit themself to a single gender expression."

"Those cases are rare among dragons," he replies. "Dragons choose the gender they prefer while inside the eggs, and they hatch once their preference is established."

"And if they change their minds later?"

"Then we refer to them in whatever way they choose, regardless of their biological appearance. It is no business of mine what parts reside in a dragon's pouch."

"And none of you have sex except during the mating season, every twenty-five years?" I ask.

"Correct."

"That would be difficult for humans. Most of us enjoy having sex often, or at least pleasuring ourselves frequently, even if we don't have a partner."

His yellow eyes blink. "How is it possible to achieve pleasure without a partner?"

He has some kind of night vision—can he see how deeply I'm blushing? I got myself into this, so I suppose I had better explain. "Men stroke their cocks with their hands to achieve a pleasurable release. And women have areas that are sensitive as well. The parts I showed you today… those are sensitive, both on the outside and the inside. Right at the front we have a tiny nub, like a very small berry, or a peaked bit of flesh. It looks different on every woman, but when manipulated, it feels wonderful."

"How is it manipulated?"

"Usually with the fingers when one is alone, or with the mouth and tongue of a partner, until the climax is reached, and then… god, it's a delicious feeling. We call it an orgasm." My own words are sending me into a state of heated arousal. I can feel wetness slipping between my legs. If I wasn't lying in a dragon's nest right now, I would be touching myself.

"And that delicious sensation would make you happy, contented, and comfortable?" asks the dragon.

He's getting far too interested in this topic. "Yes, but sexual pleasure doesn't solve problems or give lasting comfort. It's only temporary."

"All comfort is temporary. That doesn't make it worthless." His great body shifts, rustling in the nest. "Show me this part of you again. I will use my tongue to make you content and comfortable."

"No!" I squeak, pinning my legs together. "That sort of thing isn't done between dragons and humans, and certainly not between enemies."

"And why not?"

Why not? demands my body. *Why the fuck not?*

"It's wrong," I whisper. "Like it would be wrong for me to let a horse or a wolf fuck me."

"But I wouldn't be fucking you, only licking you. And I'm not a beast, not in that way. I have higher thought."

"No, I—it's not that. You're obviously very intelligent, and—shit, it's not even about mental acuity—"

"It is because we are enemies. You despise the idea of my tongue on your genitals because you hate me."

For a moment I picture myself spread wide in the nest, with the dragon's tapered muzzle between my legs, his tongue sliding out from between his jaws, slipping inside me...

My pussy flutters desperately. It's all I can do not to press my hand over it.

"You should touch yourself, if that would bring you comfort and pleasure," says the dragon.

"I can't do that with you here. It would be inappropriate."

"So many rules," he mutters. "If dragons had such parts, and such inclinations, we would take full advantage of them. Life is difficult enough without denying oneself simple pleasures."

"What qualifies as a simple pleasure for you?"

"A flight at sunset. A good haunch of venison. Plunging through the surf on the beach at dawn." He heaves a great sigh. "Vylar—my sister—she loved the beach."

"I don't know if my mother liked the beach or not. Occasionally she would send me there with a governess, some guards, and a few maids. Sometimes she let me choose a couple daughters of the local nobles to go along. But she never came with us."

We both fall silent for so long that I'm sure he must have fallen asleep. But he gives another sigh, raw with pain and restlessness. His movements in the nest are jerky, frustrated. I recognize that feeling all too well, when you crave sleep and it's cruelly elusive.

His sigh gives me a reason to yield to the wicked desires coursing through my body. An excuse to let myself do something truly perverse.

"Would it give *you* comfort, if I let you lick me?" I ask softly.

He goes still. "It would be a welcome distraction from my thoughts."

"If I let you do this, you can't tell anyone. Not your fellow dragons, or any of the captives."

"I swear on my father's bones."

My fingers find the scrap of skirt I fashioned for myself. I draw it up to my waist, then lift my ass and slip off my underwear. "Come on, then," I whisper.

The sound of his huge body moving ponderously across the nest almost makes me retract my consent. But as I arch my legs and spread my thighs, I place my fingertips lightly over my sex. It's slick and warm, so sensitive that I moan aloud.

"Did I step on you?" The dragon's voice is tinged with horror.

"No," I assure him. "I make noises like that when I'm being pleasured. Many people do."

"I've heard that dragons make strange sounds during mating, as well." His voice comes from between my bent knees, and I gasp a little, startled by how quickly he moved into position. Other than the gleam of his yellow eyes, I can only see the faintest outline of his bulk in the dark.

"Be gentle, please be gentle," I whimper. "No teeth, only your tongue."

"Only my tongue," he promises. His voice is so big, so deep, so rich with darkness and throaty fire that I quiver with anticipation. I grip my knees, holding my legs pinned back, trembling. Waiting.

His tongue slithers over my sex, and I lose my mind. A sharp cry of utter ecstasy breaks from my mouth.

He withdraws. "Was that wrong?"

"No, no, it was perfect. Do it again. Over and over. Oh fuck!" I gasp as his enormous tongue strokes me. It's *forked,* god, it's forked and it's wriggling, probing along the lips of my sex, gliding along my slit. "God, yes... Taste me, play with me..."

I'm shaking, more alive with need than I have ever been in my entire life. I've had sex with men twice—once with a nobleman's quiet, studious son whom I could trust not to boast about it, and once with the male servant of a visiting prince from the south. I regretted that second one. And I may regret this as well, but I'm not physically or mentally capable of changing my mind now. I want pleasure too badly.

His tongue withdraws again, and I whimper in protest. "Why did you stop?" Sudden uncertainty clutches my heart. "Do I taste bad to you?"

"You are the most delicious thing I've had the pleasure of savoring," he says. "But I wanted to ask you to show me the part you spoke of. The small bud you mentioned."

"My clit," I whisper. "It's here." I place my fingertip on it.

His tongue flows along my pussy again, gliding up to the place I've indicated. He splits his tongue and curls the tip of one part over my clit, while the other part strokes me gently.

"Oh god," I choke out.

His tongue vanishes. "You mention god frequently. What god do you worship?"

"This is *definitely* not the time for a religious discussion."

"Very well." He licks me again, a quick brush this time, and I vent a soft scream. I'm hypersensitive, sweating, agonized, starving for the climax. He keeps playing with me, licking and stroking until I think I will go mad, but I can't get the pressure I need.

"Put your tongue inside me," I plead. "Here. Please, here. Deep, deep."

His tongue plunges into my entrance, writhing deep inside me. I scoot toward him, grip two of the spikes on his jaw, and pull myself right against his muzzle. With his tongue rippling in my core, and the ridge of his scaly lip pressed firmly over my clit, I come. It's the crashing climax of a beautiful song, a crescendo of magnificent music, and I whimper with sheer breathless ecstasy while the dragon's long jaws nestle between my legs and his tongue flexes inside my pussy.

He rumbles low in his chest, and the vibration races into my body through that glorious tongue, teasing out every last bit of pleasure from the orgasm. I'm left nearly senseless, entirely sated, and helplessly limp as his tongue emerges. He lifts his head, his yellow eyes shining down at me.

"I felt you tremble inside. I tasted the difference in your flavor when you reached the climax you spoke of—the orgasm. Do you feel comforted?"

"I feel amazing," I murmur.

"Rothkuri said his female responded well to licking." Satisfaction colors the dragon's tone. "I'm pleased I found the right spot. We will do this often, to keep you docile."

To keep me... docile?

I'm on my feet in a second—a little wobbly from the orgasm and the springy surface of the nest—but fury holds me upright. "We will *not* be doing this again. And it's not some magic spell to make me docile."

"But—"

"You had to ruin it, didn't you? You couldn't let me enjoy the moment, you had to say something horrible and condescending. I will never let you taste me again!"

The glow from the dragon's nostrils intensifies. "I don't understand why you're angry."

"Of course you don't. You're just a dragon."

"Fuck, you're impossible," he snarls, and he vomits a sudden blast of fire at the ceiling of the cave.

I shriek and crouch down in the nest. His fire is hotter than normal—I can tell by the way my skin tightens immediately, by the way the rocks overhead continue to glow red-hot for several seconds. In that bloody light he is terrifying, his long neck and triangular head crowned by those two vicious horns.

"What do you want from me?" he bellows.

"I want you to let me go!" I scream back.

"No." He crouches, prowling closer, his eyes molten. "You are mine. I have nothing left but this—to ensure that dragonkind survives. I swore a bone-oath to my father as he lay dying. I am compelled to protect this clan, do you understand? I must do whatever it takes." His deep voice breaks. There is such desperation in it that my anger fades.

"Is this any way to start a new generation?" I ask him. "By forcing us to participate in the mating season?"

"You will not be forced. In dragon form you will feel the urge—you will be eager to participate."

"You can't see that this is wrong, can you?"

"Sometimes what is wrong is necessary. Like the war. A ruler may hate what has to be done, but he does it anyway."

I dig my nails into my palms, trying to contain my frustration. Screaming at him won't help.

"You remind me of my mother," I say quietly.

"I am nothing like the fucking Queen of Elekstan," he hisses.

"You're more like her than you want to admit."

"Enough of this." He throws himself down onto the nest, and my body bounces a little from his impact on the thick, matted grass. "Sleep."

"I will, but not because you tell me to." A childish thing to say, I suppose, but I need every bit of agency I can grasp.

"No singing," he warns.

A short silence, wherein I believe he realizes his mistake.

I clear my throat. "I once had a wife who took my life…"

11

Kyreagan

The Princess's voice lulled me to sleep last night. It grew softer after about a dozen verses, her weariness overcoming her desire to annoy me. She is still sleeping this morning when I leave my cave and fly down to the cavern on the ground, where some of my dragons have corralled their women.

Back when we used the cave for flocks, we erected a barrier of stones and fallen trees around the entrance, to keep away the fenwolves. Now the space within serves as a courtyard of sorts, big enough to accommodate the women, several dragons, and two campfires.

I land in the courtyard, startling three women who are busy roasting strips of pork on pointed sticks over the fire. On a mat of woven grass, they have set out a bowl of berries, another bowl of wild grains, and a pot of milk. One of the dragons must have flown his woman over to the herds on the south side of Ouroskelle, to fetch the milk. The sight disturbs me because it seems to corroborate what the Princess said—that the other males are caring for their prisoners better than I am.

"It's the prince," whispers one of the women loudly to the other two. All three of them bow to me, a human sign of respect. I can't deny that their deference feels good after being treated with such disdain by the Princess. I'm becoming more sensitive to the charms of human females, and these three are all pleasing to the eye in different ways.

"Are you well?" I ask them gruffly.

"Well enough," says a woman with scarlet hair. She's the one who recognized me, and unless I'm mistaken, she's the one Varex chose. He must have brought her down here to be with the rest of her kind.

Perhaps I should do the same with the Princess. Without me around, she would have to find someone else to annoy. She has vowed that I won't taste her again, so perhaps it's best for both of us that we exist separately. If I keep living with her alone, I'm not sure I can resist tasting her. Last night, when I was licking her, I experienced the most thrilling sensations in my body, especially centered in my genital area. My cock even extruded from its slit, there in the dark—something it has never done unless I intended to piss. This time the feeling was altogether different—a hard, hot, swollen, delicious ache, a need beyond words. I crave that feeling, and I crave the taste of the wetness I found between the Princess's legs.

But I must think of her well-being. Much as I might hate her, we will have to exist in the same clan for the rest of our lives, so I should try to make peace. Her mood might improve if she doesn't have me around as a constant reminder of what she has lost. As she told me so boldly yesterday, all of this is my fault. The least I can do is provide her with a more comfortable living arrangement than my nest.

I enter the cavern where the women are staying. They have lined the walls with grass pallets, one for each woman. Someone is clearly in charge here. Varex's girl, perhaps?

At the back of the cavern is a stream, one of many springs within these mountains. Its waters form a clear pool in the gloom. As I prowl forward, someone screams and several naked women scramble to cover themselves. Apparently I interrupted their bathing hour.

I whirl around and bound out of the cavern. The red-haired woman by the fire looks up at me, a smirk on her sharp, pale face.

"You didn't warn me," I growl at her.

"Who am I to tell a prince where he can and cannot go?" she retorts.

"You belong to Varex, do you not?"

Her eyes flash with vicious fire. "I belong to no one."

So this girl has the same spirit as my Princess. It might be dangerous for the two of them to live here together. With their quick minds and determination, they might figure out a way to escape their fate, after all.

Perhaps I won't leave my captive here overnight. But I will bring her here for a meal, at least.

"Save some of the food for the Princess." I leap into the air, skimming over the barrier and mounting into the sky.

Morning light fills the cave when I return. The rays don't reach the nest, but the soft glow illuminates the Princess as she lies there on her side, relaxed, one of her long legs draped over the other. I like the arch of her hip, the way her body dips down to her waist, then rises again to her shoulder. Peace smooths her brow, which is so often puckered with anger when she's awake. Her lips are plush and pink.

Mine.

The word is involuntary, and I revolt against it. She is *not* mine. I refuse to accept her as mine. When she and the others are transformed, I will neither dance for her nor surrender my body to her.

A dragon may couple with any willing partner during the heat, whether he chooses them as a life-mate or not. But I prefer my first coupling to be with someone I respect and trust. A strong, worthy warrior like Mordessa. Not this demanding princess who wishes she had been born as a farm girl. Not this perceptive woman who cuts so deeply with her words.

"Wake up!" My command is almost a roar, and the Princess nearly jumps out of her skin. She startles upright, her yellow hair sticking out in clumps, her blue eyes huge and stunned.

"Shit!" she exclaims. "What is wrong with you?"

Something warm expands inside me, swelling into a deep chuckle. Not a chuckle—a full laugh that rolls out between my jaws.

"You idiot," she gasps. "You scared me on purpose. Just for that, I'm peeing on the nest again."

"Do that, and I won't take you to breakfast."

Her interest is piqued. I almost laugh again at the look of curious hunger on her face.

"Go away for a few minutes while I take care of certain needs," she says. "I'll do it properly, not in the nest."

"Perhaps I should watch you to be sure."

"No."

I leave for a short flight, gliding up into the bright morning air and wheeling around half a dozen times before descending again.

When I return, the Princess has straightened her scraps of clothing, put on her slippers, and smoothed her hair. "I'm ready."

I lie down on the floor of the cave. "Climb up."

"Really?" She eyes me doubtfully.

"I won't offer again."

She climbs onto my back, settling herself between two of my spikes. Her light, warm weight, the squeeze of her legs around the base of my neck, the knowledge that her sensitive parts are pressed against my scales—it affects me as deeply as I feared it would. To distract myself from my cock and its immediate response, I begin repeating her cruel words in my mind.

I think you're quite possibly the worst ruler your clan has ever had. Getting them involved in a war, getting half of them killed, and forcing them to become the monstrous kidnappers of helpless women. You have failed them. And the deaths of the female dragons—that's all your fault.

It does the trick, softening the urgency of the thrills running through my belly. Still, it's best to keep this flight short.

"Hold on," I tell her, and I dive, heading straight for the ground.

The Princess grabs two of my spikes and shrieks as we plunge down. When I level out, right before crashing into the earth, she gasps and yanks on my spikes like a human rider jerking the reins of a restive horse.

"Stop it," I snarl.

"Then stop scaring me on purpose."

"I always fly this way."

"No, you don't. You flew straight down just to frighten me."

"Fine. It was a little on purpose."

"Bad dragon," she growls, and I feel another laugh glowing in my chest. I hold it in this time.

As we glide over the wall into the courtyard where the other human women are gathered, the Princess makes a sound so full of delight and longing that my heart twinges with guilt at not letting her see her people sooner.

She slides off my back before I've found my footing. The redhead approaches her first, and when she bows, the rest of the women follow her lead.

"Princess Serylla," says the redhead.

So my captive's name is Serylla. I've never heard her mentioned as anything but "the Crown Princess."

Serylla. It's a good name, with music in it. It will serve her well when she takes dragon form.

"I'm so glad to see you all." Serylla reaches out both hands to the women. "Please don't bow. Here, we are the same. Are you well?"

"Well enough, considering," replies the redhead. She glances past Serylla, straight at me. Her look is a challenge.

"What is your name?" I ask her.

Serylla whips around, frowning, and it occurs to me that I never asked about *her* name.

"I am Jessiva," the redhead answers. "Your Highness." She dips her head, a faint acknowledgement of my title.

"Call me Kyreagan." I keep my eye on Serylla to see how she reacts to my display of obvious preference for the redhead, Jessiva.

Serylla meets my gaze, then glances away, her lips pressed tightly together as if she's holding back sharp words.

A shadow falls over the courtyard, and my brother drops into its center, landing near Jessiva. Holding my gaze, the redhead takes one step backward, closer to my brother's shoulder.

So she prefers him. Fair enough.

For his part, Varex looks surprised. He glances from me to Jessiva, but he only says, "Ashvelon and Fortunix have returned."

A bolt of excitement flares through my body. "And were they successful in their mission?"

"Yes. They await us in Ashvelon's cave."

I turn to Serylla, who is watching us both with furrowed brows and folded arms. "This is my brother, Varex. He and I are leaving now. Eat, rest, and speak to your people. I will return later."

"Don't hurry back," she snaps, an echo of what she said to me yesterday evening, when I went out to hunt.

I want to hiss at her, but since we're in the presence of others, I restrain myself. With a mighty lunge, I bound into the air and rise with powerful wingbeats, taking a vengeful delight as the wind of my ascent whips her hair across her face and makes her stagger back a step.

Varex joins me in the air. "What was that about?"

"The Princess hates me. She would rather not be around me."

"Jessiva hates me too… sometimes."

"And sometimes not?"

"It's difficult to say."

I steal a sideways glance at him. There's a brightness in his eye, a buoyant joy in his wingbeats.

"You can tell me anything," I say.

He's quiet for a moment, and then, "Do you ever feel anything strange when you're with your female?"

"Explain."

"I thought the mating heat did not begin until the Rib Moon. But I have been experiencing symptoms, like Father described when he told us what to expect. Pleasurable sensations in my body, and certain reactions that are difficult to conceal." His voice drops so low I can barely hear it over the sound of the rushing air. "Is there something wrong with me? Is this because I was hatched late?"

So I am not the only one experiencing such sensations. Reluctant though I am to confess it, I must be honest with him. He needs reassurance. "If there is something wrong with you, there is something wrong with me as well."

"Then you've felt it too? With the Princess?"

"I wish I did not. Those are sensations I was only supposed to feel for Mordessa during our coupling."

My brother hums low in his throat, a growl of sympathy. "I had no Promised, so I cannot imagine the grief you are enduring—not only the loss of Grimmaw and Vylar, but

Mordessa as well. She was a magnificent creature. I would have been proud to call her my second sister."

My muscles tighten, my sore heart pumping slow and heavy as I force myself to keep flying, keep beating the air.

"Mordessa was kind and generous," Varex continues. "She would have wanted you to feel pleasure and find love with someone else." He hesitates, perhaps remembering what I told him, about not loving Mordessa as she deserved. "On the other hand, plenty of successful matches are formed without love. It is not essential. I have always hoped to feel it, but many of our kind never experience that sort of romantic passion with their life-mate."

"I am aware." I want to tell him the rest. The shameful, cruel truth I haven't spoken to anyone. But we are approaching Ashvelon's cave, and there is no time.

Varex and I sweep into the cave and fold our wings immediately, for the space is cluttered with large bags.

"The supplies you ordered, my Prince," says Fortunix with a toothy grin. "I may not be much good for battle any longer, but I can still carry a heavy load."

"And the enchantress?" I ask.

Ashvelon shifts aside. "She's here."

To my shock, Ashvelon has crafted a sort of throne at the edge of his nest and draped it with gold-fringed fabric. The enchantress reclines on the seat, clad in a purple gown that clings to every curve of her body. She's holding an ornate goblet filled with red liquid, and there's a dark bottle tucked into the nest beside her.

She lowers her lashes, peering at Varex and me with hooded eyes. "So you're the two dragon princes."

"And you are Thelise."

"Despised daughter of a genocidal sorcerer. That's me." She laughs bitterly and drinks from her goblet. "What can I do for you? This big brute said something about transformation?" She waves vaguely at Ashvelon.

"As you know, your father destroyed all the female dragons," I say.

"And you're holding me responsible." She nods, resigned. "I always knew that bastard's bullshit would come back to bite me in the ass."

"We *are* holding you responsible. But rather than ending your life, I require a spell from you. Perform it well, and you shall be set free."

"God, you really don't know much about me, do you?" She gulps from the cup again. "Right, so what's the spell?"

"I need you to turn all of the human women we have captured into female dragons. In this way, we achieve two goals—revenge upon the kingdom of Elekstan, and the survival of our race."

"No shit." She gapes at me. "That's a big spell. A big fucking spell indeed. You didn't tell me what a big fucking spell it was going to be, sweetheart," she says reproachfully to Ashvelon. "Naughty dragon. You shall be punished later."

A submissive shudder runs over Ashvelon's body. He growls softly, but there's a strange eagerness in his eyes, an almost worshipful hunger as he gazes upon the enchantress. What sort of madness has seized my clan? If I had known these women would have such an effect, I might not have brought them here. But no matter... soon they will be transformed into dragons, and their unnatural influence will be gone. They will simply be members of the clan, to be trained in our ways and incorporated into our bloodlines.

"Can you perform the spell we need?" I ask the enchantress.

She's been staring at Ashvelon with a wicked smile playing across her mouth, but when I speak, she drags her attention back to me.

"The spell you *need*," she murmurs. "That's very interesting. Yes, my Princes, I think I can provide the magic you need."

"You *think* you can? That's not good enough."

"Fine. I swear it. On my father's *bones*."

The sacred oath, coupled with the intensity of her gaze, convinces me. "Very well."

"I'll just need a little time, and a lot more wine, and my bag—you remember which bag it is, pet?"

To my shock, Ashvelon responds to "pet" with a rumble of assent. With a forepaw he moves aside a couple of the larger bags, uncovering one made of dark leather, stamped with complex symbols.

"Give me eight or nine hours, and it shall be done," says the enchantress. "There are precise calculations to be made, chants to be written, ingredients to be blended. Oh, and princelings—make sure all your people sleep on the ground tonight. Dragons and humans."

"Why?" asks Varex.

"Don't question the sorceress, darling." She clucks her tongue reproachfully at him. "And don't worry your horrible spiked heads about anything. It's in my best interest to do what you want, isn't it, since I obviously crave my freedom and want to return to my little shack in that salt-crusted town by the sea? So rest assured it will all be done exactly as you need it to be. By this time tomorrow, you and your human captives will have far more in common." She smiles broadly, then hiccups. "Fly away, sweet monsters, but remember to keep your captives on the ground and be at their sides around sunset. The change may be disconcerting for those involved. Can't be too careful."

"Very well." I leave Ashvelon to watch her, while Fortunix, Varex, and I fly outside, up to the peak of the mountain. The morning sun bathes our scales, and the sea air lifts our wings as we converse.

"Do you trust her?" Varex asks me.

"She swore on her father's bones."

"I don't know about *trust*," Fortunix says. "But she had magic enough to confine Ashvelon and me in her stable for a while."

"She kept you captive?" exclaims my brother.

"Not for long. But I'm sure she could have imprisoned us longer if she liked. She came with us willingly."

"Perhaps she wishes to atone for her father's wicked deeds," I say.

"Perhaps." Fortunix coughs deep in his chest, then says, "With respect, my Princes, a more urgent matter requires your attention. While I was on the mainland, I sent word to the King of Vohrain and requested a meeting."

My wings stiffen with surprise. "You did this without consulting me first?"

"I assumed you would want to speak with him, to ensure that our contract with Vohrain is being honored. Without the islands he promised, we will starve. Even if there are no eggs or hatchlings this season, food will only grow scarcer. The herds of wild pigs, goats, and deer have not had time to replenish their numbers, and we cannot subsist on plants alone. We must have meat."

"I understand. Did the king respond to your message?"

"He did. He sent one of his talking birds, who said we should meet him today at noon at the fortress on Ehren's Point."

"Then we should leave now."

"Yes, my Prince."

"But the women—" begins Varex.

"The women are under guard," Fortunix assures him. "Do not concern yourself any further with them. This meeting is not about human captives, it is about dragons. It's about the bargain your father made, and seeing whether or not Vohrain will honor it."

He's right, of course. My mind knows it, but my heart reacts with wild panic, with a dread approaching physical pain, every time I think about returning to the mainland. I spent weeks there while we were fighting the war, and I must admit the landscape was reasonably pleasant. I liked the forests, plains, and bluffs where my dragons and I resided in between battles.

But the memory of those battles haunts me now, not just because the last one brought about the fall of my loved ones. I think of the men and women I burned to death, the way I viewed them as insects or pests so I could cope with the reality of what I was doing. I view it all differently now that I've been so close to a human. Every person I scorched had a family, feelings, thoughts, skills, and dreams. I eliminated it all. I caused infinite pain in so many human dwellings. Those who survived had to suffer the same grief and guilt that I feel.

A bone-oath is sacred, unbreakable, and we are taught never to refuse if it's requested by a loved one nearing the moment of death. But perhaps I should have denied my father the bone-oath he asked for. Then I would not have this ponderous weight in my chest, burdening me as I fly with Varex and Fortunix west across the sea toward the coast.

The flight to the mainland takes two or three hours depending on winds, weather, and the weariness of dragons. If I were alone I would fly much slower, but once Fortunix gets going, he is a fast flier despite his age and his scarred wings, and he keeps my brother and I moving at a quick pace. Long before I'm ready, I spot the rocky point. At its crest stands a fortress of weathered stone.

My body does not want to touch the ground. It's not as if my sister fell to the earth in this exact spot—she and the others died far from here, so touching this ground shouldn't bother me. But my revulsion isn't logical.

I can't bear to plant my feet on this continent where I abandoned my sister's bones. And yet I must.

For a fleeting moment, I think of flying to Guilhorn to take bone-tribute from all those dragon skeletons. But it's too far from here. We must be back at Ouroskelle before sunset, to witness the transformation of our captives into dragons.

Fortunix and my brother are already landing atop the bluff, near the wall of the fortress. A contingent of Vohrain's guard form three straight lines, their banners and cloaks flapping in the wind. Their king stands front and center, his boots planted widely apart, one gloved hand gripping his belt. He has wavy red-orange hair, a full beard threaded with small braids, and a broad, sturdy frame. Gold beads glint in his beard and a gold ring pierces the space between his nostrils. More gold shines on his fingers and along his ears. Though he wears no crown, he is a man of wealth and power, and he likes to make it known.

I circle the fortress once, wheeling high above the group. The humans will assume I want to make a dramatic landing, when in reality I'm bolstering my courage to touch the earth.

I must do this. I am the first-born of the Bone-King. I am one of the ruling princes of Ouroskelle. The bones of Grimmaw, Vylar, and Mordessa are not in this place. My fears are unfounded and my revulsion is foolish.

Despite repeating all these things to myself, I feel like screaming, like setting the fortress alight with my hottest fire, like incinerating the King of Vohrain and his people. Perhaps I would feel better if they were ashes on the wind, like my lost ones.

But if I kill them, I will be adding to the long list of deaths for which I am responsible. I need Vohrain's king to officially hand over the islands he promised—and I need him to tell me what happened to the Queen of Elekstan. The Princess is waiting for that news.

In my mind I can see her delicate, sorrowful features. I can hear her saying, "I would be grateful."

Selfish and demanding though she pretends to be, she is stronger than I first thought. It couldn't have been easy for her, a tiny slip of human flesh, to be carried off to the home of a creature such as myself. Would she mock me if she knew how terrified I am to simply *land*? Or would her gaze soften with pity, with understanding?

She wouldn't have the heart to ridicule me. I'm convinced of that. She would encourage me in the quiet voice she used when she sat beside me in the cave mouth and told me about herself. I can almost hear her now, assuring me that I can do this.

Before I know it I'm banking, angling downward. My claws sink into the thick, tough grass of the bluff.

I landed. And I have not died, or bathed this place in agonized fire.

Rahzien, King of Vohrain, bows to me, and I dip my head to him, as do the other dragons.

"I expected to meet with you sooner," he says. "But I suppose we have both been busy. And dragons tend to be slow of thought and action—unless they're stealing wives, am I right, lads?" He glances around at his men, who laugh jovially along with him.

I choose to ignore the slight to my kind. "I trust your conquest went smoothly?"

"Indeed it did. Though I would have preferred to have your army alongside us for the final phase."

"My apologies. It was a difficult time, and once we decided to take the captives, we had to get them back to our island quickly."

"Of course, of course." The King eyes me shrewdly. "One male to another—you realize that breeding another species might be difficult when the size difference is so great."

"We're not breeding them as humans," puts in Varex. "We captured an enchantress who is going to transform them into female dragons for us."

For the first time, the King looks truly surprised. "Well now. That's something I never would have imagined. Who's the enchantress with such mighty power?"

Varex starts to speak again, but I lash my tail against his and he quiets.

"Let us discuss more pressing matters," I say. "The Middenwold Isles—"

"—are yours," the King interrupts. "Despite your absence from the final conquest, your clan helped me win the war. You upheld your end of the bargain, and I will fulfill mine. The deed has already been changed, and maps all across Vohrain are being relabeled as we speak."

I'm unsure what a deed is, but I know what maps are. I bow my head in gracious acceptance. "We are grateful."

The phrase reminds me of the other question I must ask. "What was the fate of Elekstan's queen?"

"That stubborn bitch?" The King gives a dry laugh. "She fought to the end. But she was overpowered, as all women eventually are, by a strong man. I stripped her naked and locked her into a pillory in the main square of the city. Had her whipped, too. Once the citizens had a chance to see her truly defeated and humiliated, I cut off her head. Couldn't find the daughter, though. Some say she leaped to her death from the walls of the city—others say she fled south for refuge. I don't suppose any of your dragons saw what happened to her?" His narrowed eyes scan the three of us.

Before I can stop him, Fortunix drawls, "Prince Kyreagan took the Elekstan princess to his cave."

"Did you now?" The King turns to me. "What do you want for her? I can give you access to the Parrock Banks off the Estaphen coast. Good place for fat, juicy eels. I'm sure your dragons would love those fishing areas."

The hunger in his face unsettles me. "Why do you want the Princess?"

"It seems she's wildly popular with the Elekstan people," says the King. "I'll use her to keep them under control. Maybe even marry her."

"I thought you had already chosen a wife."

He laughs loudly. "I'm engaged, yes, but nothing has been finalized. Besides, who's to say a man can't take more than one wife? Your father told me dragons mate with each other at will during your heat, and that they don't always couple with their life-mate during such orgies. Surely you can understand a man wanting to dip his dick into more than one cunt. The duchess I'm engaged to comes with a well-stocked treasury, but she has a condition that prevents her from bearing children. Maybe the ripe young womb of the Elekstan princess will yield better results."

"I doubt she would breed with you willingly," I say.

He guffaws, and his men chuckle. "I doubt she would," he repeats in a mocking imitation of my deep tone. "She won't be breeding with you willingly either, Prince. Let's be honest with each other. I'll give you the Parrock Banks and a few chests of treasure. You dragons like gold, yes?"

"We do," I admit. I have a penchant for the beauty of wrought metal and the shine of well-cut gemstones, and I'm not the only one of my kind with such proclivities. We keep our favorite pieces in our own caves, but the rest of the clan hoard is housed in a secret location.

"So we're agreed?" urges the King. "You get three chests the size of my head, full of gold and silver, and the Parrock Banks, and the Middenwold Isles. And you deliver the Princess of Elekstan to me."

Fortunix murmurs agreement. Varex is silent, and when I glance at him, he gives me no indication of what he's thinking.

It might be a relief to be rid of the Princess's incessant demands and complaints. I picture giving her to the King of Vohrain, imagine his big hands mauling the small, sensitive places that I licked, imagine him shoving his cock inside her while she screams—fuck, no. That will never happen. No male, either human or dragon, will touch her, and no one will take her body except me.

I said I would never dance for her during mating season. But I think I was lying to her and to myself, because I cannot bear the thought of her mating with anyone else. The charming, irritating, delicious, fiery little Princess will take dragon form, and she will be mine. She will be winged and powerful and glorious. I will fuck her full of my seed, and she will bear my young.

"We have a deal?" repeats the King.

"No," I growl, and there's fire in the sound. My nostrils are glowing, smoking.

"No?" The King frowns.

"I will take the islands, as we agreed. But I'm keeping the Princess. Our bargain is now concluded."

Without a bow or another word, I whirl and take off.

Varex catches up to me in a few moments. "That was rather abrupt, even for you."

"He was planning to harm her," I snarl. "But she is mine."

"Nevertheless, you could have ended the meeting more gracefully. Fortunix stayed behind to smooth things over."

"Good for him. You'll come with me. We're going down the coast to fetch a few things before we return to Ouroskelle."

"Things?"

"Blankets," I tell him. "And some fucking tea."

12

SERYLLA

"No, that won't work either." Jessiva drops her head into her hands, her red hair tumbling around her shoulders. "God, why is this so difficult? There must be a way."

She and I have been strategizing with the other women for hours, I would guess, judging by the angle of the sun. The dragons have left us alone, for the most part, so we've had time to sort through all the options for escape.

One of the women, Brenée, suggested building rafts that could take us back to the mainland. But that would require eliminating the dragons first. There is no way they would allow us to construct rafts right under their noses.

So we moved on to the next problem: defeating the dragons. If armed airships couldn't take down one dragon, a couple dozen women armed with rocks certainly can't destroy a whole clan of them.

Someone else mentioned poison, and I contributed my knowledge of the poisonous vines I encountered when I was near the lake with Kyreagan (and fuck him for telling Jessiva his name before he told me). But again—how are we to gather enough poisonous vines when we are watched constantly by at least one of the dragons? Not to mention the fact that the vines would cause *us* harm if we touched them.

"We can harvest the vines at night, when most of them are roosting and there are only one or two on guard," says Brenée. "We could cause a distraction, and then some of us could slip out through the wall and head for the lake."

"Whatever we decide, we must remember that not all of us are being kept here in this cavern at night," I say. "Others are imprisoned alone in the higher caves." I think of the plump, rosy-cheeked woman I saw in Rothkuri's lair. The one who loves being licked.

"There's something no one has mentioned," puts in a slim dark-skinned girl with a white streak in her black hair. I think one of the others called her Gweneth. "Some of the dragons do not agree with the prince's plan. They didn't want to kidnap humans in the first place. What if we focused on finding those dragons and forming a rapport with them? Maybe we can persuade some of them to rebel against the princes, and then the rebel dragons can fly us home."

Murmurs of interest and agreement ripple through the group of women.

"There's one problem with that plan." I rise from the rock I've been sitting on. "It would take time we don't have. Do you all know what they plan to do with us?"

"Kill us? Eat us, rape us? Keep us prisoners for life? Does it really matter?" says Brenée.

Jessiva's pale skin turns a shade whiter, and instantly I realize that she knows the truth. She knows the fate the princes have planned for us, yet she has chosen not to tell the other women. I'm not sure why. Maybe she doesn't want to cause a panic.

"My mother was never fully honest with our people about the state of the kingdom," I say slowly. "But I believe honesty is important, especially when the decisions being made affect everyone. So I will tell you now, what the dragons' true purpose is. They have captured an enchantress—the daughter of the Supreme Sorcerer. When the princes flew away from here, they were going to meet with her. They want her to turn all of us into dragons."

The women gasp, and two of them start crying.

"In less than a week, the mating season begins," I explain. "It occurs once every twenty-five years. Every dragon on this island will be compelled to mate. They will give us a choice of partners, but my understanding is that the compulsion is so strong, we'll want to participate in the heat, if we're in dragon form. Some of us will lay dragon eggs as a result. We will be mothers to the hatchlings of our kidnappers."

"No," moans Brenée. "No, this can't be happening."

I turn to the black-haired girl, Gweneth. "Your plan is a good one. I just don't think we have the time to make it work."

"We could try." Her tone is threaded with desperation. "We have to try *something*."

"We could run," suggests another captive. "Leave this place, spread out across the island. They'll waste time hunting all of us down, and maybe some of us can gather the vines to poison them."

"Gather them how?" says Jessiva. "The vines can poison us, too. We can't touch them with our bare skin. And how would we persuade the dragons to ingest poisonous vines? They don't consume cooked food, and we have no pots in which to cook it. Even if we did, they would see us putting the vines into the food."

"The water supply?" suggests someone.

"There are water sources all over this island. We can't poison them all."

"Talking is getting us nowhere. We must choose." I speak firmly, clearly. "Those who wish to run, go now, while there's only one of them watching us. Run to the beach—maybe there's a swamped boat that's still somewhat seaworthy. Run to the forest—maybe you can find a weapon. I'm not sure whether they need us to be present for the spell, or whether it will be cast over the whole island, but if you want to flee, do it. If you want to fight, think of a strategy. If you want to stay and try to convince your dragon to take you back to the mainland and set you free, use every charm, every persuasive argument."

"It would be best if we worked together," Jessiva counters.

"But we can't. We don't agree on the best course of action, and none of our schemes seem likely to succeed. For my part, I think I'll run. Maybe if they can't find me, they can't include me in the spell."

Jessiva shakes her head. "Spells like that can be cast from a distance, targeted to a specific group of beings," she says. "Hiding won't protect you from the change."

"It's better than nothing. At least I won't have to deal with the fucking Prince of Dragons anymore."

Gweneth steps forward. "I'm running too."

A few more of the women chime in with their agreement.

"I'm staying," Jessiva says. "But we'll distract them for you, so you can slip past the wall. Maybe it will take them a while to notice you're gone. Be careful, though. Varex has spoken of creatures that inhabit this island and come out at night—dangerous predators that occasionally bring down the dragons themselves."

The idea of something scarier than a dragon makes me think twice about my escape plan. But the other women who want to run have already gathered around me, and they seem to be looking for me to make the first move. So I swallow my apprehension and say, "Let's find a place in the barrier where we can squeeze through. Then the rest of you can distract *him* somehow—" I point upward to the bronze dragon circling lazily in the air, high above the courtyard.

"I know what to do," says Jessiva. "They want us for breeding, right? Which means they want us healthy, uninjured. So if we start a fight, and make it vicious—" She's eyeing one of the other women, a tall, gorgeous, grim-jawed blonde with rich brown skin. Antagonism flickers between them, and I suspect they've had words, if not blows, before this moment.

"I will gladly help you make it look real," says the blonde through her teeth.

"Very well." What can I do but agree? Their private dispute isn't my business. And I'm feeling the same rush of nervous energy that sent me to the city wall when the dragon alarm sounded. I need to *do* something, and since I have no weapon to fight the dragons this time, I will run from them.

"There's a gap over there," mutters Gweneth. "We've heard creatures snuffling around the wall at night, but they were all too large to squeeze through the barrier and not strong enough to leap over it. One of them shifted a log, though, and I think we can make it through."

I start to ask if they glimpsed the predators at all, but enraged screeches from the far side of the courtyard interrupt me. Jessiva and the blonde are grappling with each other. The fight has begun.

The yelling catches the attention of the dragon guard overhead. He descends sharply, the wind of his wings stirring the loose dirt within the enclosure.

By good fortune, his back is to us as he faces Jessiva and the blonde. He begins speaking in Dragonish, then remembers they can't understand him and switches to the Eventongue. I barely hear his reprimand to the quarreling women, because I'm too busy squeezing through the barrier behind Gweneth. Branches scratch my ribs, my arms, and my legs—new injuries added to my bruises. But with a little writhing and wriggling, I burst through with a lurch and a stagger. Gweneth grabs my arm, steadying me.

"Good luck to you, Princess." Her dark eyes hold mine. "Keep to the trees." Then she whirls and runs off into the forest like a deer leaping for freedom, her long legs easily clearing the undergrowth.

I glance back once to ensure that the others are making it through unnoticed. But I can't help them now. Every woman must find her own fate.

Taking a deep breath, I start running.

Instead of racing full-out, I maintain a steady jog. I'm used to riding, walking, shooting a crossbow, and swimming occasionally, but when it comes to running, my stamina is poor. I need to pace myself so I can cover as much ground as possible before I have to rest.

Several times, I think I hear light footsteps behind me, too light for a dragon, too heavy for a rabbit or fox. But when I glance back, I don't see anyone.

At last I venture close to a bubbling spring that empties into a shaded pool. I creep toward it, staying beneath the overhanging boughs of a huge oak so no dragon flying overhead can spot me.

My heart pounds from exertion, and my body is damp with sweat. I braid my hair swiftly and tie it off with a long piece of tough grass. Then I sink to my knees by the pool, bathing my skin with the cool water. It smells fresh, so once I've caught my breath, I bend over to drink from the rippling surface.

A scuffle of running feet. A hand slams against the back of my neck and shoves my face into the water. I choke out a garbled cry of surprise, bubbles slipping from my mouth.

I fight to sit up, but the hand holding me down carries the frenzied strength of anger. I feel it in the violent clutch of the fingers, the rigid force of the arm that's drowning me. I claw backward, behind me, but I can't seem to find my attacker's face.

Frantically I lurch and try to roll aside, but my attacker flings their entire weight on me, pinning me down.

I have precious little air left, and my panic is a force of its own. But through sheer strength of will, I stop fighting. I make myself go utterly limp, even as my body demands that I struggle. My killer needs to think I have already drowned.

In my head I count the seconds. *One, two, three, four, five, six, seven, eight, nine—*

The weight on my back lifts, and the hand disappears from the back of my neck.

I spring up instantly, gasp a raw breath, and fling myself aside to avoid the attacker as she yells with shock and lunges for me again. Choking and coughing, I dodge behind the great oak and seize a dead limb above me. My weight makes the branch crack free, and I swing my new weapon on sheer instinct, with all the strength of both my arms in the blow. The branch smashes into my attacker's face as she rounds the tree.

Blood spurts from her mouth. She reels and crashes to the ground.

She's spasming, twitching, while blood drains from her mouth into the soil. My blow mauled the lower right half of her face, broke her cheekbone and her upper jaw. I can see white teeth and bone protruding through torn red flesh. Her skull is probably fractured.

"Oh fuck." I drop the branch and kneel beside her. I vaguely remember seeing her among the girls who wanted to run. "Why did you do this?"

Grief and rage leak through the pain in her eyes.

"My mother," I whisper. "That's why, isn't it? You lost someone in the war, maybe more than one person, and you blame the royals. This was vengeance."

Her head moves a little. Almost a nod. Her hand forms a claw against the ground. Blood is flooding her right eye, and her body continues to jerk as her damaged nervous system tries to cope with the wound.

"I'm sorry," I manage through my tears, through my clenched teeth. "I'm sorry."

It's not enough. I can never atone for everything my mother did—for everything I failed to do. I can tell myself it wasn't my fault, that my mother pushed me aside and wouldn't let me get involved—but I *allowed* her to push me aside. I amused myself with babies, horses, dogs, and various domestic tasks, like a child at play, while she sent droves of citizens into the jaws of death.

But I wasn't a child. I was a fucking adult. I kept myself busy in my own world, and I did *nothing* to stop the carnage.

I should have tried harder. No… I should have *tried*. But I didn't. Not at all. I thought my private conflict with my mother's policies was enough, that I was being subversive by quietly agreeing with the servants and guards when they condemned her rule. What must they have thought of me, the spoiled princess who thought herself powerless to enact change, when in reality I always had more power than any of them—I just didn't claim it, or use it. I used my privilege to express mild dissent or to stay out of the way.

"I've been a lazy fucking cunt," I whisper to the dying girl. "I didn't fight my mother on any of it. Just sulked about things occasionally, and that did no one any good. It's too late to fix what happened, but I swear—I vow to you, I will never again stand idly by and watch someone be harmed without trying to stop it. I wish you'd talked to me, before it came to this."

Why did I swing that branch so hard? Everything happened so fast, I couldn't think. I just *survived*.

All I can do now is witness her passing.

I don't hold her hand. She wouldn't want that. But I stay beside her until her spirit goes, leaving her eyes empty.

I cover her body with branches as best I can. Then I wash my hands in the stream, drink my fill, and keep running.

Nausea bubbles in my stomach when I think of the dying girl's smashed face. But she's gone now—she's not the immediate threat. I need to find the coastline, locate a place to hide, and start thinking about how I can make a seaworthy raft. The horror of what I've done will have to wait.

The dragons will come for us, that much is certain. I will hide, scheme, struggle, and do everything I can to stay out of their grasp. If I escape the effects of the enchantress's spell, I will live in the deepest thickets of the forest until I figure out a way to cross the stretch of sea between this island and the mainland. If they change me into a dragon, I will fight them tooth and claw until they regret that choice.

It strikes me that perhaps the males haven't considered the potential danger to themselves once the women become dragons. They assume that once the change is complete, we'll be resigned to our fate, happy to join the clan. As dragons, the females will still be outnumbered, but we'll be far more powerful. Able to fight back and take our revenge.

Of course, we'll be new to our dragon bodies. We won't know how to fly right away, and if we have fire, it may take a while to learn how to use it. Perhaps that's what the males are counting on—that time and training will ease any residual rage we feel after the transformation. Perhaps they hope that the mating frenzy and the subsequent hatching season will tame us, domesticate us.

I hope to god they're wrong. I'm determined to hold onto this anger, no matter what happens. I won't forget what the dragons have done to my people, and if I do become one of them, I will repay those wrongs ten times over.

13

KYREAGAN

"What do you mean, she's not here?" My bellow echoes across the courtyard, reverberates into the cavern. "You were supposed to be watching them."

Gosrik recoils, his bronze tail dragging and his head lowered. "The women began fighting, my Prince. I feared they would injure each other. While I was intervening, several of the other captives slipped through the barrier and ran off into the forest. I called for Rytar and Ixione immediately, as they were the nearest. They went to hunt for those who escaped, while I remained behind to watch the other women."

"You hoped you could retrieve them before I found out."

He cringes lower. "Yes, my Prince."

I glance over at Varex. He's sitting in front of Jessiva while she stares at him defiantly.

"She masterminded this," I snarl.

"It could just as easily have been *your* woman who planned it," Varex retorts.

"Remove Jessiva from this enclosure, where she can't cause any more trouble," I command. "Take her far from here, but remember what the enchantress said. When she transforms, she won't know how to fly yet. She will need you there to teach her."

"I heard," he snaps. "I was there. Fortunix and Ashvelon are already spreading the word that everyone must roost on the ground tonight. Don't you think it a strange rule—"

"I think it strange that I am still here, talking to you, when Serylla is roaming the island unprotected." With a final roar at the cowering Gosrik, I take off, catching a swift breeze from the ocean and using it to speed across the belt of forest near the women's enclosure.

I don't bother checking the broad, open fields or the cliffs that make up most of our island's geography. Serylla is clever. She'll keep to the densest parts of the forest where it's harder for me to spot her, where I can't fly in to grab her. I'm a good hunter, but only because I know the habits and patterns of my usual prey. An intelligent, defiant little human will be much harder to track.

"Fuck!" I vomit the curse on a stream of orange flame.

For hours I hunt her, landing occasionally to sniff the grass and the trees, trying to discern her scent among the myriad of odors. For some reason, I can't smell her anywhere. I waste time following a trail that smells sweetly human, only to find a girl with coppery curls huddled beneath a stand of fir trees. She looks petrified, but I merely huff an angry breath and take to the sky again. Let someone else take care of that one. My sole concern is the aggravating little princess.

A few times I spot dragons with thrashing bodies grasped firmly in their claws, flying back toward the clan caves. Despite my satisfaction that some of the women are being retrieved, I'm annoyed as well, because I can't seem to find mine. The sun is sinking, and still there's no sign of her anywhere.

Finally I land on the north beach and prowl along the treeline, peering deep into the gloom beneath the branches. I even stalk into the forest, cursing every time branches drag at my wings.

I keep going, until at last I wedge myself through a tight gap between tree trunks and find a steep, grassy slope ahead. Jutting rocks and lumpy ridges of turf scar its surface, and among those ridges and rocks are large holes, half-hidden by long clumps of grass.

I forgot there was a voratrice nest here. Fuck.

We should have been more forthcoming with the women about the dangers of Ouroskelle, like the poisonous vines, and the wolves who hide in caves too narrow for us and come out at night to steal our prey. Worst of all are the voratrix. Each voratrice is something between a titanic earthworm and a carnivorous plant. It cannot move through the earth, but must stay rooted in one spot. Deep beneath the ground, all the serpentine appendages of the creature share one bloated stomach, and during the night, its long necks extend, carrying its many mouths closer to the surface. Each wormlike neck emerges through a separate tunnel, like the many stalks of a single plant—and on the blunted end of every writhing neck-stalk is a toothy maw which can shoot out several long, tongue-like feelers. Those feelers are the true danger to dragons. They can reach far into the sky, and are so transparent they're nearly invisible until it's too late.

Once prey is caught, the voratrice swallows the victim down one of its gullets into the shared stomach. The creature can live on one deer or dragon carcass for weeks. They reproduce rarely, sending out runners to form new cores only once every ten years or so. Old cores are tough and fibrous, nearly impossible to destroy, but when we discover a new core, we send fire down its throats and burn it out while it is still young and vulnerable.

The voratrix are only active at night, so in most cases we can avoid them. But there have been a handful of dragons killed by the voratrix during my lifetime—most notably the Bone-

King's life-mate, my mother. She went out for a night flight with Varex and was caught by the feelers of a core no one had spotted. Vylar and I mourned her deeply, but my brother's pain was worse. He had to watch her die; in fact he nearly perished himself, trying to save her. All he brought back was her claw, which had been ripped from her foreleg as she struggled to free herself.

After Varex reported my mother's demise, the Bone-King took several dragons with him to the spot, and they spent a day and a night vomiting fire down the voratrice's tunnels. They even dug deep into the earth, trying to locate the core. But the creature was old, massive, and deeply buried in rocky soil. It never emerged, and the dragons could not find its root. My mother was gone.

The sun hangs low in the sky, and its golden glow bathes the slope, throwing the hollows and holes into sharp shadow. The voratrix always emerge at dusk. In moments this monster will be active, eager for prey. I should go.

As I start to turn away, the skin beneath my scales tingles with a sudden awareness. My nostrils flare, catching a faint scent mired beneath a layer of foulness. The heavy odor is dragon dung, and the scent beneath—it's unmistakable. It's *her*.

Whirling back around, I peer at the slope again, scouring every shadow.

There she is. She appears to have smeared her arms and legs with dragon scat, to camouflage both her pale skin and her scent. She is a disgusting, clever little creature.

And... fuck me. She's sitting in the entrance to one of the voratrice holes.

A chill of violent horror sets my scales on edge. Any moment now, the monster's sinuous necks will slide up those tunnels, at a speed faster than dragon-flight, and one of its mouths will scoop her up and carry her back to the underground stomach, to be slowly digested while she remains conscious. She won't last long in that corrosive acid, with her soft skin, but she'll be alive long enough to suffer agony. I cannot think of a more gruesome death.

"Princess," I say quietly. "Please, let me speak to you."

She retreats a little way into the tunnel. "Don't come any closer. I know you can't fit into a space this narrow, and if you approach me, I'll go deeper."

"That would be a mistake," I growl. "You're perched in the entrance to a voratrice tunnel. It's a predator that even the strongest dragons fear."

"I don't believe you. You're just trying to get me to come out."

"Look at the sides of the tunnel. See the texture of the earth, how it has been smoothed by the nightly emergence of the creature?"

She looks around, worry tightening her features. She's too smart not to see the signs herself, now that I've pointed them out. But she doesn't yet fear the unknown monster as much as she fears returning to me.

"There are more holes in this slope," I tell her. "Most are nearly invisible, draped with grass, but some are large enough to accommodate a dragon, once its wings have been broken. That's what this beast does. It catches a dragon with its tongues, tears off the scales, breaks the wing bones, and swallows the whole dragon down its gullet. But it will accept other prey, too, not just dragons. You'll be a delicious treat for it. I doubt it has ever tasted human flesh."

Serylla glances nervously down the tunnel.

"They come out at sunset," I continue. "Any moment now the creature could emerge. You'll be swallowed before you can run."

She crawls forward to the entrance and remains there, poised in a crouch. "If I come out, you're going to take me back to your cave, or to that pen where you keep the others."

"Yes. You'll be safe there."

"You're going to destroy this body, *my* body, the one I was born with, and turn me into something else, against my will."

"We've been over this. I have reasons, compelling reasons." My voice rises, strident with frustration and fear. "Come out at once, and live. Or stay there, and die."

The ground murmurs faintly beneath my claws. It's not so dramatic as a tremor, but it's movement for certain.

The voratrice is coming.

"Serylla!" I roar, and I leap forward.

She's already moving, springing out of the tunnel. Too slow—she's jerked backward, screaming. I can barely see the slimy transparent tongue wrapped around her ankle.

I dive in, slicing at the tentacle with my claws. It's tough, stretchy, difficult to cut through, but my talons do enough damage to make it let go.

Serylla crawls away, her leg bleeding from the tiny hooks embedded along the tongue's surface. Those hooks are perfectly evolved for prying off a dragon's scales.

I open my wings, catching the air as I seize her body in my front claws. But before I can soar upward with her, several tongues wrap around my tail and legs, while more of them coil around the joint of my left wing.

I bellow, straining to break free, but several of the worm-heads have gripped me with their feelers, and their strength is inexorable, like the sucking pull of Varex's void magic.

Understanding rushes through me like black, icy water.

I'm already dead. But maybe the Princess can live.

With all my might, I throw her forward into the forest. Her body crashes into the undergrowth as I fight to stay aloft, my wings pummeling the air.

"Run!" I roar. "Run, you foolish human, run!"

14

SERYLLA

Five writhing, wormlike necks protrude from various holes in the rocky slope. Each one's blunted tip gapes open, showing rings of teeth, and from those hungry mouths emerge the clusters of long transparent tongues that coil around the dragon's back legs, his tail, and his wings. All of the worm-things are working together to bind and break him.

Kyreagan strains against them, every muscle in his powerful body surging, his magnificent wings flared wide. He twists around and sprays focused bursts of fire at some of the tongues, but they don't seem to be affected. More tongues rake along his back and sides, their tiny hooks tearing out his scales, leaving raw red wounds.

The dragon crashes to the ground, caught in a web of tongues. Two of them coil around his throat and tighten. He chokes out a snarl.

Frantically I hunt for a weapon, for anything I can use to help him. There's no question of leaving him behind, enemy or not. I can't watch him die. It's not that I care about him—I don't. But he doesn't deserve *this*.

I find a sapling with a pointed end and run back up the slope. Instead of trying to cut through the tongues, I head for one of the mouths and jam the stick sideways into the monster's gullet. A stray tongue darts out at me, and I barely avoid it. I'm lucky that most of the voratrice's feelers are occupied, or I'd be in one of its throats already.

Only one of the five worm-things is big enough to swallow something of Kyreagan's size. That's the one I need to focus on.

The voratrice is wrapping Kyreagan's wings with its tongues. I can sense what's about to happen, how it will constrict those beautiful wings, how the bones will snap and crumple. Kyreagan is panting, agony threaded through each strangled breath.

"No!" I scream as I heave up the biggest rock I can manage and beat it against the blunted head of the largest worm. "No, fuck you! You can't have him! If anyone is going to kill this bastard, it's going to be me!"

The skin of the monster is thick and ribbed, apparently fireproof and tough as old leather. Nothing I'm doing is working. I'm not strong enough to hurt it.

The tongues around Kyreagan's wings tighten. He bellows in anguish, but his voice changes mid-roar—

And so does his body.

A flash of searing purple light explodes outward from him, and then he shrinks so abruptly it's like he's there one second and gone the next. The tongues fall limply to the ground as the giant wings they were clutching vanish altogether. They begin to poke around blindly, as if searching for the dragon they had in their grasp. Although I can't see eyes or nostrils, they must have some sense of heat and movement, or perhaps they taste the air like a serpent does—but the blast of magic seems to have dulled their ability to sense prey.

In the center of those writhing tentacles stands a tall man with long black hair, graceful horns, and light brown skin.

I know it's Kyreagan instantly, and I don't question it. Survival is paramount. Everything else can be sorted out later.

He seems stunned, so I rush to his side, hopping over the confused tentacle-tongues, and I drag his arm around my shoulders. "You have to run," I tell him. "Forget everything else. Run!"

His long legs are clumsy, but with my help he hobbles down the slope. We reach the treeline just as two tongues scrape against the backs of my legs. I scream and shove Kyreagan forward faster, until we're out of reach. When I look back, the tongues are prodding the trees and wiggling through the undergrowth. I hope their seeking senses are permanently damaged.

"Come on." I grip Kyreagan's arm and hustle him through the woods.

"What just happened?" The words sound garbled, like he's struggling to form them with his unfamiliar teeth and lips.

"Don't talk yet. Keep moving."

We don't stop until we're on the beach. His legs give out then, and he collapses on the sand. I take off my ruined slippers and keep going, desperately, determinedly, until I reach the surf, where I wash the dragon shit off my arms and legs and scrub my skin with handfuls of wet sand until I feel clean again. The saltwater stings my scrapes, especially the cuts on my leg, but I welcome the pain. I want that area thoroughly purged of the voratrice's touch.

I can't deal with Kyreagan yet.

I can't deal with any of it.

He *transformed.*

He fucking changed into a human—or mostly human.

Could he always do that? I highly doubt it, judging from his reaction. This must be new.

The enchantress arrived today. Maybe she promised to perform the spell the dragons wanted, and instead she did something *else*. Something unexpected.

My limbs are finally clean, but I'm also soaked from the neck down, and the chilly ocean breeze raises goosebumps on my skin. Still, I remain where I am for another long minute. I stare at the flat gray sea and follow it to the horizon, where it blurs into the deep gray of the oncoming night.

Finally, inhaling a deep breath, I turn around, and I face the dragon prince.

He's sitting where I left him, bare-ass naked on the sand. Dark blood stains his brown skin in several places, and a streak of grime marks his left cheekbone. In the lingering glow of dusk, he looks like a beautiful, wounded god who washed up from the sea. His ebony hair cloaks his shoulders, strands of it lifted by the breeze.

With quick, tense steps I walk toward him. My heart hammers in my chest as it sinks in—the reality of what happened, and what *almost* happened. He nearly died, and the transformation saved him.

"You're human," I announce breathlessly.

"So it would seem." He shapes each word carefully, his tone hollow with shock.

"*Why* are you human?"

"The enchantress, Thelise." He tries her name a few times before managing to pronounce it correctly. "She tricked me. There's no other explanation."

"Do you think she only changed you, or all the dragons?"

"All of us, I suspect." He's adapting quickly to his new mouth—his words become clearer as he continues speaking. "She warned us to stay on the ground with our captives tonight. Made it sound as if it was for *your* benefit, so you would be safer and more comfortable during the change, but clearly she didn't want us transforming in midair, falling out of the sky, and smashing ourselves to bits. A small mercy, I suppose."

I snort. "And why did you trust her to do this spell?"

"We told her if she didn't, she'd remain our prisoner forever. I promised that as long as she did the spell correctly, she would earn her freedom."

"What if she had performed a spell like the one her father cast, and killed all the male dragons?"

"The casting of that spell killed the Supreme Sorcerer, and I assumed she would not want to die."

"Well... at least you *tried* to think it through."

He looks up at me, annoyance in his eyes—lovely dark eyes. Human eyes, in a handsome face. God, he's beautiful. Why did the enchantress have to make him gorgeous? Broad shoulders, mounded pectorals with tight beaded nipples. A defined abdomen, a large cock, strong thighs—I rip my gaze back up to his face as warmth rushes into my cheeks.

"Is it a permanent transformation?" I ask.

"Not entirely, I think." He places long brown fingers over his chest. "I can still feel my dragon form and my powers, inside, though I don't know how to access them."

"Right, and you still have the—" I gesture to his horns. "I wonder how long this form will last."

"I don't know." A muscle in his jaw flexes.

"You should get up and wash the sand off, otherwise it's going to be very uncomfortable for you later."

"Very well."

Fear must have galvanized him into action before, because when he tries to get up this time, he wobbles and keels over immediately.

I can't help a small laugh, and he shoots me a glare that could incinerate stone.

"Do you want some help?" I ask.

"It's the sand," he growls. "It won't—I can't—how do you humans exist with such wretched narrow feet?"

Stepping closer, I hold out both hands. After several curses and failed attempts, he gives in, grips my fingers, and manages to haul himself upright. His tall, lean body sways against mine, the hard planes of his chest bumping against the softness of my breasts.

Images tumble into my mind—the dragon's face between my thighs, his tongue stroking into me. I remember the sensation when I rode on his back—the thrill of having such a powerful being under me. I felt wickedly aroused by him then, and I hated myself for it. But now he isn't a dragon anymore. He has a broad, warm chest, and muscular arms, and *fingers*—god, such strong fingers, tipped with dark claws. When he moves, there's a shimmer to his skin, like a faint gleam of the dragon-fire buried deep within.

I'm in such deep shit.

"Let's get you cleaned up," I say crisply. "Watch your step. Take it slow."

We wade into the ocean until the water is up to his knees. As we walk, he keeps glancing down between his legs at the very fine penis swinging there. The sight of it seems to displease him.

"What's the matter?" I ask.

He gives me a tragic look. "It's so small."

I choke out an incredulous laugh. "No, it is most certainly not small. Maybe compared to your dragon dick, but in human terms, that is a very large cock. A rather nice one, too—" Shit, I need to stop talking. "We'll go a bit deeper so you can wash yourself, and then we should find somewhere to get out of this wind."

"I feel so tiny and naked," he says, shuddering.

"You *are* naked."

"It's more than the lack of clothing. I feel weak. Unprotected. Vulnerable. How do you live like this? You must be frightened all the time."

"Sometimes. Especially when I'm being seized by a huge dragon and carried away from everything I know."

"Point taken," he mutters.

We wade out farther, until the water reaches his waist. He holds himself steady with one hand on my shoulder while he rinses the sand from his lower half and bathes the blood from his torso and arms. He grimaces at the sting of the saltwater, showing a row of white teeth with wickedly sharp canines.

He has a few raw patches on his skin. Apparently some of the wounds where his scales were torn out have transferred to his human body. But they don't look as deep as they did in dragon form.

A large wave rolls in, so I plant my feet and help him remain steady until it has crashed over both of us and skimmed on, toward the beach.

"The waves could so easily wash us away," he says. "With this thin skin, there is almost no defense against the elements."

"And now you understand our affinity for clothing."

He looks at me, a gleam of realization in his dark eyes—almost admiration. "It takes a unique kind of strength to survive in a body like this. To make something out of your life, to find joy, when you are so weak and helpless."

I roll my eyes. "We're not as helpless as you think."

We wade to the shore again, and I lead him up the beach to a large, flat stone partially shielded by another huge rock, which juts out over it at an angle, forming a sheltered hollow. I sit cross-legged beneath the angled slab. Kyreagan sets his butt down beside me and folds his long legs awkwardly into a similar position. After a moment he scoots forward to give himself more headroom, so his horns don't scrape against the rock.

"This is a dream," he says matter-of-factly. "I've been swallowed by the voratrice, and I'm dreaming this while I'm digested in its belly."

I reach over, take his nipple between my thumb and forefinger, and twist.

"Fuck!" he exclaims.

"That's proof you're not dreaming."

He looks down at himself, then touches his own nipples. "These are strange. They are like your teats. Do they give milk?"

"I will give you every piece of jewelry I'm wearing if you never say the word 'teats' again. And no, you're male, so you won't be nursing anything. *God*."

"Another mention of 'god,'" he says. "Do your people worship a god?"

"More like an idea of a god. The Maker. An entity of power who set the world in motion. He has mostly been reduced to a curse word at this point."

"We believe in the Bone-Builder." Instead of elaborating, he starts touching his cock. He lifts it, peering at his balls. "What is that?"

I press one hand to my forehead. "Why? Why *me*? Why do *I* have to explain this to you?"

"I have been forthcoming with information about my species," he says coldly. "You may as well return the favor."

"That's your ball sack. When you climax, that's where the cum originates. The, uh…"

"The seed," he says.

"That's nearly as bad as 'teats,' but yes."

"These parts are internal for dragons," he comments.

"The Maker left them outside when he formed human men, so us women would have something to kick."

Kyreagan doesn't answer. He's inspecting the head of his cock.

"I don't think I should be here for this." I start to rise and knock my skull against the angled stone slab. "Ow! Shit."

"Seeing my genitals is making you uncomfortable," he says. "Even though I've seen all your parts, and tasted them, too."

"That's beside the point," I gasp, holding the top of my head. "God, this hurts."

"I hurt too." He shifts his position, sighing. "Pain and discomfort seem more intense in this form. No wonder you are always so unpleasant."

"*I'm* unpleasant? You're the impossible grouch. If I'm occasionally unpleasant it's because I've been stolen from my home by an arrogant dragon who thinks he has the right to claim me and determine my fate."

"In war, such rights go to the victor. I claimed you. I own you."

His voice isn't quite as deep as it is in dragon form, but when he speaks those words, my body instantly heats. It's rebellion, yes, but it's something else, too—a perverse delight that ripples through my stomach, tinged with guilt because I shouldn't like it when he says those horrible things.

"You don't own me." The words don't sound nearly as strong or defiant as I hoped they would. "You can't own a person, a soul."

But he's distracted again, running his fingers along his sinewy forearm. It's flecked with hair, like his chest and legs. Right above his cock, there's a light dusting of curly dark hair as well. He's far less hairy than most men, but the mere presence of the hair seems to fascinate him. He takes a handful of his silky black locks and examines that, too.

"I don't like this form," he states. "I can almost feel my wings, but they aren't there. I am *stuck* to the ground, like a slug on a stone. And I'm so small, like a rabbit that must hide under rocks. Still, I'm larger than you. How tiny you must feel! How defenseless."

"Keep calling me weak and defenseless, and I'll show you how it feels to be kicked in the balls."

Despite the deepening gloom, I can tell he's looking at me with sudden interest, his attention transferred from his own body to mine.

Without warning, his fingers glide up my bare thigh. His hand is deliciously warm, as if he's being heated by a furnace within, and I'm cold, so I don't protest.

"Your skin," he murmurs. "So soft. I can feel it much better now."

He picks up my arm and traces the bones of my wrist and fingers. I barely breathe, charmed by the curious, careful way he handles me.

"Am I frightening you?" he asks.

"No."

"Your heartbeat is quicker than usual."

"I'm not scared."

"Angry, then?"

"At you? Always."

He chuckles, then shakes his head. "My voice sounds different."

"You still sound like yourself. Just not so huge. You don't have lungs the size of rowboats anymore."

His hand clasps my neck suddenly, and I gasp. But it's not a chokehold or a caress. He's still exploring.

His palm moves lower in the dark. Glides down my neck to my collarbones, along my chest. And then... over my breasts.

I don't know why I let him do things to me in the dark that I would never allow in the light. Night softens my reason, awakens every bit of my skin and makes it exquisitely sensitive. Besides, it's cold out here under the rocks, on the beach, and he's warm. So deliciously warm.

He pulls up the band of pink fabric around my chest and cups my naked breast with his bare hand.

My pussy thrills, warm and swollen and wet. My nipples tighten, both from cold and arousal.

"You did not run from the voratrice," he whispers. "You stayed, and you tried to help me. I cannot deny that I was moved by your sacrifice."

"I still hate you," I breathe. "And you hate me."

"Of course." But there's something in his tone that makes me want to be sure.

"And I'm still the last one you would dance for at the start of mating season," I prompt him. "If such a thing can even happen now."

He pauses for a second, then resumes fondling my breasts, almost absently, as if their smoothness and weight are a comfort to him. "There will be mating. I have felt the first signs of the heat coming upon me, and I feel it even now. We know that the enchantress can alter forms. I simply have to visit her again and impress upon her the importance of doing *exactly* what I asked. She will reverse this spell, and perform the one I requested."

"And if she doesn't?"

His hand slips lower, traveling down my stomach. "Then we may have to mate in this form and see what results from the coupling." He moves aside the cloth I tied around my waist, slides his hand into my underwear.

Fuck, he's going to touch my clit. I lean back on my hands, trying not to whimper as his fingers creep nearer.

"Careful," I breathe. "Your claws. Please…"

"I will not hurt you." He angles his hand so that only the pads of his fingers touch my pussy lips. "I like the feel of these. Ah, here it is. The special place." He taps my clit with one finger, and a tiny whimper escapes me.

"You sound so small and tender, Princess." Though it's dark, his voice betrays that he's smiling. "I like you this way. Gentled. Ready to be mated."

"That isn't—oh…" I release a shrill sigh as he strokes me, clumsily at first, then gently, rhythmically, his fingers wet and slippery from my arousal.

"The wetness is lubricant for breeding, is it not?" he murmurs. "These human fingers of mine can feel everything. It's one advantage to being in this form."

"Enough." I grip his wrist and move his hand away. "Don't touch me there."

"But you enjoy it."

"I enjoy the stimulation, yes. But I don't want to do this with you. I let you lick me once, and that was a mistake. I won't make it again."

I can't see his expression in the dark, but I feel the visceral tension between us, the thrum of need in the air. I swear I can smell him, the heat of his body, the musk of arousal. I imagine that long cock slipping inside me…

"We should rest," he says. "My night vision is gone, so we can't travel in the dark. Besides, it would be dangerous with the fenwolves roaming the forest. They rarely come to the beach, so I think we will be safe here."

"I hope so." I shiver at the thought of wolves coming upon us in the night—two naked, weaponless humans. We'd make an easy meal for them.

"You're cold?" he asks.

"Yes."

"Then we will lie together, and I will provide you with heat."

I can't think of a good reason to say no. The night will only get colder, and without his warmth, I could suffer severely from exposure.

"I suppose we must," I murmur.

We settle in with him on the outside, his back toward the beach and the ocean. I face inward, toward the slanted rock, with my back against Kyreagan's chest—and my ass pressed to his crotch. He's half-hard, and as I move cautiously closer, I feel his length twitch.

Carefully he wraps his arm around my waist, pulling me tight against him. "This is more pleasant than I expected. Do you have enough warmth?"

My arms, feet, and nose are cold, but the rest of me is incandescent. I've never lain with a naked man like this. Both my previous trysts were fairly quick, with no time to cuddle afterwards lest we be discovered and serve as fuel for palace gossip.

"My arms are cold, and this rock is uncomfortable," I whisper.

"Still complaining." His tone isn't frustrated, though. It's tinged with humor, or... affection.

"You're taking this change relatively well," I say.

His body tenses. "To be truthful, I'm furious, and I'm afraid. And yet doing this—experiencing the sensations of skin—it is pleasant."

"Even though you're injured?"

"Even so."

We lie in silence for a while. Being held by him is like snuggling with a massive wall of packed muscle and satin skin. His heat envelops me, warming me down to my bones, and if I tuck one arm under my head, the rock isn't so uncomfortable. It dips in a couple places, and I'm able to find a good spot for my hip and shoulder. In fact, I might be able to sleep... if my stomach would refrain from growling. I haven't eaten since the breakfast I enjoyed in the women's enclosure, before we started plotting our escape.

My belly growls again.

"Your body is loud," Kyreagan comments.

"I'm hungry. And yes, I know I'll have to wait for food."

He shifts a little closer, and pauses, inhaling.

"Are you smelling me?" I whisper.

"Yes." His lips brush my shoulder, and soft warm breath bathes my skin. "I must learn your scent better, so I can find you more quickly if you run from me again."

I forgot that I intended to run, to hide, to fight him, to do everything possible to keep from being back in his power. None of that seems so urgent now, with his big arms encircling me and his strong legs woven with mine.

He has burned people alive, Serylla, I tell myself sternly. *So many of Elekstan's forces, incinerated by him and his dragons. Picture it. Feel it. Don't yield to this foolish desire, this false sensation of safety, of rightness. Nothing about this is right.*

Kyreagan's voice reverberates through his body and mine. "You told me you know other songs, not just the annoying one."

"Yes."

"Your voice is soothing," he murmurs. "I thought you might sing a while. Perhaps one of the songs you created yourself."

Killer. Kidnapper. "No."

He rumbles low in his throat. "Sing for me, captive."

"No."

With a louder growl he sets his teeth against my shoulder, biting lightly. A bright thrill traces through my clit.

"Stop being so feral," I gasp. "You're better than that. Go to sleep."

He doesn't ask for a song again. I assume he has gone to sleep, because he's motionless for the longest time. Hours pass, yet the most I can do is doze restlessly. Every time I shift my position even slightly, I'm hyperaware of the thick, hard cock pressed between my ass cheeks. The cold, his heat, my hunger, his dick… it's all too distracting for me to rest. And the rock has become uncomfortable again.

There is nothing quite so torturous as a long night when you desperately want to sleep, need to sleep, and you *can't*. I've experienced such nights often throughout my life, but at the palace I had tea or wine to help me drift off. Here, there is nothing.

Tea... it's been so long since I had a good cup of tea. I think I miss it more than my own bed. Tea was my main indulgence, my one religion...

I'm jostled suddenly by the abrupt movements of Kyreagan as he disentangles himself from me and scrambles out from beneath the slanted rock. I scurry out as well and follow him as he staggers drunkenly across the sand.

Moonlight shines on the beach, highlighting the crests of the ocean waves and glowing on his body—the smooth curves of his ass, the valley of his spine, the broad muscles of his back partly obscured by the swinging sheet of his black hair. Starlight glints on his long, tapered horns.

He keeps falling, catching himself with his knee or his hand, pushing himself back up, stumbling onward.

"What is it?" I exclaim. "Did you hear a predator?"

"I can't do this." He's hauling in great, frantic breaths. "I need to fix it, now. I need to find the enchantress."

"Not at night! Not with wolves around. Kyreagan, stop." I dart in front so I can face him.

His eyes are wild, his jaw gaping as he struggles to breathe, but his breaths are too shallow, too quick.

"Grab your thighs and bend over," I tell him. "Put your head down. That will make it easier to breathe."

He obeys, his hair swinging over his shoulder. His skin shines with sweat, and he's shaking so hard it's a wonder he can stay on his feet. Cautiously I place my hand against his back, between his shoulder blades. I can feel his heart thundering at a frightening pace.

"You'll change back," I tell him.

"What if I don't?" he chokes out.

"Then you'll learn to live in this body."

"No. I have no power in this form. I can't bear it."

"You were going to force such a change upon me," I murmur.

"A change for the *better*. You would have been stronger, bigger, more glorious. This is a change for the worse. I should never have trusted that enchantress."

"Probably not."

"I shouldn't have told my people to take captives."

I hesitate, stunned. It's the first time he has admitted that capturing us was wrong. "No, you shouldn't have."

"I should have told her I loved her. Even if I didn't mean it." A harsh sob explodes from his body, and I put my other hand on his back, too.

"Your Promised?" I ask gently.

"She told me she loved me, shortly before the Guilhorn battle. And I did not reply. She did not mention it again, but I know my lack of response pained her. Her heart was like a mountain, strong and thriving. Mine is—like this." He picks up a worn shell with ragged edges.

"I don't think that's true. Yours isn't the kindest heart I've known, but you have your good qualities. You care about your clan."

"I told my brother and sister I would rule with them. Equal partners. But I kept making the big decisions, the important ones, and they let me. I have done what my father wanted, what I swore to him I would do, and yet things keep getting worse. And now *this*." He straightens, drops the shell, and stares at his hands. "Look at me."

"Could be worse." I step back, tilting my head. "At least you're pretty."

He stares at me, incredulous.

"The enchantress could have turned you into a fish, or a frog," I point out. "Or a bat. But she chose to give you this chance. I think she wants you to understand us better. To examine your choices."

"She didn't really seem like the type for such philosophical purposes."

He's still trembling, so I place my palm over his heart to check its pace. It has slowed somewhat, and seems to be returning to a safer speed.

When I glance up at him again, he's watching me, his eyes stormy with emotions I can't decipher.

"Safe to say we won't be sleeping," I tell him. "Maybe we should try to find something to eat."

"There are some roots that grow near the beach, just within the treeline. I used to love them when I was a hatchling. I rarely take the time to dig for them now."

"Let's hope they're edible for humans."

We pass the pre-dawn hours hunting for the tubers, which luckily are topped with huge feathery greens that make them easy to spot. Once they've been washed in seawater, they're good eating, if a bit starchy.

After we've sated our hunger, I gather some clumps of seaweed and weave a loose sort of loincloth for Kyreagan. The weaving takes a couple of hours, and by the time I'm done, the sun has risen.

The loincloth doesn't cover everything, particularly not in the back, but it forms a screen for his privates so my brain doesn't immediately scream *gorgeous cock* every time I look at him.

"Thank you." He nods, apparently pleased with the result. "Now we must go back to the others."

I hesitate, remembering my personal vow to stay out of the dragons' clutches. Of course, the situation has changed since then. If this transformation is permanent, our captors will be easier to defeat. I should return, at least to consult with the other women, and to find out more about the spell.

"Come, Serylla." Kyreagan's voice is low, firm, and compelling.

I approach him, but instead of letting him lead, I stalk past him, heading for the trees. "Don't say my name like that."

"Like what?"

"Like you expect to be obeyed." I pick up the slippers I discarded yesterday. They're damp and smelly, worn through in places after my forest trek, but slippers with holes are better than walking the woods in bare feet.

Kyreagan has no footwear, and when he steps into the undergrowth, he winces. He hides his discomfort immediately, assuming a grim expression. The concept of walking straight seems to baffle him, and he keeps veering from side to side and grabbing trees for support. I allow myself a giggle at his expense.

"We must be sure to avoid the voratrice's den," he says haughtily, ignoring my mockery.

"Before we go any farther, I need to relieve myself. You should as well."

A look of dread passes over his face.

"Don't be scared. Everything works similarly to your dragon parts. If you take a shit, just make sure to clean yourself with leaves, grass, whatever is available. If we were in my palace, there would be a privy with a porcelain toilet, soft cloths for cleansing, and perfumed soaps. Oh, and hot water. And towels."

"Seems like an overcomplication of simple bodily functions," he mutters.

"Of course you would think that, dragon." I walk away from him and duck behind a large tree to do my business.

Once I'm done, I wait while he curses, mutters, and stumbles around. I'm not sure what he's struggling with, exactly, but I let him figure it out, cupping my hand over my mouth to stifle the laughter.

At last he calls irritably, "Well? What's taking you so long?"

I rejoin him with a prim little smile. "I feel much refreshed."

He looks somewhat frazzled, but he seems to have avoided soiling himself or the loincloth, so that's promising.

Despite not traveling on foot through the forest very often in my lifetime, I've done a good bit of riding, and I'm decent at remembering landmarks and retracing paths. Kyreagan and I travel for most of the morning, until both our stomachs begin to growl again. We still haven't spotted anyone, human or dragon.

When we approach the area where I killed the vengeful girl, I take care to skirt around that spot and take us upstream for a drink. The day is warm, and I've been sweating from exertion, so when Kyreagan staggers off into the undergrowth growling something about taking a piss, I kneel on a flat stone by the stream, remove the band of pink cloth around my breasts, and bathe my heated skin. Judging by his earlier struggles, Kyreagan won't be back for several minutes, so I take my time.

I love the way the clear water ripples over the rocks, like rounded glass. I love the dark colors of the pebbles at the bottom of the stream, and the dappled light of the sun filtering through the leaves. Everything looks fresh and new this morning, and so beautiful I could almost forget about the ugliness of war, and the fact that I've seen three people die in the span of a few days.

The warrior. Listor. The vengeful girl.

"May the Maker accept their spirits," I whisper.

Near the rock I'm kneeling on, there's a patch of earth thick with rich green moss, dotted with tiny pale flowers. I stroke the moss with my fingertip, then pluck one of the flowers. Its stem is barely thicker than an eyelash, and the miniscule bloom at the top entrances me with its delicate perfection.

Gently I lay the flower in the water, watching it whisk away between the rocks. It's one of many flowers in that hollow, so I shouldn't feel guilty for picking it, but I do.

Is that how Kyreagan views me? One of many humans, frail, disposable? Easily crushed, or plucked for his pleasure?

The crack of a twig shocks me out of my reverie. I reach for the bit of pink cloth I discarded, but it's not where I left it.

It's in Kyreagan's hand, and he's standing right behind me.

15

KYREAGAN

I watch the Princess take the tiny flower gently between her fingertips and admire it. Her yellow hair pours over her shoulder, and her bare back curves as she kneels on the stone. As she lifts her arm and lets the flower go, I glimpse the side of her breast, smooth and round and tempting.

Slowly I bend and collect the garment she discarded. I'm not sure why, nor do I understand the heavy heat in my body, the sweet ache in my heart, the sudden thrill in my belly when my foot cracks a twig and she whirls around.

She is breathtaking when she's startled. Her eyes flare wide, alert and defiant. Such boldness in one with so little means of defense. I will never forget the courageous look on her face when she tried to save me from the voratrice.

I would have died if not for the enchantress's trickery, and I couldn't have stumbled away from the voratrice den fast enough without Serylla's help. I owe both of them my life, in different ways. I must remember that.

Serylla covers her breasts clumsily with one arm and snatches at the pink scrap of cloth I'm holding. "Give me that."

Without really thinking, I lift the pink garment above my head, far out of her reach.

Her eyebrows rise. "Really?"

My heart pounds hotter, and my mouth curves in a half-smile I can't suppress.

"You take human form, and now you act like this?" She gives me a reproachful glare. "Do I have to kick you in the balls?"

I consider risking her wrath. But then she says, "Kyreagan," desperately, and something inside me comes alive.

My name, from her mouth, in that breathless tone of both pleading and command, is everything I need.

I lower my hand, and she snatches the cloth. She turns her back to me and begins fumbling with the scrap, struggling to tie it in place—but apparently her fingers won't cooperate. When I step in beside her, I notice that she's trembling.

All thought leaves my brain, and I become a creature of emotion and instinct. Guided by them, I place both my hands over hers.

Her fingers go still. She lets the knot slip free, lets the pink silk flutter down to the rock. Looks up at me.

My hand slides around her wrist, drawing her fingers toward my chest so she can feel my heart beating, nearly as fast as it did last night. Serylla's lips part, and her gaze dips to my mouth.

She rises on tiptoe. Tilts her face up. And softly closes her lips over mine.

I don't know what to do. The sensations coursing through me are immense, overwhelming, and among them are strong currents of grief and guilt. Yet the most important thing in my world seems to be the silky lips touching my mouth, and the lovely body pressed against mine.

She tips her head back slightly. Smiles. "You don't know how to kiss."

"Kiss?"

"Of course... dragons don't kiss. This is kissing." She cups the back of my neck and takes my mouth with hers again, more firmly this time. The tip of her tongue slips out, stroking between my lips, probing into my mouth. With one hand she pulls my lower jaw down, and I open for her.

My tongue is shorter in this form, but still forked. I'm lucky that speaking has come easily to me, despite the change. Tentatively I meet Serylla's kiss, winding the twin sections of my tongue around her round, blunted one. She hums into my mouth and moves closer.

That's when I realize that my human cock is poking straight out, burning hot and painfully sensitive. Serylla sways her lower body inward, pinning my length between us.

My hands find her waist, drift up her smooth sides, glide up her back and plunge into her hair. All the while, she keeps her mouth on mine, and our tongues dance until my entire body is a column of searing flame, of violent, incandescent need.

My fingers clasp the back of her head while my other hand drops to her lower back, crushing her hips against mine. She responds with equal force, dragging my head down so she can kiss me more deeply.

But in that cacophony of roaring emotion and surging need, I sense a change. A ripple of magic pouring over my skin, trickling along my veins, vibrating in my bones.

I stagger back from her. "Fuck..."

"What?" Her mouth is scarlet and swollen. "What is it?"

"Something's happening. I'm... aahhh!" My voice changes to a throaty roar, and with a burst of energy, I am transformed, returned to my huge, scaly body, with wounds that feel deeper and more painful now that I'm back in this shape.

Besides the injuries, all the parts of me are as they should be. I have my long, spiked tail, my four clawed feet, and my wings—fuck, my wings are getting tangled in the trees. I snarl in frustration.

"Here, let me help." Serylla darts forward and holds back the branches until I can fold my wings close to my sides.

Once again, I am a dragon. Fire surges in my belly, warm and accessible should I require it. My tongue is its usual length, to match my jaws.

I am the same… and yet I am forever changed.

"You're back." Serylla looks disappointed. She bites her lip, pressing her thighs together. Then she picks up the pink cloth and ties it around her chest. When she speaks again, her voice is stiff and cold. "I suppose you can give me a ride now?"

Of course she hates me again, now that I'm not like her. The closeness of our bodies during the night, her kindness when I panicked, the fragile moment we shared just now—and the kiss—it's all over.

I crouch low on the bank of the stream. "Climb on. But be careful of the places where the voratrice ripped out my scales."

I half-expect her to step on those places anyway, out of sheer spite. But she doesn't.

When we return, the women's courtyard is in an uproar. Apparently one of the males transformed when he was standing near the barrier and smashed part of it when he regained his dragon shape. The women chatter together while the dragons skulk around the outside of the barrier, looking confused and chagrined. I don't see Ashvelon or Fortunix anywhere, but I spot Varex and I head straight for him, with Serylla still on my back.

"Did it happen to you too?" he asks frantically.

"Yes."

"She tricked us. Thelise tricked us."

"I know. Where is she?"

"Still in Ashvelon's cave."

"Were there any casualties? Do you know if anyone fell from the sky when they turned human?"

"Not that I've heard of. Most of us were on the ground with the women. Some dragons were stuck in their caves all night, as humans, and they flew down here to join us as soon as they reverted to dragon form."

"You and I must address the clan," I tell him. "First, however, I will confront the enchantress. You stay here and keep everyone earthbound and calm until we know if the change will happen again."

"Agreed," Varex says. "Do what you must to get the answers we need. But Kyreagan—don't kill her."

"Not until I find out what she has done to us." I leap into the air, and Serylla gives a little yelp of surprise.

"Warn me before you take off next time," she snaps. "I nearly fell."

"You should always be prepared when you're on a dragon's back. It's a dangerous place to be."

"*You* should always be considerate when you have a rider."

"I see you've returned to your usual mood."

"What's that supposed to mean?"

"Nothing," I growl. "Only that you were different, in the forest. You treated me more kindly when I was in human form. Perhaps because I was less of a threat. Weaker, softer."

"I wouldn't say softer," she mutters. "You felt pretty hard to me."

Heat and shame roll through me, and Mordessa's image rises in my mind. What would she say if she knew how I was behaving, so soon after her death? She would scorn me for desiring a human. How could I thus dishonor the memory of the one who loved me?

I dive abruptly, and Serylla shrieks.

"Don't mention that again," I command her. "Not to anyone."

"Asshole," she gasps as I resume a normal flying pattern. "So you got hard when I kissed you. You don't have to be embarrassed about it."

"I should not have such feelings prior to mating season. Especially not for *you*."

"How do you think *I* feel? I kissed the dragon who ripped me away from my home, threw me into a cave, and intends to use me as breeding stock." A wretched laugh bursts from her.

"Perhaps we both went a little mad, after we came so close to dying," I concede.

"And with the unexpected change of your body—it was confusing," she adds.

"We can forget it. Pretend it never happened."

She shifts restlessly on my back. "If that's what you want."

"It's what both of us want, is it not?"

"Of course." A pause, and then she says, "But in such troubled times as these, if we seek physical comfort, it does not necessarily have to mean anything deeper. Two people can despise each other and have no intention of being together long-term, yet still use each other for mutual benefit."

"Use each other... sexually?"

"Yes. Humans do it all the time. For instance, we could say that if you're ever in human form again, we're allowed to use each other purely for physical relief, without liking each other at all. No emotions or promises involved."

She falls silent after that. I can feel her waiting for my answer, her legs pressed tightly to my scales.

Something ravenous inside me leaps at the opportunity she offers, its greed overwhelming my guilt. "If it's a common arrangement among humans, I may as well follow that custom when I'm in that form."

"Right," she says eagerly. "In dragon form, you follow dragon customs, and in human form—well, no one has to know what we do."

The subversive nature of those words appeals to the dark, wild part of me. "And it changes nothing between us. I can still feel distaste for your spoiled behavior, and you can hate my plan for mating season."

"Exactly. It doesn't change a thing."

"Very well. But it's unlikely I'll ever be in human form again. I fully intend to force Thelise to do the spell properly and transform the women into dragons, as I intended."

"Of course," says Serylla brightly. "And I fully intend to despise you for it."

I rumble agreement. Yet oddly enough, now that we've made our little arrangement, I find myself hoping that last night wasn't my only time in human form. I rather wish it would happen again.

When we land on the ledge of Ashvelon's cave, I'm surprised to see him pinning the enchantress down with one huge, dark-gray claw. Her purple skirts are tangled around her thighs, her arms are flung outward, and her hair is strewn across the rocky floor. One of his claws is hooked into the bodice of her gown, tugging it so low her breasts are nearly exposed.

As I prowl forward, Ashvelon retreats swiftly from the enchantress, snorting and chuffing with embarrassment.

"Oh god," murmurs Serylla. "Was he about to kill her or fuck her?"

I choose to ignore her comment, but the enchantress stands up, adjusting her neckline, and says, with a sly half-smile, "I was wondering that myself. Hello there." She flutters her fingers at Serylla. "I'm Thelise."

"Witch," I snarl. "What have you done to us?"

I expect to have to torture the information out of her, but she only laughs and pats me on the nose as if I'm a wayward yet beloved puppy.

"It's quite simple, really." She sashays over to Ashvelon's nest, where several bottles are tucked among the grasses. While she's speaking, she uncorks one and pours herself a drink. "I didn't have the supplies or the power to do what you asked. Transforming small creatures like humans into giant hulking dragons would take an immense amount of energy, if it can even be done. I doubt even my rat-bastard of a father could have accomplished it. Killing something—now that's easier. Although taking down all you male dragons would have ended me too, which was out of the question since I prefer to exist. I doubt the afterlife has such delectable wine."

I growl, and Serylla advises, "I'd get to the point. He's extra impatient today."

"Says the most impatient creature I know," I retort.

"You two are charming, really," chuckles Thelise. "As I was saying, I couldn't transform women into dragons, so I did the next best thing. Dragons into men. Dragon-shifters, to be precise. It's based upon a handy bit of spellwork I tested once upon a time, transforming chickens into rats. This particular spell is a thing of beauty—my crowning achievement, really. I wrote it all down, thought of every detail. You should be thanking me."

She hesitates a moment, as if she's actually expecting thanks. When I snarl, she shrugs and continues. "Last night was your longest period in human form since everything was getting adjusted and taking effect. From now on, your time as humans will be shorter—eight hours a day or so. You won't be able to control the change at first, it will just happen, so I'd take short flights, and don't go too high. When you start to shift, you'll feel the change coming on, so you should have just enough time to land, if you're in dragon form, or strip off your clothes really quickly, if you're in human form. Eventually you'll learn to transform at will, though your daily hours as a human will still be limited."

Thelise gulps more wine. "You'll be able to fuck, too, anytime you like. You're welcome. But as a species you're still mostly *dragon*, so you'll have a mating season as usual, when you're fertile. From what Ashvelon tells me, when dragons mate, their genetic material combines in the female's womb, and then the shell of the egg forms around that little blob. My spell keeps that process intact, but the eggs will be somewhat smaller, for the benefit of the girls who have to birth them." She winks at Serylla, who says "fuck that" in a strangled, incredulous tone.

"The mating, incubation, and hatching schedule might be sped up a bit," continues Thelise. "But when it's all said and done, there will be a crop of little dragon shape-shifters hopping around. I've arranged it so they'll be hatched as dragons, and they won't be able to change forms for the first six months. Of course, all this is subject to the vagaries of the spell. I planned everything meticulously, as I said, but sometimes the magic does have a mind of its own." She giggles again, as if it's all the best joke in the world.

I know that her spell saved my life, and yet, for a moment, my anger overcomes my lingering gratitude. Her levity on the topic infuriates me.

"You will reverse this," I demand. "Or you will die."

Ashvelon growls low in his throat. "You will not kill her."

"If she does not cooperate, I will."

He paces forward, squaring his great shoulders, his wings lifting and arching in defiance. "No. I won't allow it."

I arch my wings and my neck as well. "I am your prince, Ashvelon. You will do as I say."

"Obeying you got us into this mess. Shedding her blood will rectify nothing."

"Boys, boys." Thelise walks unsteadily between us, holding up one hand with the goblet and waving the other hand as if to pacify me. "There's no need for this. The spell isn't reversible—you can kidnap any other sorcerer you like and ask them. They'll tell you it's impossible. I couldn't undo it if I wanted to. Let's focus on the good news." She pats my nose again, and I bristle. "You can still have the mating frenzy that you're all looking forward to so desperately, and you'll get to enjoy hatching season. The offspring that come out of the eggs might be a bit different than what you expected, but the whole point is to continue the dragon race, right? So as long as the traits are preserved in some form—"

I leap forward, swinging my head into Thelise and knocking her off her feet. Her body crashes into the wall of the cave much harder than I intended.

Serylla slides off my back, running to the enchantress's crumpled form, right before a blast of bluish-white frost-fire explodes in my face.

Ashvelon roars with all the might in his body, a direct challenge I can't ignore. We're mostly immune to each other's fire—it would take a lot for one of us to kill the other—but death isn't the point of such challenges. Dominance is.

With a snarl, I attack.

16

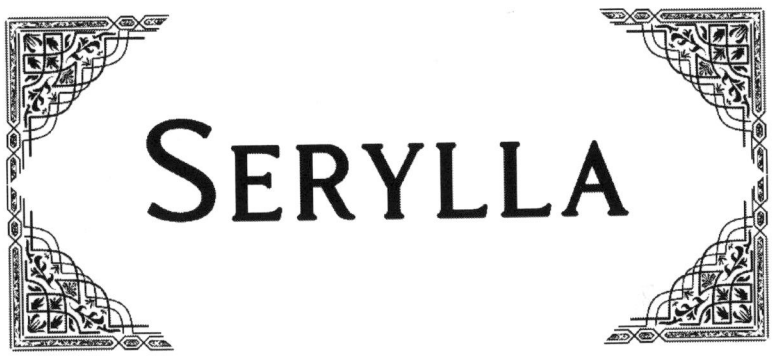

SERYLLA

"I'm fine," gasps the enchantress, brushing away my concern. "I want to see!"

She cranes her neck, peering around me at the two dragons, who are bellowing, biting, and clawing at each other's scales and wings.

Ashvelon is dark-gray and massive in the shoulders, with an extraordinarily long neck and a blunt head that give him an almost snake-like appearance. Long spikes jut from his spine, starting behind his head and running all the way back to his tail. Unlike Kyreagan's warm orange fire, Ashvelon emits bursts of frost-fire, which freezes and burns at the same time.

Kyreagan is huge as well, but his body is sleeker, not so thick in the shoulders and haunches. I like his triangular head, and the glossy black of his scales, and the wicked spikes that tip each bone of his wings…

"Don't crush the supplies," calls Thelise, as the two dragons thrash and roll through the cave. "Watch out for the wine! Please, god, not the wine."

I can't help chuckling. I liked her before I met her, simply because she made the dragons trust her and then turned on them. And now I think I like her even more, despite her egg-laying comment.

Thelise collects her now-empty goblet and pouts at the spilled wine, which is soaking swiftly into the rock. "Such a pity. I'm going to pour another. Do you want some?"

"Please," I say fervently. "My beverage of choice is tea, and I've felt dreadfully deprived. Wine will do the trick nicely, though."

She tilts her head. "So that's what Ashvelon meant. On our way here he was upset, kept saying that he'd forgotten to 'do the tea' or 'ask about tea' on behalf of his prince."

"It's alright. These dragons don't know what they're doing half the time."

"Much like human men." She gives me another wink.

"You're not wrong."

Keeping an eye on the battling dragons, the enchantress crawls over to the wine bottles and refills her cup. I watch Kyreagan leap on top of Ashvelon and pin the other dragon's neck to the floor. Ashvelon bucks, but Kyreagan maintains the hold and snarls a warning right in the other dragon's face.

"I will not yield," chokes out Ashvelon. "Unless you swear not to kill her. Otherwise you will have to slay me, too. Are you prepared to do that, Prince?"

Kyreagan lifts his head, arches his neck, and glances over at me and Thelise. His yellow eyes narrow before he looks back at Ashvelon.

"You care for the enchantress," he says.

Thelise grins, her eyes fixed on the frost-fire dragon.

Ashvelon twists, writhes. "Is that a crime?"

"Only if caring for her makes you a traitor to your kind. Did you know what she was planning to do?"

"No. I swear it on all the bones of my ancestors."

"Very well." Kyreagan's lips pull back in something that startlingly resembles a wicked smile. "I will promise not to harm her, if you swear, right now, to take her as your life-mate. She will be your responsibility, and your burden."

"Life-mate?" exclaims Thelise. "Wait a goddamn second—"

"I will," Ashvelon says immediately. "I do."

"And you, Thelise." Kyreagan swerves his great horned head back toward her. "Your one chance of survival is to pair with this dragon, the one who would defy his prince to ensure your well-being. As his life-mate, you will have protection from everyone in this clan who may wish to harm you—and trust me, I am not the only one enraged by what you have done. Do you agree?"

The rosy wine-flush drains from Thelise's cheeks. "I suppose I must."

"Then I declare you bound forever. We will perform the bone-knitting ceremony after hatching season. Come, Princess."

But I hang back. "I want to stay here and drink wine, and look through the supplies. Maybe there will be soap."

"There is," Thelise assures me.

"Then I'm staying. You go and speak with your people—your dragons, I mean."

Kyreagan jumps down from Ashvelon's still-prone body and stalks toward me, his head lowered, his yellow eyes penetrating mine. Blood rises to my cheeks under that possessive glare.

"When will our human forms return?" he asks Thelise, though his eyes never swerve from mine.

"Fuck if I know," she says.

"Give me an estimate."

"Might be another ten or twelve hours? Things are still settling. But like I said, take short flights, stay low when you can, and if you feel a strange buzzing sensation, land immediately."

"I'll be back in six hours, Princess," says Kyreagan. "Be ready for me."

Those last four words carry a significance and meaning that sends a chill up my spine. He agreed with my impulsive plan, that we should use each other physically when he's in human form. I get the feeling he's looking forward to it.

Kyreagan heads for the entrance of the cave, throwing an order over his shoulder. "Ashvelon, you're with me."

Ashvelon heaves himself up off the floor of the cave. He dips his head to Thelise, then to me, before flying away with the dragon prince.

"He really likes you." I elbow Thelise lightly.

She laughs. "He's a good boy. Does what he's told, for the most part. Though I rather like it when he decides to assert himself."

"Is that what he was doing when we arrived?"

A shadow crosses her face, and she turns away. "Shall we investigate the contents of these bags? Ashvelon and Fortunix didn't think it worth distributing the goods to the women since they were going to be transformed so soon. Now that the captives are staying human, much of this will be given to them. But as the Crown Princess, it's only right that you should have first pick. You can take all the best things."

There's a faint edge to her tone, and I get the sense that this isn't just kindness or friendliness—it's a test. She wants to see if I'm a greedy, spoiled bitch. I intend to prove I'm not.

We take our time going through the bags, organizing the supplies into piles—clothing, blankets, cosmetics, jewelry, perfume, wine, and various herbs and salts.

"You had all this readily available?" I ask.

"Oh no." She laughs. "When the dragons came to get me and said they needed supplies for other captives, I made them wait in the stables while I sent a messenger to buy the rest of the things at the market. I tried to think of everything a civilized person might miss if they were being housed in a dragon's cave."

"Back up a moment. You made two dragons wait in the stables?"

"I bound them there. With magic."

"Then... you could have overcome them both and escaped."

She wraps a flamboyant scarf around her neck. "Of course."

"So why did you let them take you?"

She looks at me soberly for the first time. "Days before my father's last act, he sent me a letter describing what he planned to do. I didn't believe he'd go through with it, so I did nothing. I told no one."

"You came here because you felt guilty?"

"Not guilty, exactly. I don't believe in guilt. But I suppose I felt some responsibility. The dragons didn't specify what spell they needed, but I figured I should go along and see what I could do to mitigate the situation."

"And you weren't afraid you might make it worse?" I wince. "Forgive me, but I heard that your spells don't always go as planned."

"You heard I'm a terrible enchantress. Powerful, but unpredictable and careless."

"Well... yes."

Thelise smirks. "That's the beauty of gossip, darling. I have never performed a spell that didn't turn out exactly as I intended. But I did perform several that produced very strange results, whereupon I pretended to be shocked and embarrassed. You see, if you're powerful *and* skilled, people never stop bothering you to do magic for them. But all you have to do is deliberately mess up a few times, and they leave you alone."

"You're brilliant." I sip the wine, cradling its smooth richness on my tongue.

"Best mistake I ever made on purpose was when a man came to me, asking for a larger dick. And I made an extra dick sprout out of his head."

I nearly choke on the wine, but I manage to swallow it. "You did not."

"Oh yes. Nearly got myself run out of town. But I pacified everyone and I paid for a number of very fine hats so the man could hide his new… protuberance. You should have seen it— this big soft cock just flopping around on top of his head…"

I'm laughing so hard I nearly spill the wine. "God, the dragons are lucky you didn't do something similar to them."

"I considered it. But my aim here is to bring peace and harmony, not foment more anger."

My smile fades. "You made them beautiful so we would want them."

"Yes. Does that make me a monster?"

I'm not sure how to answer, so I bite my lip and pick through the assortment of soaps. Finally I select a bar that smells like fresh oranges.

"I understand what you're doing," I tell her. "But I'm not sure it will work. The dragons are so different from us. And most of the women are terrified. They just want to go home."

Thelise snorts. "Do they? Or are they simply pretending they do? What about adventure? What about romance? What about birthing a new race?"

"I don't want to birth any new fucking race."

"Yes, well…" She rises, straightening her skirts. "You'll have a choice, of course. The dragons' human side should soften the effects of the mating frenzy a bit. But I'm sure they will be very insistent and persuasive nonetheless. You may find yourself yielding against your better judgment."

"Do you have any contraceptive herbs?"

She purses her lips. "I do. Not enough for everyone."

"I want some."

"I can spare enough for two doses. Beyond that, I must reserve the rest for others."

Perhaps she expects me to argue, but I don't. I take the paper packet of herbs that she gives me, along with soap, a comb, a tin of salt, some new underthings, and an orange dress that precisely matches the color of Kyreagan's fire.

"I have some men's clothing, too," offers Thelise. "I didn't know the prisoners were all female. It's mostly castoffs from ex-lovers of mine. This one is rather princely, don't you think?" She holds up a black cloak with dramatic epaulets. "Might suit Kyreagan in his human form. There are boots too, somewhere in these bags. Everything got jumbled together."

Eventually we locate the boots, as well as a pair of black pants and two shirts, one black and one ivory. I find a second dress as well—a pink one with sleeves down to my elbows and a ruffled neckline. It looks like something a farm girl might wear on a special day.

Thelise brings over an old bedsheet from one of the bags, and she helps me create a bundle containing the cloak, the clothes, and the other supplies. Then we recline on her throne-like chair together, sipping wine and talking of the women we have known, the men we have kissed, and the dragons who have claimed our future.

17

"There is nothing we can do!" I repeat, for the hundredth time, to the group of male dragons. They cluster around a jutting rock on which Varex and I have perched, with Ashvelon and Fortunix flanking us. "The spell is permanent."

"We should kill the enchantress!" bellows Saevel, a dragon with green scales. "She has ruined us and doomed our race!"

A growl rips from Ashvelon's throat. Fuck, he's enamored with that woman. I don't understand it.

"Ashvelon has claimed the enchantress as his life-mate," I announce. "I bound them myself. Therefore she is under the protection of the clan and may not be harmed. He accepts full responsibility for her future actions."

"Including any other damaging spells she may do?" shouts Hinarax.

Fuck—I hadn't thought of that. What's to stop Thelise from continuing to meddle in our lives with her magic?

"I accept full responsibility for everything pertaining to her," says Ashvelon. "If any dragon wishes to challenge me, he may do so."

"He is a daunting opponent," I add. "I would not challenge him lightly."

The other dragons rumble their discontent.

Varex steps forward, his claws scraping the rock. "My brothers, let us calm ourselves and give each other time to adjust to this new reality. We should talk together, share our experiences in our human bodies, and think of the benefits that might accompany this shift in form."

"Benefits?" someone snarls.

"Yes, benefits." Varex's voice holds a note of eagerness. "We can care for livestock better. Plant gardens and fields. Forge armor, craft machinery, create books—"

"You mean change our culture?" Fortunix shoves his way between my brother and I, his scarred wing scraping my shoulder. "Become more like the humans we hate, the humans who perpetrated this act of devastation upon us? Forgive me, young Prince, but I find that intolerable. Who here recalls the days of the dragon hunters? Precious few of us, because so many died during that dark time. Then we endured the plague. Next, the war and the murder of our females. And now we are supposed to ponder the *benefits* of assuming frail human flesh for several hours each day? I cannot view this event as anything but what it is—an assault on the very nature of dragonkind. An affront to the Bone-Builder himself. If we accept this, we are pissing on the skulls of the ancestors—on your own father, Varex. The Bone-King, Arzhaling himself. What would he say to this?"

A low growl ripples in Varex's throat. "Keep my father's name out of your mouth. You will refer to him by his title, or not at all."

"You would teach *me* the rules of honorifics, hatchling?" snarls Fortunix.

"Enough!" I bellow, with sufficient force to send both of them back a step. "As my brother wisely said, we need time to consider all aspects of this change. It's difficult for everyone, but squabbling is foolish and futile. We need each other more than ever."

Silence falls over the gathered dragons. And then Varex says, "Was anyone else's human cock frighteningly small?"

An instant rush of exclamations surges from the group, mostly horrified agreement. Pride swells in my heart as I watch Varex leap down from the rock and pace among the others, commiserating with them about the strange human genitals. There is some mention, too, of accompanying sensations, but I don't take the time to listen, because my focus is on Fortunix. He's flying away, probably to cool his temper.

Perhaps I should not have spoken so harshly. He is an elder, after all. And he helped Ashvelon bring the enchantress here, so perhaps he feels somewhat responsible for what has happened.

I leave my brother to handle the clan, and I fly after Fortunix, intending to apologize.

But he isn't heading for his cave. Instead he soars over one of the peaks and banks sharply northwest. In that direction lies the area most heavily populated by voratrix and fenwolves. What reason could he have to go there?

Instinct tells me I should avoid his notice until I find out his purpose. With the help of a strong wind, I gain altitude and use the misty clouds as cover to partly conceal myself as I follow him. He's flying low, heeding the warning which I communicated to the clan.

Is he seeking solitude? Hunting? Looking for a predator to battle, to burn off some of his anger?

I can empathize with his fury. I'm angry and confused myself. But Fortunix has more cause than most to hate humans. My father told me that when Fortunix was young, he was blessed with the love of two life-mates, a male and a female. Their trio shared a passion that was legendary among dragonkind. During the dragon hunts, both of his life-mates were killed and skinned.

Since the hides were separated from the carcasses before dawn could return them to ash, the hides and scales remained intact. Such trophies would fetch a high price among wealthy humans.

Skinning or dismembering a dragon's corpse is a sacrilege of the worst kind. It is said that such an act prevents the dragon's spirit from returning to the cycle of the universe. Small wonder, then, that Fortunix carries such hatred for humans.

Perhaps he has his life-mates' bones hidden somewhere and he is going to visit them, in which case I should not spy on his grief. I'm about to turn around when I see him dive into the Necrocleft, a dark crack where a mountain once split in half. Dragons rarely go there because it's almost too narrow for wings, and because it is a cursed place, where dreadful tragedies have occurred. Venturing into the Necrocleft is like begging the Bone-Builder to curse you with bad fortune.

Swooping lower, I dive into the crack as well and follow Fortunix at a careful distance, gliding as much as I can and beating my wings when he does so he won't hear my approach.

I have no reason to pursue him like this. No reason not to trust him. And yet… he set up the meeting with the King of Vohrain without being requested to do so by Varex or me. He stayed behind to "smooth things over," and he hasn't told me what was said after I left. He undermined Varex and me just now, in front of the clan. And instead of remaining with everyone else to discuss our predicament, he is here, navigating the Necrocleft.

When the chasm narrows more, Fortunix lands, folds his wings, and continues on the ground. I land as well, creeping along far behind him until he begins to claw his way up a sheer rock face. About halfway up, he disappears. There must be a hidden cave that I can't see from this angle. Rather than confront him directly, I continue along the chasm past the spot where he vanished.

Up ahead, a pile of rock chokes the canyon. It's the very avalanche in which Mordessa's first family perished. Some say their spirits never rose from the rubble of the rockfall, and that their souls remain trapped with their bones, forever groaning under the weight of countless boulders.

My father told me Mordessa's parents came to this place for alethia, an herb which, when consumed, causes a dragon to see the world in rainbows of rippling color, and to imagine the most fantastical things. This chasm and a few others like it are the only places on the island where such herbs will grow.

In the other places where alethia thrives, the fenwolf packs are too numerous for a grounded dragon to face. Like the older voratrix, the fenwolves of Ouroskelle have developed fire-resistant hides, and our magic barely damages them. So Mordessa's mother and father chose to collect the herbs from this narrow chasm, where even fenwolves fear to go. A foolish risk for a few plants.

Perhaps Fortunix has come here for alethia? I spot clumps of iridescent leaves along the edges of the rockfall, but I can't be sure it's the right plant. My father outlawed alethia after Mordessa's first family died, so I have never seen it.

A giant slab of rock rests at an angle against the cliffside. I crouch beneath it and wait until Fortunix emerges, crawls down to the ground, and returns the way he came, without glancing in my direction. Then I claw my way up the cliff to the place where he disappeared.

Sure enough, there is a tunnel into the mountain, concealed from below by the angle of the rock. It's just large enough for a dragon of Fortunix's size to squeeze down it.

After a dozen paces or so, the tunnel widens into an oval-shaped room. Several chests stand against the walls, some of them overflowing with treasure. This must be a private hoard. Usually dragons keep a small selection of their favorite jewelry and contribute the rest to the clan hoard, but Fortunix has been holding back many valuable items. Selfish, perhaps, but not traitorous.

I'm about to leave when I hear a tinkling, scuffling sound. Near the back wall of the room sits a wooden crate filled with wide-mouthed glass jars, each covered with a piece of leather speckled with holes and secured with a metal band. It's odd that Fortunix would own human-made items other than jewelry—but that's not what surprises me. The clinking and scuffling sounds come from the shell-like wings of blood-beetles bumping against the glass.

Every jar holds about a dozen beetles, each one a deep reddish-black. They crawl over and over each other, now and then trying to fly away only to bump against the thick glass. Their serrated pincer mouthparts move incessantly, and the sharp tube between those pincers jabs up and down, seeking flesh to impale.

Blood-beetles mostly attack warm-blooded animals, but occasionally one will get into a dragon's mouth or genital pouch, or dig into the hollow of a joint, causing pain and distress. The insects are capable of consuming a shocking amount of blood and they can swell up to five times their size. Animals or dragons bitten by them often become infected by other diseases as a result.

I have no idea why Fortunix has concealed this treasure, or why he's keeping blood-beetles as pets. But I've indulged my curiosity long enough. I must return to the others and remind them to take short flights and stay near the ground. We should hunt and gather food for ourselves and the women before the change occurs again. Then I have a private errand of my own to complete, after which I must go back to Ashvelon's cave to collect the Princess. She and I won't be returning to my cave tonight—I have a different spot in mind.

18

SERYLLA

Clinging to a dragon's back while holding a large bundle is more difficult than I expected. Fortunately, Kyreagan flies slowly, staying nearer to the ground than usual, as Thelise suggested.

"We're not going back to your nest?" I renew my grip on one of his spikes and clench my thighs around his neck as tightly as I can. My free arm circles the bundle, holding the precious clothing and supplies close to my chest.

"I'm taking you to a different roost for the night."

"What about dinner?"

"There is food waiting for you."

"Good boy," I croon. "You're learning."

He scoffs and swoops down, making my belly jump even though we're not far above the open meadow. We're skimming toward a series of low foothills at the base of another mountain. It amazes me how complex and varied the geography of this island is. I suspect parts of it are not entirely natural—probably built from dragon bones or carved by their claws, and then the land reclaimed those places, spreading moss, earth, and grass over it all.

Kyreagan zips through a gap between the hills, then glides over a shaded valley where glassy pools lie beneath gnarled, flowering trees. Spring is in full force here, with frothy pink blooms festooning the trees and rich purple violets coating the damp, gloomy hollows.

The beauty of it makes my heart ache.

"This place is so pretty it hurts," I murmur.

Kyreagan hums low in his chest, and I know he feels the same way. Deep in that wild dragon-heart of his, there's a softness I find appealing. I can't help it.

It's dangerous being out here alone with him, because I'm beginning to forget that I'm supposed to hate him.

To bolster my inner resistance, I summon the memory of him knocking Thelise into the wall. She wasn't hurt, and I don't think he intended to do more than frighten her a little, but the act of violence still angered me.

And he killed Listor. Grabbed him and flung him off the wall. But that was war, and the rules were different—he was angry, grieving—

No, Serylla. Stop making excuses for him. He has burned people alive. Soldiers by the scores, maybe even hundreds. He killed relatives of your servants, your guards, your friends...

Kyreagan glides over several round pools, each rimmed with crystallized rock. Steam rises from them, misting the air with heat. The crooked trees arch over the pools, as if drinking in the warmth, and their pink petals float through the air like fragrant snow, settling on the water and collecting in rosy drifts along each pool's edge.

This is a hot spring. He has brought me to a *hot spring*, and my skin immediately cries out to be submerged in those heated pools.

"This is a sacred place," Kyreagan says. "We come here on certain moons to ask the Bone-Builder for wisdom, and we bring our hatchlings here to be cleansed during the third moon cycle after their hatching. No human has ever been allowed to visit these hot springs."

"Then why am I here?"

"Because I wish it." He lands on a strip of mossy rock beyond the pools, in the entrance to a shallow cave. When I peer inside the cave, I notice two more pools within its shelter. They're glowing a faint bluish-green.

"The crystals in the rock glow at night," he explains.

As if this place needed any more beauty to make me adore it. I've never seen anything so lovely.

"Wait here." Kyreagan enters the cave and blows his superheated breath on a few cube-shaped rocks stationed at intervals along the floor. Each rock begins to glow bright orange, and unlike regular rocks, the light doesn't fade. They must be uniquely adapted to hold the heat.

As the rocks' glow floods the cave, it illuminates two worn blankets spread upon the rough stone floor. Set out upon them are three bowls—one containing some very stale-looking rolls, the second holding dried, salted fish, and the third boasting a wedge of golden cheese, coated with mold along one side.

But the thing that catches my attention is a small stone cup, the perfect size for my palm, obviously chiseled by a dragon's claw. It's half-filled with water, and a large, cold clump of tea leaves are swamped in the center of the liquid, like a pathetic island.

My heart seizes up as laughter, shock, and sweet pain collide in my chest.

Somehow I manage to compose my features as I point to the cup and ask the dragon, "What is this?"

"It's tea." He looks so smug. So proud of himself.

I stare at the cup, my throat swelling with tears and my heart with—no, it's not affection, or gratitude, because I can't feel those things for a monster, for the slayer of my people. I've betrayed my kingdom by letting the dragon lick me, by kissing him… I can't go any farther down this road.

"This isn't tea." I make a disdainful face at the cup. "This is just water and leaves."

"But that's what you said…oh, fuck, I forgot!" His long neck snakes down and he blows a concentrated breath into the cup. The water immediately begins to steam. "There! Tea."

Warmth spreads through my whole chest, and a smile teases at my lips. "Where did you get all this?"

"From a large house along the coast. I asked for the best they had."

Whoever he spoke to must have been terrified at the appearance of the monstrous black dragon, and yet they were defiant enough to give him stale bread, salted fish, and moldy cheese. Kyreagan didn't know any better—he took it all in good faith. He has to stop trusting people so readily.

The dragon looks at the food, then back at me. "Is it wrong?" Uncertainty threads through his deep voice, and fuck, I can't bear it.

"It's perfect." I force the two words out. It's a betrayal of my country, a concession greater than the dragon will ever understand. I care enough that I can't disappoint him, not when he flew all the way to the coast to get these things, knowing they would please me.

"Wait…" I turn toward him. "You went to the mainland? Did you meet with the King of Vohrain?"

He swallows, pins his sharp ears back slightly. "I did. Yesterday."

"You said you would ask about my mother."

"I planned to tell you about it when I returned, but you escaped, and then—"

"The voratrice, and the transformation," I finish. "But you could have told me during the night, or this morning."

"It didn't seem like the right time. Nor is this the right time. You should eat, enjoy your tea."

"Kyreagan." I step up to him and place my hands on either side of his long muzzle. His yellow eyes flare wider at my touch. Then they shift aside, avoiding my gaze.

"Kyreagan, tell me."

He huffs out a warm breath. "The news will distress you."

"I can take it. It's harder *not* knowing. Please—"

At my plea, his eyes swerve back to mine. "She ended her life," he says, low. "When the Vohrainian forces invaded the palace, they found her dead on the throne."

But his eyes shift again as he says it.

"You're lying, and you're not good at it. Tell me, dragon. Right now." I clutch the spikes along his jaw, desperate for the truth.

"She fought." Kyreagan's voice is a doleful growl. "She fought back until they took her weapons away. The King of Vohrain stripped her naked and had her beaten in front the people. Afterward he cut off her head."

My hands drop from his spikes. I turn and stumble away from him, my vision glazed with tears.

My mother, who never stepped out of her rooms without face powder, rouge, and lip stain flawlessly applied; my mother, who wore grand, sumptuous clothing even on days when she didn't have court or meetings; my mother, whose hair was intricately coiffed for every occasion—for her to be stripped of all her layers, her personal armor, and subjected to a beating in the city square—it's an image I wasn't prepared to handle.

"The tea was supposed to help," Kyreagan says quietly.

"Tea?" I wheel around, shaking. "That fucking blob of leaves in water? That's not tea. It's disgusting, and so is the stale, decayed food you brought me."

He shuffles back a step, his neck arched. His horns and spikes look more like a crown than ever, and I hate him for it. I hate that he's so beautiful and regal, that he looks so hurt and yet so concerned for me.

"I loved my mother." The words nearly choke me. "I hated her, and I loved her, and she was a wretched, careless woman who spent lives like coin, but she didn't deserve to suffer like that. She didn't. She must have been so humiliated, in so much pain—she needed me, and I wasn't there, I wasn't—"

"The same thing would have happened to you, or worse," Kyreagan replies. "The King of Vohrain offered me three chests of gold and the Parrock Banks in exchange for you."

"Why the fuck?"

"He says your people love you. He plans to use you to control them, and he wants to breed you as well."

"And what did you say to him?"

"I considered the offer, but decided not to accept it."

"How unexpectedly wise of you," I say through clenched teeth. "Maybe you're finally beginning to understand that your ally is a bigger monster than any dragon. He has used your clan to do despicable things. He leveraged your desperation and turned all of you into the agents of his cruelty. You can't trust him, or his rewards. If you do, you're a fool."

The dragon's lip hitches with a quiet snarl. I hurt him by telling the truth about the food and the tea, and now I've stung his pride. But I'm too full of helpless anguish to care.

"You gave my people into the hands of a terrible man," I tell him. "The families I care about, the people who were kind to me—they're in his power now, and that's your fault. I can never forgive you for that."

He snarls louder and shuffles back another step, his wings sharply arched and his spiked tail lashing.

"I'm surprised you didn't hand me over," I say. "You've done far worse things, like commit widespread carnage in exchange for new hunting grounds. Why not take the treasure and the Parrock Banks or whatever the fuck, and give me to him? You could always fetch another girl to take my place. Some meek little thing who wouldn't annoy you, who would be happy to take your cock and birth your eggs."

He paces toward me with his head lowered and his eyes aflame. Every word shows his long teeth, gleaming in the low light. "I don't want another girl."

A thrill pulses through my heart, but that only makes me more desperately angry. I can't manage the towering thunderstorm of emotions in my body, so I grit my teeth and punch his scaly snout, right between his nostrils.

Kyreagan chuckles darkly. "Feels as if a fly landed on my nose."

I screech with frustration and haul back to hit him again, but before I strike, he inhales sharply and shudders.

A burst of light obliterates him for a second, and when it fades, he's the tall, toned man from before, with the light-brown skin, sharp horns, and a waterfall of inky black hair.

I punch him hard in the left breast, and he staggers back with a grunt. The violence eases my frenzied pain a little, so I hit him again, in the ribs. My knuckles ache, but that discomfort is nothing compared to the agony of my flayed heart.

Kyreagan steps back, snatches a blanket, and wraps it hastily around his waist, tucking it rather than knotting it. I suppose he has no idea how to tie things. He's a bit steadier on his legs this time.

When he turns back to me, his dark eyes glow with earnest regret.

"Go ahead. Hurt me," he says. "Your anger is raw and fresh, and it requires violence. When one dragon is responsible for another's death, whether by intent or accident, the killer is chastised by one of the deceased dragon's relatives. I have caused you unutterable pain and loss. No matter what my motives were, you deserve reparation. Tear my skin, bruise me, beat me—I will not resist. My body is yours."

I stand motionless, galvanized by his words, so unlike the ones he spoke after snatching me out of the air by the city wall.

Back then he said, *Your will, your future, and your body are mine.*

And now he is giving his body to me. Yielding to pain for my sake, even though he, too, has experienced unimaginable loss. I can't forget his voice when he told me of his Promised, his grandmother, his sister. I can't unsee the tooth and the claw, set with such care on the ledge in his cave, inscribed with the names of his parents. I can't deny the wordless testimony of the meal he planned for me, and the tea, the stupid fucking tea…

"Did you hear me, Serylla?" he repeats. "Enact your vengeance upon me. Use me."

Heat rolls over my skin, burns at my core, singes my veins, my fingertips. Blood roars in my ears.

Use me. Use me…

I leap for him, grab his hair, drag his face down to mine. My mouth tears at his, teeth and tongues, frantic, hungry. My body is starved for touch, for warmth, for anything except the constant, wearying uncertainty. I'm so fucking tired of hurting, of being sad and stressed and frightened. I need the hot, smooth skin of his chest, the compact muscle of his abdomen, the ridges of his hips. I need the strong arms that fold tentatively around my body as my fingers dig into the broad expanse of his back. He's unsteady on his human feet, so I push him back toward the other blanket and we collapse onto it, knocking aside the lumpy tea and inedible meal.

"You said I could use you." I manage the words between violent kisses. "I want to use you to feel better. May I?"

"You need my tongue." He darts it out suggestively, and it's adorable, and I laugh. I *laugh*, and then my face falls because my mother is dead, my mother was beaten and beheaded and *god what is wrong with me*—I stop kissing him, press my forehead against his shoulder, and close my eyes against the oncoming tears. I hold them back so hard I can't breathe.

My whole body spasms, the violent proof of my pain. Kyreagan's hands tighten on my sides.

"Perhaps you don't need my tongue right now," he says quietly. "Perhaps you need rest."

"No." I rake my teeth along his thick collarbone, bite down until his breath hitches. "I need you to make me stop thinking, stop hurting."

"Physical pleasure can achieve this?" The ache in his voice strums a string in the very depth of my soul.

"For a little while."

"Then do what you like with me. I said it, and I meant it."

I sit up, astride his waist. I'm still wearing my underwear and my skimpy wrapped skirt, and he's wearing the blanket—but even through the material, I can feel his erection.

Enemy though he is, I don't want to take him beyond what he's prepared to do. He's a virgin, after all. "If you don't like something I'm doing, tell me, and I'll stop."

"I will like it all." He's flushed, staring up at me like he's terrified and wildly excited at the same time.

That look on his face blurs all the awful truths and shifts them to the back of my mind. In this moment, there is only him, with his reckless, volatile dragon's heart, and the clawed hands holding my waist so carefully, and the beautiful black silk of his hair spread across the rug.

I pull off the pink wrap around my breasts and throw it aside. His face changes, intensifies to something like worship, and I nearly laugh again. I've never quite understood the fierce fascination some people have with breasts. I like mine, but damn. Kyreagan looks as if he wants to build a monument to them.

"You've seen them before," I murmur. "Touched them before."

"Yes, but..." *But this is different.* He doesn't have to say it—I feel it, too.

Removing the other scraps I'm wearing takes but a moment, and then I seat myself on his hard stomach again. I take his wrists, but instead of placing his hands on my breasts, I move his arms aside while I scoot forward. Carefully, a little awkwardly, I plant my knees on either side of his head, and I curl my fingers around the roots of his horns. His mouth is right below my pussy.

"Show me that tongue," I whisper.

He's already opening his mouth, already lifting his head, eager to taste me. I use his horns for leverage, to adjust the angle of his face as I settle onto it.

Kyreagan groans, his deep voice rippling between my legs.

"Fuck." The word jerks out of me as I rub myself against his jaw, his mouth, his nose. His forked tongue tantalizes me, swirls over my swollen, sensitive lips before lapping firmly, rhythmically.

"Oh... oh... oh..." I pant the same sound, over and over, squirming against him. Shit, I'm already so close to coming, and I don't want to, not yet. This can't be over so soon—I can feel the shadow of grief waiting to close back in, and I can't bear it. I need this to last.

When I try to move away, I realize he's grasping my ass cheeks, holding me to his face. He's loving this, truly relishing it.

"Let me go, or I'll come too soon," I gasp.

"Can you come more than once?" He speaks the words right against my clit, and I squeal helplessly, trembling right on the edge of a climax.

"Yes," I whimper. "Yes, yes..."

"We will count, and see how many times you come for me."

When he says *come for me*, with his lips brushing my clit, a hot flare of bliss shoots through my core. My legs shudder, and I haul convulsively on his horns, pulling his face tighter between my thighs. I ride his face helplessly, prey to the thrilling sensations.

Kyreagan digs every one of his nails into my ass, not hard enough to break the skin, but enough to let me know he's fully invested in my bliss, fully supportive of me suffocating him with my pussy.

"Easy," I pant, releasing my grip on his horns. "I'm going to move off you now."

His fingers relax, caressing my bottom in slow circles as I rise on my knees to let him breathe.

"I was mistaken," he says. "Human bodies are glorious."

When I slide off him, I notice that his cock is pointing straight up under the blanket he wrapped around his waist. I unwrap the blanket and lay it aside, leaving his body entirely bare.

"You're so fucking beautiful," I whisper. "Like this, and also the other way."

He sits up, his gaze locking with mine. "You think I'm beautiful as a dragon?"

"You know you are."

He starts to smile. And then something hits him—I see it, I know the feeling because it just happened to me. I know that guilt in his expression, I know it so fucking intimately. The feeling that I shouldn't ever be happy again, because people I care about have been hurt or killed.

His handsome face tightens, stricken with such pain that I hurt too, for *him*.

I reach out and cup his jaw in my hand. "What is it?"

"I shouldn't feel this way." His breathing is heavy, his chest surging with emotion. "This is how I was supposed to feel for my Promised. She told me she loved me, and I couldn't answer her. She deserved my love, and she received death instead."

"You feel guilty." I run my thumb across his lips.

"I feel other things, too. For you."

There's something soft and passionate in his eyes, something tender and intimate. A warning blares in my mind, like the dragon alarm from my home city. Abruptly I clamp my hand across his mouth. "Don't say it."

He pulls away. "You asked why I didn't want the King of Vohrain to have you—"

"Kyreagan, stop!" I lunge for him and press both hands over his lips this time. "Hush, silly dragon. Or must I silence you with my pussy again?"

He imprisons my wrists in his big hands. "Is that what it's called?"

"That, and other words."

"Are you afraid of words?" He cocks an eyebrow at me. "You seem to be."

I squirm, trying to tug free. "Some words, yes."

"I was only trying to tell you—"

With a sharp curse, I jerk one hand free and wrap it around his erection.

His eyes go blank instantly, and he makes a strangled sound, half-gasp, half-moan. I allow myself a triumphant smile and circle my thumb over the head of his cock, glossing it with his arousal.

"Don't talk," I murmur. "Unless you want me to stop."

With my hand still curled around his shaft, I scoot in closer to him, leaning into his space, his heat. My lips hover near his, our breath mingling as I begin to stroke him. I love how dazed he looks, as if his brain has been wiped clean of everything but the sensation of my fingers gliding along his length. His tanned cheeks glow rosy and his breath quickens as I trace the side of his cock, following the line of a thick vein.

Gently, with one fingertip, I coax the sensitive spot right beneath the head of his cock. His length bobs against my hand, leaking more arousal.

"Serylla," he whispers.

"Do you want me to stop?"

"No."

"Good." I shift my position and bend over his lap. When my tongue caresses his cock head, he hisses, "Fuck," and leans on his hands, throwing his head back, his dark hair spilling onto the ground.

The other two penises I've tasted were unwashed and smelled rather sour, but Kyreagan tastes salty like the ocean and fresh like wind-blown grass, so I take him fully into my mouth.

He comes immediately, with a harsh cry. I almost choke, but I manage to adjust the angle of my head and throat to swallow his cum. There's so much of it that I nearly give up, but I keep drinking until every bit is safely in my belly. While I'm swallowing, I keep one hand on his thigh and caress his tensed stomach with my other hand. Through my palm I feel the strain of his muscles, the harshness of his breathing, the vibration of his groans, the surge of heat from the fire locked within him.

When he's done coming in my mouth, I sit up and comfort his cock with my hand, guiding him through the end of the orgasm. I watch his face—eyes shut tight, black lashes painted against flushed cheeks, his sharp jaw flexed, his lips parted. He's so powerfully built, even in this form, and yet he looks so vulnerable, and so lovely I want to kiss him again.

I haven't felt this genuinely happy in a long time.

"You came for me," I say softly. "Good dragon. Your first time."

His eyes blink open, and he sits up straight, carefully removing my hand from his dick. I can't read his expression now.

"Are you alright?" I ask. "Are you—do you feel bad about it, because of *her*?"

He reaches for me and trails his claws through my hair. "I have questions for myself. But I don't regret it."

19

KYREAGAN

That was… fucking amazing.

Dragons are not supposed to experience sexual fervor except during mating season, but I'm no longer just a dragon. The rules have changed. And what I experienced felt so incredible I refuse to tarnish it with regret.

Serylla touched me, pleasured me, and yet she would not let me speak the truth of my heart, or tell her how my feelings toward her have altered. So I keep silent while she lies open for me on the blanket. With my mouth and my fingers I cherish her, until she comes for me again, with the prettiest of little cries.

"Again?" I ask, ready to keep licking her—but she says, with a giggle, that twice is enough for now. Then she rises, collects the wedge of cheese, and walks out of the cave toward the nearest pool.

Serylla dips a toe in the steaming water and makes a breathless sound of delight. When she turns back toward me, I'm stricken senseless by the shape of her lithe form, uplit by the glow of the crystals from the pool. She looks radiant, unearthly. Almost divine.

"Come on, dragon." She beckons to me as she breaks pieces off the huge wedge of cheese. She's removing the bluish growth on its surface, bit by bit, until all that's left is creamy yellow.

There's a stretch of rough rock between me and the pool, which I'll have to navigate on these skinny human limbs of mine. I managed to stumble through sand last time—surely I can traverse the cave floor with reasonable skill. I must try to walk gracefully and smoothly, like she does. Making a fool of myself certainly isn't the way to win the Princess's affection.

I start to rise, but my legs tangle and I sit back down, hard. It seems that this body works best when I'm not thinking about walking, talking, eating, or pissing. The spell that changed me must have included a certain level of instinct to aid with such functions. If I start thinking about the movements too much, I become clumsier. Not ideal for someone like me, who tends to overanalyze most things.

Maybe I should crawl to her. I'm used to walking on all fours. It might be less awkward than staggering and wobbling across the uneven floor of the cave.

I begin to crawl, and realize quickly that it is *not* less awkward. This body was not made to crawl. The edges and bumps of the rock hurt my knees, and my feet drag oddly behind me.

Serylla's eyes are bright with amusement, her lips pinned tight as though she's trying not to laugh. She sets the cheese on a stone and comes to the brink of the pool, propping her arms on a smooth part of its crystalline edge. "Here, dragon. Come on, boy. You can do it."

"Why do I feel like you're mocking me?" I growl.

She makes a saucy little kissing sound with her mouth. "Here, boy. Good dragon."

"That's 'Prince Dragon' to you." I swing my legs into the pool and lower the rest of my body into it. My hair spreads out over the pool's surface, soaking up the liquid instantly. I gather a handful, inspecting the soggy clump.

"The water feels good, doesn't it?" asks the Princess.

"Yes, but I suspect its heat is less dramatic for me, since I regularly exude so much heat on my own."

She shrugs, breaking a piece off the hunk of cheese and popping it into her mouth.

This water doesn't sting as badly as the ocean did, but I still have a few wounds from the voratrice. They're no longer raw, but covered with a sort of scaly, darkish material.

"Don't pick at that," Serylla warns. "It's part of the healing process, a protective covering so the skin beneath can repair itself. The scaly part will come off on its own, once the healing is complete."

I inspect my palms, one of which suffered a scratch from a rough bit of rock. "This skin is so ridiculously thin, like the skin of a berry."

"We're vulnerable, it's true," she says quietly. "That's the price we pay for feeling all the good things. You can't be armored *and* sensitive to touch at the same time."

"So to feel the most exquisite pleasure, one must also be exposed to the most horrific agony."

"That's what it is to be human." She lays a palm flat against the water's surface, then lifts it and watches the glittering drops rain from her fingers.

I copy her movements, enjoying the sensation of the rippling water. "In dragon form, my scales are sensitive to pressure, but it's impossible to feel all the textures of objects, unless I use my tongue. And even that is far different than using these." I hold up my wet fingers.

But a sorrowful thought must have entered her mind, because she barely acknowledges my comment. Her lashes sweep gloomily lower, shading her blue eyes, and her lips droop at the corners. She's hurting again. But now I understand that there are ways to circumvent the pain when it becomes too terrible.

I move toward her through the water. "Shall I make you come a third time?"

"Um..." She flushes, glances away. "Not right now."

"But you're sad. Pleasure can fix it."

"Pleasure is a distraction, like wine or food. It doesn't eliminate the sorrow." She plucks another bit from the cheese. "Open your mouth."

I rear my head back, eyeing the food cautiously. "It smells odd."

"You eat raw animal carcasses."

"This is different. I don't think I will like it."

She rolls her eyes. "Have you tried it?"

"I don't want to."

"Dragon." She takes my jaw in her hand, her blue eyes wide and intense. "Open your fucking mouth. I drank everything you gave me—the least you can do is eat what I feed you."

I retreat farther. "Will you be alright, after drinking so much of my seed?"

"Your *cum*," she corrects me. "I'll be fine. I'm certainly less hungry now, since there was so much of it. And it tasted better than human cum, actually."

Heat flares in my chest. "You've tasted another male's seed?"

"Yes."

At her admission, I growl, low in my throat.

Serylla's eyes widen with surprise. "You don't need to be jealous. I didn't belong to you then—I could be with whoever I wanted. So you have no right to be upset."

"What did you say?" My heartbeat kicks up.

"I... um..."

"You said you didn't belong to me *then*."

"Nor do I belong to you now," she amends swiftly.

It's my turn to pursue her, and her turn to retreat through the steaming water. But my legs are longer, and I manage to corner her. I realize I'm grinning widely. I hope it doesn't look too terrifying.

"I'm not yours." Her protest is faint and breathless as my fingers curl around her upper arms.

I lean down, intending to kiss her—but she pops the bit of cheese between my lips and sinks beneath the water.

The unfamiliar taste paralyzes me for a moment. Rich, creamy, nutty flavor, edged with a sharp tang. I chew slowly, exploring the firm yet crumbly texture.

Cheese.

Serylla resurfaces at the other end of the pool. "Well? Do you like it?"

"I don't know yet. I think I need more."

"We'll share." She sweeps over to the rock where she left the wedge and divides it in half, handing me one chunk. For a few moments all is quiet except for the gurgle of the pool, the soft noise of chewing, and the whisper of the night breeze through the flowering trees overhead. Between the light from the dyre-stones in the cave and the glow of the luminous crystals, I can see the Princess clearly, even without the night vision I possess in dragon form. Flower petals fall from the blooms above, drifting silently down to float on the glimmering water. Never have I experienced a moment so peaceful—

"You're chewing very loudly." The Princess stares intently at me. "I know you're not used to your teeth and tongue yet, but could you *try* to chew with your lips closed? I've always hated the sound of lips smacking."

"Ah, so you don't like this?" I begin chewing louder, smacking my lips emphatically.

"Asshole."

I take a large bite of cheese and chomp it noisily while speaking. "You're not the only one who can be an irritating little shit."

"Let's be clear—you're calling *yourself* that."

"And what would you call me?"

"Big horny bastard."

"It's almost as if you had that title ready and waiting."

She laughs, but the sound fades almost instantly, along with her smile.

"What is it?" I keep my voice low. "What did you remember?"

"It's nothing. Only... my mother had a few names for me. She'd save them up and use one occasionally, under her breath so no one but I could hear. They weren't flattering." She draws in a breath, lets it out slowly. "But then I would go down to the kitchens, and the cooks and everyone made me feel so welcome. The head cook, Myron, was a big, burly fellow who loved a good story or song, so there was always someone spinning a tale while everyone listened and worked. Or one of the staff would teach us a new song, and we'd sing it together. Myron always said, 'Stories and songs make labor lighter.'"

"You are anxious for his well-being."

"I'm worried about all of them."

"I'm sure they miss you as well."

She's playing with the floating petals, stirring them with her finger, and all the while drifting closer to me. I'm not sure she even realizes she's moving in my direction.

"What about you?" She cups water in her hand, blows lightly on the petals to make them flutter. "Tell me some of your good memories."

"You don't care about the lives of dragons."

"Maybe I didn't before," she says softly. "But now I do."

Reluctantly, I begin to speak of Varex's hatching, of how my siblings and I learned to fly, of the patience with which my mother instructed us. Once I begin, it's difficult to stop, and I tell her of Vylar's affinity for strategy, how she would invent countless games for us hatchlings to play. I reminisce about my father's fondness for eels and the lengths to which he would go to catch them. I tell her about the flights my mother would take with Varex, how she enjoyed lightning storms and moonless nights.

Even after we leave the pool and wrap ourselves in the blankets, I can't seem to stop telling her everything. I recite a stanza of a poem Grimmaw composed, roughly translated from Dragonish, and I tell her how Mordessa and I became Promised at the urging of our families.

Between my stories, she shares more of hers—tales of the fierce hunting dogs in the palace kennels who would lick her hands and whine for her attention. Tales of plump human babies and toddling children whom she seems to love almost as much as their own parents do. Tales of sneaking around the palace, performing mundane tasks with the servants because she enjoyed being busy, feeling useful, and helping to lighten the burden of their duties.

As we sit side by side in the cave, with our memories between us, our losses become a little easier to bear. And when we finally lie down, overcome with weariness, Serylla scoots close to me in her blanket and begins to sing a haunting tune about wings and teeth, wind and sea, whispers and darkness. Without asking, I know it's a song she crafted herself, after I brought her to this island. My throat tightens, because she told me she never sings her compositions for anyone, and yet she is singing this, for me.

Tears slip from my eyes in the gloom—tears of affection, of admiration, of wonder, because never have I heard a song that more perfectly embodies the wildness, the danger, and the beauty of Ouroskelle.

I wake in the middle of the change, with magic vibrating along my limbs. Hastily I scramble away from Serylla and lunge out of the cave, just as my dragon form bursts into existence.

There is a half-instant, during the transformation, when I am bodiless. I am nothing. It's the most frightening thing I have ever experienced—akin to death, I imagine.

When it's over I shake myself, flaring my wings. The wounds where the voratrice tore out my scales are healing, and they don't pain me anymore, but it will take weeks for the scales to grow in completely.

Frustration clamps its burning claws onto my spirit, and I whip my tail savagely, opening my jaws and spewing a trail of fire across three of the pools until steam rises from them in great plumes. Singed petals flutter through the air, crumbling to ash.

Nothing is going as planned. Since my father died, there's been one disaster after another, and every time I try to regain control of the situation, I fail. I'm sick of it. I'm not used to slogging through so many emotions at once; I can't sort them like shells or line them up like bones. I've tried to tuck them away, like dark treasures in the back of a cave, but they come roaring back out, swamping me, weighing me down. I slept, and yet I'm exhausted. We had a blissful evening, Serylla and I... yet in the light of the new morning, now that I'm back in my usual scaly skin, our time together seems as distant as a dream. The quiet peace I felt evanesced during my abrupt waking, and now all I feel is rage.

Serylla shuffles to the cave opening, flushed and sleepy, wrapped in a blanket. "You're a dragon again."

"Obviously."

She frowns. "You're grouchier than usual."

"I don't like this," I snarl. "I hate being forced to switch between bodies. It's unnatural. I should have punished the enchantress."

"Beyond forcing her to be Ashvelon's life-mate?" She quirks an eyebrow. "I think that was punishment enough."

"It was for her own good. And he's in love with her, can't you see that? You're human—you should be able to read the fucking signs and understand when someone is violently, horribly, wretchedly in love."

"Goodness." She blinks at me. "You make it sound so terrible."

"It *is* terrible. Pack up your things. Let's go."

"I want to bathe in the hot spring again."

"No."

Both her eyebrows go up this time, and her head lifts, haughty defiance overtaking her features. "You can't tell me what to do."

"You're my prisoner. Of course I can."

Her fingers flutter to her mouth in exaggerated surprise. "I'm your *prisoner*? Really? I had completely forgotten about that. Tell me, dragon, do all captors put their tongues inside their prisoners?"

"You said that sexual pleasure would not change anything between us," I reply. "When I am in this form, you'll do what I say, when I say it."

She shoots me a rebellious glare and stomps back into the cave. At first I think she's planning to obey me, because she puts on a simple white dress and packs everything else into a large bundle, ready for travel. But when the packing is done, she leaves the bundle near the mouth of the cave and walks farther inside.

"Serylla." I prowl after her. "Come here."

She keeps walking, all the way to the back of the cave, where there's a short tunnel.

"That tunnel is a dead end," I warn her.

"So?" She retreats down it with a satisfied grin. "You can't follow me in here."

Shit.

I leap for the tunnel and push my head and neck inside as far as I can, but she's right—my shoulders won't fit through, and I can't reach her. My jaws clash, a vindictive snap that makes her jump and gasp, but then she laughs. She fucking *laughs*.

"You need water and food," I tell her. "You'll have to come out for that."

She plops down on the floor and crosses her arms.

"Fine. Stay in there and starve," I growl. "One less mouth to feed. It's not as though we have much food to spare anyway."

"Because of the plague," she says. "I still think it's strange that it would travel from island to island like that. It would have to be carried by something, like birds, dragons, insects—and if it was insects, it would probably be the biting kind, like—"

"Blood-beetles," I say faintly.

"I don't know what those are, but they sound disgusting."

I whirl away from the tunnel entrance, spring to the cave mouth, and take to the sky.

Tell me I'm wrong, Fortunix. Tell me I'm wrong, tell me...

He had blood-beetles in that cave, inside those jars. Why would he keep so many? Certainly not as pets. There had to be a reason, a darker purpose. Blood-beetles infected with plague. If my suspicions are correct, he set them loose months ago, knowing they would decimate our prey, knowing they might even take down a few dragons.

Why?

Because once our prey became scarce, we'd be forced to look for new hunting grounds. Fortunix must have known my father wouldn't steal new islands. Ancestral land is sacred to dragons, and we would never forcibly take earth with a prior claim on it. Fortunix knew the Bone-King would bargain for the land—bargain with Vohrain, the kingdom that held the nearest, richest hunting grounds. And in bargaining with Vohrain, we became their allies in the war against Elekstan, the nation Fortunix has hated ever since their dragon-hunting days.

It makes sense, and yet I can't believe he would orchestrate something like this. Surely there's another explanation. It has to be coincidence, or a paranoia gripping my mind, born of grief. An elder would never put other dragons in danger.

Fortunix's home is a triangular cave near the top of a craggy peak. He has lived there ever since I can remember. As a hatchling, I dreamed of the day I would be able to fly that high. When I finally gained the strength and confidence, I used to visit him often. He always had a few fat eels on hand for hungry young dragons.

I'm wrong about this. I'm paranoid, I've concocted a demented theory that couldn't be farther from the truth. Asking him about it, doubting him to his face, after all we've been through—it would be cruel. He'd be hurt that I questioned his loyalty, even for a moment.

And yet…

I sweep into the cave, rapidly folding my wings.

The space is just large enough to shield him from the elements, so I can tell at a glance that he isn't there. There's no sign of fresh kill, no food anywhere, and his scent is stale. He hasn't been here for hours. Perhaps he stayed on the ground last night.

What does his human form look like? He never mentioned it during the clan meeting. Perhaps it is an aged form, weaker than most, and he's ashamed for anyone to see it.

His absence chafes me. I want to settle this now. A moment ago I thought myself cruel for suspecting him, and now I can't bear leaving this place without answers. Fuck, my mind is like a school of fish, swerving first in one direction and then the other. I can't decide what to do.

I burst from the cave again, roaring my frustration to the sky. An answering call echoes from a nearby peak where two dragons are circling, probably enjoying the sun before they hunt. Instead of going to greet them, I head for the hot springs again. I left the Princess there, but I'll be damned if she thinks she has won. I'll *make* her come out, and I'll take her back to my cave, where she will wait until I decide what to do with her, with Fortunix, with everything.

But as I wheel toward the southeast, I spot a bank of dark clouds along the horizon—a dense, forbidding line that stretches as far as my eyes can see.

I've seen a cloud bank like this once before, and I've been warned about it many times. What I'm seeing is the Mordvorren, a massive, slow-moving storm whose thunder cracks rock and whose lightning can pierce even a dragon's armored body. It is a cosmic hurricane composed of many storm cells—an unnatural, sentient weather phenomenon—a condensed loci of unstable magic. It is destruction.

My father warned my siblings and I about the Mordvorren countless times. "If you see it approaching, gather all the food you can find and take shelter," he would say. "The Mordvorren is no friend to dragons."

We were fortunate last time. The Mordvorren passed us by, and Ouroskelle only took the edge of its fury. This time, it's headed straight for us. Although its enormous size will slow it down, the Mordvorren will reach us by nightfall.

It's nearly the Rib Moon, and the Mordvorren can last for days. Which means our mating frenzy won't be a joyful, passionate orgy out in the sunny green fields, under a spring sky. Instead it will happen while we're all trapped in caves, waiting for the lethal lightning and rock-shattering thunder to abate.

A sour laugh escapes me. Of *course* this is how my first mating season would go. It fits with all the misfortunes we've suffered lately.

My questions about Fortunix will have to wait. There is no time to spare. I must warn the clan so we can gather enough food to last us through the storm. Then each dragon must decide where he will shelter, and with whom.

20

SERYLLA

Blood-beetles.

He said that inexplicable word and then he left me here all day.

At first I stayed in the clammy stone tunnel, convinced that he was just pretending to be gone and would snatch me up in his claws the moment I poked my head out. But after a couple hours I sidled out of the passage, stripped down, and sank into one of the steaming pools for a soak. Later I poked around for food, but the ants had dismantled the stale bread and the remaining cheese. Lucky for me, I had a bag of sugared nuts Thelise sneaked to me right before I left her cave. No thanks to Kyreagan. With him as my caretaker, I would have gone hungry all day, or been forced to try some berries from the nearest bushes, on the off chance they weren't poisonous.

I make up a song about him while he's gone, an angry ballad with as many spiteful words as I can think of. I'll sing it to him sometime, when he's exhausted and trying to sleep.

Fuck him. I thought we had turned a corner, he and I. We shared things—not just sexual things, but emotional ones. I thought... never mind what I thought. It was foolish.

To amuse myself, I put on the orange dress I selected from the clothing Thelise brought. It has no straps or sleeves, but the bodice fits me perfectly once I manage to get it mostly buttoned. There's one button I can't reach by myself. Three tiny gold chains are stitched along the waist by way of a faux belt, and their ends fall free, glittering against the voluminous orange skirts. I love the dress, more so because my mother always said orange wasn't my color. Wearing this feels like a tiny rebellion against her control, and I feel guilty for it because of how she died, but I'm also recklessly angry enough not to care. I'm furious at her for not surrendering during those final weeks, when she might have been spared. If the King of Vohrain had agreed in writing to spare our lives, as part of the terms of surrender, he would have had to keep his word before his people and ours. But when he entered as a conqueror, to subdue the former queen, there was no such bargain.

I wish I could kill him for killing her. I wish I could turn back time and stop the Supreme Sorcerer from performing his final terrible curse. I wish I could stop myself from climbing the wall to that tower. I wish I'd run away across the southern border and disappeared. I wish I'd been able to get closer to my mother, to understand the strange partnership between her and the Sorcerer. I wish I could hate Thelise for being his daughter. I wish I didn't like her so much, and I wish I didn't care about a certain cranky black dragon.

As the afternoon progresses, the sky begins to look strange. There's a yellowish, almost greenish cast to it, which disturbs me, and instead of the air feeling soft and fresh like it did this morning, it seems almost brittle, strung taut like a bowstring that's been tightened too far and is ready to snap.

"Kyreagan, where are you?" I mutter, staring up at the sky.

Moments later his shadow crosses me, almost as if he heard my summons. I race for the cave, intending to dive back into the tunnel and defy him again, but he's too quick for me this time. He darts into the cave entrance, blocking my path, and nudges my bundle toward me with his nose.

"Grab your things and get on," he orders.

I was ready to fight with him again, but the terse urgency in his tone changes my mind. Clutching my bundle, I climb onto his back without further protest.

He takes off with a lurch that nearly dislodges me. "Idiot!" I snap, and he bites out a curt, "Sorry."

"What happened?" I ask as we rise into the air. "You said 'blood-beetles' and then you—oh my god—what the fuck is that?"

A towering cliff of churning black clouds has devoured the horizon, and it's nearing Ouroskelle. This is no ordinary storm—it's a ruinous cataclysm. Countless branches of purple lightning flash silently beneath its threatening bulk.

"The Mordvorren," says Kyreagan. "You've heard of it?"

"In school," I breathe. "It destroyed part of our capital city decades ago. And then it passed near the southern coast again when I was young, but it turned away and went back out to sea."

"We won't be spared this time. It will be here in two hours or less, and judging by the tales, it might last several days. The other dragons and I have been hunting all day, storing up fish and game to see us through. The women have been foraging for many hours as well."

I grip my bundle more tightly against my chest. "You left me there, at the hot spring. I could have come with you. I could have helped."

"I left because I had something else to deal with," he says. "But when I saw the storm, I knew the other matter would have to wait. Our survival takes priority. I didn't have time to pamper a spoiled princess who would rather sulk in corners than do as she is told."

"If you had come back and explained the situation, I would have come out. But maybe you thought I wouldn't be much good at foraging, since I'm such a weak, spoiled brat."

"Enough!" He nearly bellows the word, and my heart jumps. "The dragons and humans are gathering as we speak. Once you and I arrive, we must determine where everyone will shelter."

"Oh fuck," I exclaim as realization dawns in my mind. "The mating heat will occur during the storm, won't it?"

"Yes."

"What will happen?"

"I don't know. But last night was the end of our time together. Since you despise me so thoroughly, you will choose another dragon with whom to weather the Mordvorren."

His words sting me more deeply than they should. "Fine. I'll stay in the big cavern with the other women."

"No one can remain in that cave. It floods during hard rains."

"What if the women stay together in another cave, farther up the mountain?" I ask. "Just humans, no dragons."

"Wherever prisoners are housed, there will be at least one dragon. We will not leave any group of prisoners unprotected during this time."

"Unprotected?" I vent a derisive laugh. "We're far less safe with you brutes around."

He doesn't reply. The wind has picked up, and it whips my cheeks as we soar over fields laid with fresh dragon bones, over jagged spires of rock, back to the mountains where the dragons' caves lie. We glide over the damaged enclosure where the other captives had their campfires. It's empty now, not a soul to be seen.

"They're waiting in Conch Valley," Kyreagan says. "It is a gathering place for dragons. If one stands on the stone slab in its center, everyone in the valley can hear what is being said."

I don't answer him. I'm breathless, tears flying from the corners of my eyes thanks to the fierce wind. Besides, I'm furious with him. He rejected me, so I have to choose someone else. No matter what I do, I can't be sure that I'll be safe, and I can't protect any of the other women.

"You must promise me that no one will be forced to mate." My voice, thread-thin, barely cuts through the wind. But Kyreagan hears me.

"I have already declared a penalty of death upon any dragon who does such a thing."

"Oh." It's a relief, I suppose, but a small one. None of us really know how the mating heat will affect the dragons, now that they can shift between forms. Will the urge be too strong for them to control themselves?

"None of this is safe, or right," I choke out. "You did this, by bringing us here, by kidnapping Thelise. You put all of us in this position. Whatever happens will be your fault."

"Of course it will," he snarls. "No one else bears any responsibility. All of it is mine. But there is no escaping it now— not the storm, not the spell, not the mating heat. We must manage as best we can. I daresay you'll be glad to be rid of me."

He dives, and I shriek at the abrupt descent. But I've grown skilled at holding on with my knees and thighs. It's like riding an extremely large and restive stallion.

I tucked up the orange gown when I mounted him, and its fiery skirts billow around me as Kyreagan lands in a violent thunder of black wings. I slide off him clumsily, clutching my bundle, conscious that dozens of dragons and humans are all staring at me. Thank god I chose the orange gown instead of the white shift.

The eyes of an audience hold little terror for me. I'm used to parading before others, used to being scrutinized and applauded, criticized and worshiped. I'm used to people examining everything I wear and everything I do, from the smallest of actions to the slightest change of my expression.

Calmly I lay down my things, smooth my skirts, and stand beside Kyreagan, my palm pressed lightly against his neck. He tenses as if he might swerve away from my touch, but he doesn't.

We're standing on a large slab of rock, almost like the platform on which a queen's throne might sit. The rest of the dragons and humans gather slightly below us, on the floor of the valley.

A slender black dragon leaps from the crowd onto the rock slab and sidles closer to Kyreagan. It's his brother, Varex. He speaks quietly, but his voice resonates through the valley, clear and audible.

"The males want to perform their mating dances, brother," he says. "I told them we would allow it."

"There's no time," growls Kyreagan. "The storm is nearly upon us. We must choose our companions quickly and take shelter."

"We have a little time." Varex lifts his head higher than Kyreagan's. "This is an important tradition, a ritual handed down through generations. To save time, instead of each dragon performing alone, we can perform the dances together, all at once."

"That isn't how it's done," Kyreagan replies.

"It's called a compromise." Varex's voice deepens, and purple light flickers in his nostrils. "This is important to me, and if we truly share the rulership of Ouroskelle, you will allow me to make this decision. I respect every choice you have made, and I support you in all of them. Support me in this."

It's shocking to me how they're having this frank conversation in front of everyone. My mother would never allow us to appear in public as anything but a devoted parent and dutiful daughter. If I even hinted at disagreeing with her in front of our people, I knew I would pay for it later in long tirades, vicious slaps, and reduced privileges. Even once I passed age twenty, she made it clear that I belonged to her—that I was an asset, an object, not a partner.

Watching the partnership between Kyreagan and Varex makes my heart ache—even more so when Kyreagan dips his head to his brother. "I support you."

"Then we will have music," calls Varex. "Ladies of Elekstan, you may have been captives at first—spoils of war, prey to our vengeance—but I believe I speak for every dragon here when I say, you have become far more than that to us. You are honored guests, beautiful friends, cherished companions. You are our salvation. As my brother proclaimed earlier today, not one of you will be forced to mate with any dragon, in any form. But if you would deign to honor us with your affection during this season, we will worship you as you deserve and cherish you as long as you allow. No pairing during the heat will be binding. It is a time of joy, and yes, of breeding, but the eggs, once laid, will be the males' responsibility alone. You will be free to live as you like, with or without the dragon you choose today."

I elbow Kyreagan's neck and mutter, "Why couldn't you have said it like that?"

And of course, my words are transferred throughout the valley. Everyone hears them.

Hot blood rises to my face as I realize what I've done. I humiliated Kyreagan, questioned his leadership abilities in front of the whole clan and all the women.

"My brother has a tongue of gold," Kyreagan says loudly, with humor in his voice. "I am fortunate to serve the clan with him."

It's a graceful admission that he's less skilled at public speaking than his brother. The other dragons chuckle at his comment, and Varex takes over smoothly, directing the women to back up and move together, calling the dragons to gather around the central slab of stone.

I don't see Thelise or Ashvelon anywhere. But Jessiva approaches me, reaching up her arms, so I toss her my bundle and manage to scramble down from the slab without hurting myself.

The noise of the dragons fills the valley—the beat of their wings, the impact of their feet, their voices growling in Dragonish as they quickly plan their performance. Under cover of that noise, Jessiva faces me, with the bundle between us, and says, "Each of us was given fresh clothes today, and soap, and a few other supplies."

"I'm glad." I try to take my things, but she holds onto them. Beneath the cover of the blanket-wrapped bundle, she's giving me something. I touch a sharp edge, and my eyes flash up to hers.

She mouths the next words distinctly. *Kill the prince. With this.*

Her fingers press mine around the object. It's a curved knife, or maybe a claw. Useless against a dragon, but for a human, it could be deadly.

She's giving me a weapon. She wants me to kill Kyreagan with it, when he's in human form.

"He won't choose me," I whisper.

"You can choose *him*," she says. "I'll choose his brother."

Her fierce look leaves no doubt in my mind. She's determined to remove the leadership of the dragon clan, in the hopes that the resulting upheaval will permit us to escape.

Jessiva steps back, leaving me with the weapon and my things. I manage to slide the claw-knife into a fold of the bundle before setting it beside a nearby rock. I'll retrieve it once I determine which dragon I'll be leaving with.

Last night, I thought Kyreagan was on the verge of confessing his love for me. Obviously I misunderstood what he was trying to say. I acted like a fool, covering his mouth, panicking over a declaration he never intended to make. Today he has made it obvious that he doesn't feel any affection for me at all.

Kyreagan and Varex both said the women can choose their jailers, guardians, partners—whatever the dragons are calling themselves now. I could pick Kyreagan, against his will. But that seems wrong to me. My best option is to choose another dragon, someone who is kind and intelligent, but already has his affections set on a different captive.

The blue dragon, Rothkuri, seems like the obvious choice. I'm confident he would take care of me and protect me during the storm. And judging by how his captive was stroking his shoulder a moment ago, the two of them are still deeply fascinated with each other. He'll be fucking her for sure. Maybe I can offer her some of the contraceptive herbs I got from Thelise, in case she wants sex but doesn't fancy squeezing dragon eggs out of her vagina.

I almost laugh, standing there in the group of women, thinking such outrageous thoughts. This situation is beyond ludicrous, beyond anything I'd ever pictured myself having to endure. I thought my best chance at a decent life might be a reasonably attractive prince from a neighboring kingdom, who would hopefully treat me well, with whom I could enjoy friendship if not love. I was fully prepared to have babies with said theoretical prince, and make those babies my entire life's purpose.

What's laughable is that I have been claimed by a prince, and he *does* need a mate to father his children. But in my fantasies, such a life came with certain luxuries—clean, well-appointed rooms in a fine palace, excellent dining every day, lovely gardens in which I could play with the children and the pets. A home to manage, not a cave. Tailored clothing, not scavenged gowns. Food that has actually been cooked on a proper stove.

The dragons are doing their best, I suppose. I have to admit, the other women look decently cared for—they're much cleaner now, clad in fresh clothing. None of them are weeping, nor do they look quite as desperate as the first time I encountered them. I wonder how many of them have grown close to a particular dragon—or more than one. After all, there are more dragon males than women. Some might be left without a mate, which, according to Kyreagan, means that their magic may be diminished.

Five of the male dragons have withdrawn to the side, apparently more interested in each other than in the performance. Two of them seem particularly affectionate. As with humans, I suppose some dragons discover that the love and fulfillment they crave lies beyond a male-female pairing—or beyond the confines of any gender.

Someone touches my arm, and I turn to see Gweneth, the woman who ran into the forest ahead of me.

"So you were recaptured as well," I murmur.

"No," she replies. "I returned on my own. Once I saw more of the island, I realized the dragons were my best option for survival. And I discovered…" She bites her lip, her eyes soft and distant. "They're not as terrible as I thought. They need us. And to be needed, wanted… *craved*… that is worth something to me."

Her words strike deep. I want to talk to her more, to ask questions, to unpack some of the feelings clashing within my heart—but before I can figure out what to say, the dragons begin their song.

First a low, resonant hum, deep in the chest of every dragon. Some form a circle around the great central slab, others perch upon it, and about a dozen of them take to the air, beating their wings in perfect sync. Meanwhile the dragons on the ground stomp their feet, a rhythm interspersed with the thump of huge tails.

The thunder of their moving bodies pounds deep into my very bones, quickening my heart. Music has always affected me powerfully, and there's something about this primal rhythm that weakens my knees. Wind rolls from beneath majestic wings, tossing the hair of the women. Every dragon's eyes are alight with fervent fire, jaws bared, necks proudly arched, horns gleaming.

"Fuck, they're beautiful," whispers a woman behind me.

As the stomping, humming, and thumping continue, groups of six dragons separate from the others and begin to dance. Some of them are rather awkward, whipping their wings, bobbing their heads, twisting around and around as if they're chasing their tails. Others have a natural grace that makes even the silliest movements seem sensual. I try to pay attention to Rothkuri, who eagerly flaps his blue wings and jives in a merry circle, nodding his sleek head. But Kyreagan is in the same group, and I can barely take my eyes off him.

He dances as if he's fighting. His neck snakes forward, jaws snapping in time to the beat. He whirls like he's going to pounce, slashes his claws as if he's attacking prey. Every line of his body, from his narrow yellow eyes to the tip of his tail, screams rage and passion and need. He is sinuous, glorious, wicked. I'm utterly mesmerized, and when his group retreats to make way for another, I'm disappointed.

He doesn't want me. He said so. I need to make the best choice for myself, for my safety. Besides, I'd rather not make a decision about whether or not I should kill him.

What am I thinking? I *can't* kill him. Despite every bad choice he has made, and the way we treat each other sometimes—I simply can't. Perhaps, as the Crown Princess, I'm responsible to look out for the other captives and ensure they get home, but I won't do it at the expense of his life. I refuse. If Jessiva wants to destroy the two princes, she'll have to do it alone.

Should I warn Kyreagan that Jessiva plans to kill his brother? He might roast her on the spot. Perhaps I should tell Varex directly, so he can be on his guard. But is that a betrayal of my own people?

Once each group of dragons has had a turn to dance, the resonant hum grows louder and more compelling as the dragons break formation and stalk toward their audience. Some of the women squeal and clutch each other, but I hear breathless giggles threaded through the feigned terror. Now that they've seen the dragons in human form, everything has changed. The very air tingles with possibility, with power, with desire.

I wonder what the other dragons look like as humans. Surely none of them can be as handsome as Kyreagan. That doesn't mean I want him—it's simply an objective judgment. He is handsome. There's no sense trying to convince myself otherwise.

The dragons continue to stomp and hum, but they pin their wings against their sides as they prowl around our group, like predators circling prey. With a short final roar and stamp, they all stand still.

"Our guests will now choose their guardian for the duration of the storm," declares Varex. "Once everyone has chosen, you will have a moment to collect your things before your dragon takes you to his cave."

I spot Rothkuri's girl heading straight for him. He greets her with an affectionate nuzzle of her cheek.

If I'm going to choose him, I'd best be quick about it. But I need to speak with Varex first, before Jessiva gets to him. She's talking in low tones with one of the women, so I weave my way through the other captives until I reach Varex.

He was watching Jessiva, and my appearance seems to surprise him.

"Princess," he says with a respectful dip of his head. "I thought—I expected you and my brother to—"

I seize one of his jaw spikes and pull his head down so I can speak quietly in his ear. We're not on the central stone anymore, but I want to make sure my voice doesn't carry.

"Be careful of Jessiva," I tell him. "She wants you dead."

When I let him go, he lifts his head, pain flooding his amber eyes. "You're wrong."

"I hope so. Just… be careful."

A large, spiked mountain of black scales and leathery wings enters my peripheral vision. "You've chosen *him*?" Kyreagan's growl is strained with disbelief, tinged with hurt. "You're going to shelter with my brother?"

"No, I'm not! I'm going with Rothkuri."

Kyreagan towers over me, looking down his long snout with majestic disdain. "Rothkuri?"

"Yes."

"No." The word thunders from his chest.

"What do you mean, *no*? You said I could choose—that I *had* to choose. It's either Rothkuri or Varex. Or maybe that one." I point to a white dragon with sapphire scales sprinkled over his body. "Oh, the red one is lovely, and he danced well. Maybe I'll choose him."

Kyreagan snarls, his jaws wide, fire glowing at the back of his throat. Varex has slunk away, and the others are giving us a wide berth—all except for a pretty black-haired girl who approaches Kyreagan. "If I may… I'd like to choose you, my lord." She smiles shyly. "And we can… you know. I'm willing to—"

"Oh good. Yes, please take him," I cut in. "He could use someone sweet like you. Look at that adorable body of yours! I'll bet she's a good fuck, don't you think, dragon? Carry her off to your cave, and I'll go find Rothkuri."

As I turn and start to walk away, Kyreagan gives a strangled roar. The next second I'm snatched up between his jaws.

I go hot and cold at once—freezing dread in my veins, shock heating my skin.

Kyreagan is holding me carefully, cradling me with his lips and tongue, but I don't dare move for fear of impaling myself on his sharp teeth. His breath comes fast and frantic, not hot enough to burn me, but it stings. That panicked, rapid breath tells me he's reached his limit. The immense weight of everything he's been forced to carry is breaking him. He's beyond rational thought right now, and only raw instinct is left.

I want to help him, but I can't do that while I'm in his mouth, in such imminent danger of being sliced to shreds on his dagger-like teeth.

"Kyreagan!" I gasp. "Put me down."

Varex appears right by Kyreagan's head, speaking in a low, urgent tone. "Brother, what are you doing? Release the girl, right the fuck now."

Kyreagan hisses, but he lowers his head and lets me roll out from between his jaws. Before I can scramble away, he's on top of me, his great chest pressing against my front, not firmly enough to crush me, but it's a definite warning to be still. He licks my throat, and a compulsive shudder rolls through him, along with a groan of need.

"Fuck," I whisper. Heat flares between my legs, roars through my body. Despite the fact that everyone is watching, it's all I can do not to rake up my skirts and beg him to use his tongue on me.

He wants me. He really does. And with that realization comes the full understanding of *why* he tried to push me away.

"Be very still, Serylla," Varex warns. "Give him a moment." Then, in a stern voice, he orders, "My brother, if you don't get your shit together, I will have to battle you myself, right now. You said yourself that no woman would be forced by a dragon."

But Varex doesn't understand. None of them do. They don't realize that Kyreagan was my first choice, my only choice, and if he hadn't stubbornly insisted on a separation, I would have picked him from the start. They don't understand that Kyreagan's behavior in this moment isn't a sign of mating frenzy, but of a devastated heart, an exhausted mind, and a soul in conflict.

Fine… maybe a little bit of mating frenzy.

"It's alright," I call out. "He's not forcing me into this. I choose him. I'm going with him."

The other women murmur to each other as the dragon prince shifts back to a sitting position, letting me rise. His breathing slows, but his golden eyes still churn with pain, panic, and humiliation. I need to get him away from here so he can recover.

"Sorry," I tell the shy girl. "You'll have to choose someone else. The prince is mine."

She looks disappointed but not devastated as she wanders off toward the scarlet dragon.

"He'll be alright now," I say to Varex. "Thank you."

He bows to me and turns to greet Jessiva, who is approaching him with a bright smile. I could swear she was his devoted lover, instead of the woman planning to kill him. At least he has been warned. He can choose to weather the storm with her, or not.

"Wait here," I tell Kyreagan. "I'll get my things, and we'll go to your cave."

21

KYREAGAN

I leave my brother to supervise the remaining matches and ensure that everyone reaches their caves safely. It's difficult for me to yield leadership entirely to him—I can think of a hundred things he will need to check on or deal with before the Mordvorren hits. Since we'll be sheltering for several days, everyone must be reminded to keep their caves clean of offal and discard any meat that begins to spoil. Those with a water source inside their cave must take precautions against flooding.

But Varex knows all this. My brother is wise and capable, and he'll do his best to protect the clan. He must, because I'm in no state to lead. I've made a fool of myself in front of dragons and humans alike, all because I hunger so desperately for the girl sitting on my back.

My cave looks quite different than it did this morning. Two animal carcasses hang in the cool darkness at the rear of the cave. Along one wall I arranged our share of the food the women foraged today—berries, mushrooms, seaweed, cresslily stalks, nuts, seeds, and plenty of large, starchy roots like the ones we ate raw during that night on the beach. With my claws, I widened and deepened the channel of the spring, so we'll be at less risk of the trickle becoming a stream that overflows its usual groove in the floor.

I know Serylla sees it all, understands the provisions and precautions. But she doesn't mention any of it. She slides off my back, tosses her bundle into the nest, and walks around to my head, her expression serious. "Are you alright?"

"No," I reply.

"You have the right to be… *not* alright." Her eyes hold so much sympathy, so much kindness I can hardly bear it. "Kyreagan, you went off to war while you were still grieving your father—"

"His war," I say.

She lifts her eyebrows.

"His war. He made me swear a bone-oath that I would uphold his bargain with Vohrain. Bone-oaths cannot be broken."

"Oh shit," she whispers. "Ky, I'm so sorry."

I blink at the shortened version of my name. I think I like it.

"So you joined your father's war, as a new ruler, still grieving," she continues. "You slaughtered hundreds of people. You lost loved ones. And while you were grieving them, you made some terrible choices, out of revenge and necessity. Those choices didn't turn out as you planned, and you had to adapt to Thelise's spell, to this unexpected shifting between bodies. And *now*, the Mordvorren. A catastrophic storm. The weight of everyone's safety and your race's survival falls on you and your brother, but I think you feel it more deeply than he does."

"He has his own wounds," I say. "But he handles dire situations and public speeches better than I do."

"I'm used to most things being beyond my control." Serylla places a hand on my muzzle. "Not that I like it, but it's familiar for me. You, however—you've always been respected. You've always been given responsibility and choices, even before your father passed, so the loss of control has been harder to manage than you thought. That's why your body keeps reacting like this. And then there are your feelings about Mordessa. You cared for her, but she *loved* you, and you feel guilty that you didn't love her back. You feel guilty for surviving. You don't think you deserve to experience the kind of love she wanted from you. So you're fighting against what you need, as hard as you can, and it's hurting you."

I rear back, staring at her in utter disbelief, my wings draped limply on the stone floor.

I thought, once we were alone, she would rage at me for being so fickle, for rejecting her and then claiming her in front of them all. But instead of chastising me, she's being unutterably kind. And she seems to understand me better than I understand myself, which is both wondrous and unsettling. The emotions that I've been struggling to untangle… she picked them neatly apart and laid them out for me. It was the work of a moment.

Noting my surprise, she laughs a little. "I never thought I would be able to get inside a dragon's head like that. Was I close to the target?"

"Dead center," I manage.

"Good." She smiles, pats my nose. "Get some rest before the storm hits. And dragon—don't ever grab me in your jaws again."

"I won't. I'm sorry. Did I hurt you?"

"You were very gentle. But I was scared. I mean, your teeth are huge." She pushes up my lip with her small hands. "Look at these things. Each one is the size of a butcher knife. Open up."

I obey, feeling that low thrill in my belly again. There's something oddly intimate about the matter-of-fact way she's handling my lips and jaws. When I open my mouth, my tongue twitches automatically. I can taste the crackle of the oncoming storm in the air.

"I remember you," the Princess says softly to my tongue, and my whole body thrills. I try to suppress the shiver, but I think she notices, because she smirks and closes her fingers around my tongue. It's a handful for her. Is she thinking about the way I probed inside her body and coaxed her to climax? Because I can't think about anything else.

She tugs on my tongue gently, and my cock hardens inside my body. But then she lets me go, and she ambles away, swishing that little round ass of hers as she proceeds to inspect the food I've stocked.

"This will last both of us for several days?" she asks.

"It should last through the worst of the storm, at least. As a dragon, I can go without prey for days if I must. We'll make it work." I don't tell her that stocking our caves for the storm wiped out much of the remaining game on Ouroskelle. We had no time to travel all the way to the Middenwold Isles, so we had to make do with the available prey, including our cows. It's a loss, but it had to be done.

After the storm, we will switch to hunting solely in the Middenwold, allowing the animals on Ouroskelle to replenish their numbers. And I have some thoughts about exterminating the fenwolf population, now that we can shift into human form and enter their dens. We will have to train first, develop ourselves as human warriors before we attempt to cull the wolves.

Serylla throws me a keen glance. "I told you to rest, but you're planning and worrying. Stop thinking."

"I don't understand rest anymore," I grumble as I crawl to the nest and settle myself within it.

She laughs. "I enjoy work, but to do the work well, one must get a decent rest. Close your eyes, and I'll sing to you while I unpack the things I got from Thelise. I'm also going to rearrange the food supplies—they're in a dreadful jumble."

The cave lends a faint echo to her sweet voice, and the melody she sings is so soothing I don't even realize I've fallen asleep until a giant explosion of thunder sends me startling out of the nest, with my spikes bristling and a snarl on my lips.

For a moment I thought the mountain cracked in half. But my cave is still here, still solid. Torrents of rain shatter on the ledge outside and gush off its brink into the void below.

Serylla crouches in my nest. She's wearing the white shift dress now—she must have put the orange gown away for later. I should have told her how much I liked that flame-colored dress, but she looks just as adorable in this one. She's frightened, though. The Mordvorren brought utter blackness down upon us, and she can't see in the dark like I can.

"Kyreagan?" she says faintly.

Before I can answer, a blazing bolt of white fire streaks down from the sky, so close I can hear it sizzle. Serylla shrieks. A sharp, acrid smell assaults my sensitive nose, as if the air itself is burning, despite the sheets of thundering rain.

"Kyreagan!" cries the Princess.

"Wait a moment."

I locate my two dyre-stones and push them into the center of the cave. With my breath I heat them until they glow like lanterns. Then I climb into the nest and curl my body around hers. She crawls right against me and shivers against my armored belly. I ache to be in human form right now, to be able to feel more than the pressure of her body. I want her skin under my fingertips, her breasts beneath my palms, my lips on hers. I crave that nearness so badly I find myself holding my breath.

A buzzing sensation jolts through me, and suddenly I'm *him*—my other self, so much smaller and leaner than my dragon form, yet still larger than the Princess—large enough to provide her with security and comfort.

Serylla falls backward into the straw when I change, as my bulk vanishes from beneath her. She sits up, looking flustered. "What just happened?"

"I did it." I sit up too, grinning. "I wanted to change forms, and I did."

"So I see." She reaches out, strokes my long black hair out of my face, and disentangles a lock from my horns. Her lips part to say something else, but the wind outside rises suddenly to a shriek that sounds so human her eyes flare wide with terror. The shriek goes on and on, rising and falling, a fierce keening wail that veers between mourning and madness.

"I've never heard anything like that," she whispers, crawling closer. "Hold me."

I'm sitting in the nest with my knees arched, and she scoots back against me with her rear pressed to my hip and her body tilted against my chest. I wrap both arms around her and thank the Bone-Builder for every bit of her skin that touches mine.

"It's a living storm, threaded with strange magic," I murmur against her hair.

"Yes, they mentioned that in school," says Serylla. "I wish I'd paid better attention, though."

"We have a long poem about it among our historical orations."

"Recite it for me."

"Unfortunately I don't remember it well. I didn't always pay attention to my instructors, either."

She giggles. It's a sweet, soft, feminine sound, and my cock jumps. I can't help tensing at the hot rush of blood through its length.

Serylla twists and looks down between my legs. "Do you want some pants? I chose a few things for you, from Thelise's stash."

I don't want pants. I want to bend her over onto her hands and knees and push this new cock of mine inside her.

Did I want to fuck her that first day, when I saw her standing on the wall, aiming the crossbow at me? I think perhaps I did, though I wouldn't let myself admit it.

"I should have some pants," I grit out. "Yes."

Serylla tilts her head, with the mischievous half-smile I've come to adore. "First, a lesson."

"A lesson?" I can barely manage the words.

"If you're going to be a man, with all a man's desires, you should know how to handle them on your own when you need to. How to give yourself relief. You remember what I did for you, back at the hot springs?"

I swallow as my cock bobs again. "Yes."

"This time I'm not going to touch you. You're going to do everything yourself."

Whatever blood isn't throbbing in my cock rushes up to my cheeks.

I've touched my genitals since I first shifted, of course. I inspected my cock carefully, and I've used it to piss. But I didn't really think of it in this context, didn't realize what it meant, that I can touch myself like humans do. It means that if I have the inclination, the desire, I can pleasure myself whenever I want. Essentially, I am now my own source of sensual entertainment.

And that opens up a whole new realm of possibilities.

Serylla tugs at her plump lower lip with her teeth and winks at me. "Open your legs a bit wider."

With my heart pounding as loudly as the rain, I obey.

"Now put your hand around your cock, right at the base."

It feels good, warming my sensitive length with my fingers.

"Move your hand up, keeping it wrapped around your cock. It should be tight enough, but don't squeeze. Slide it up, then down. If you want things to be a bit more slippery, you can use some of your precum, that liquid beading there, at the tip. Spread it around."

I examine the tiny slit that's oozing clear liquid. Slowly I rub it over my cock head and my shaft until both are glossy and slippery.

"How does it feel?" The Princess sounds a little breathless.

"It feels good," I murmur. But when I look up at her, everything I'm doing suddenly feels not simply *good*, but exquisite.

Her face is flushed, her eyes starry. The low neckline of the simple white dress shows a generous amount of her breasts. Her fingers are tucked between her thighs, pinning the material there as if she's trying to stifle the sensations in that delicate place.

She was in control of this a moment ago. But not anymore.

With a half-smile of my own, I speak to her in my deepest voice. "How does it feel for *you*, Princess?"

22

SERYLLA

I was lost the moment he grabbed his cock.

Seeing him sitting there, his strong legs open to me, every sleek surface and defined groove of his muscled body lit with the dyre-stone glow—it was too much for a mere mortal to cope with.

His spine curves as he examines his cock, and his stomach muscles tense as he follows my directions and slicks precum along his shaft. There's a studious look on his face at first, but the velvety rose of his lips and the color in his cheeks is the most debauched thing I've ever seen. I have to press my hand over my pussy to keep it from quivering.

When he looks up at me, his face changes, an instant transformation from obedient exploration to grinning dominance. In that deep dragon voice of his, he croons, "How does it feel for *you*, Princess?"

His big hand keeps caressing the full length of his cock, while his gaze ensnares mine. He's learning much too quickly.

I snatch my hand out from between my legs.

"This is about you, not me," I retort, but my voice trembles a little. "Explore yourself. See which spots are most sensitive, what rhythms give you the most pleasure." I glance away.

"Look at me, Serylla."

My breath hitches as I turn back to him, drawn by that powerful voice. His eyes are like dark stars, and his black hair glimmers in silky strands over his broad chest and shoulders. His ebony claws catch the light as he strokes his thick length steadily.

"Am I doing this right, do you think?" he rumbles.

"Yes… um… do you… do you feel the pleasure building, like before, when I touched you?"

"You mean when I came in your mouth?"

My eyes nearly glaze over, and I clench my thighs more tightly together. "Yes."

"You didn't answer my question," he says. "How are *you* feeling?"

"Hot," I whisper.

"And?"

"Wet."

"Show me." He growls it, fiercely. It's not a request, but a command, and god help me, I love it.

Propping my back against the edge of the nest, I pull up the skirt of the shift dress. I didn't put on any underwear when I changed, because deep down, I knew exactly where this was headed. I want him to fuck me. The only question that remains is *when*, and whether or not I'll use the contraceptive herbs afterward. Whether or not I'll let him fill me up with his seed, as he calls it. Whether or not I'll be birthing his eggs. Thelise seemed to think it was not only possible, but safe. Then again, I'm not sure Thelise's word is very reliable.

For now, Kyreagan seems dazed enough by the sight of my damp pussy that he doesn't ask for anything else. He strokes faster, his gaze traveling up my body to my eyes and back down again. He's relishing all of me, including the expression on my face. He's finding his pleasure by witnessing my arousal, my emotions.

Tentatively, I press two fingertips to my clit. My body responds with a dramatic flutter, and I can't help squirming. I circle my clit feverishly, occasionally sliding two fingers down to dip inside myself.

Kyreagan's eyes blaze hot, searing me, flooding me with a more visceral need than I've ever experienced. I need this orgasm like I need air.

Another giant column of lightning snakes down the cliff, past the cave. It startles both of us—I scream faintly and Kyreagan lets out a deep groan. Fear sharpens our pleasure, and those involuntary cries loosen our inhibitions. I let myself gasp aloud, shrill and breathless, and Kyreagan lets out the prettiest dark moans, lovely male sounds that send my pulse skittering into pure delight.

"You... come first," he rasps. "I want to see it."

My hand flies faster, and I focus on the surging pleasure, winding it up in my mind, working myself to the breaking point. I tilt back my head with a whimper... almost there... I take one more long look at Kyreagan's flushed face, his swollen cock, his heavy balls, strong thighs framing it all...

"Fuck!" I scream as it hits. Fingertips pressed to my clit, I force myself to keep my legs open, to let him see the spasming flutter of my pussy. My fingers and my inner thighs glimmer slick in the warm light.

"Serylla... Serylla..." Kyreagan groans heavily, and white cum flies from his cock, sprinkling my leg and the compacted grass of the nest.

"Keep going," I gasp. "Give yourself some more pressure, until it's enough."

He groans again, stroking firmly a few more times. Then he falls onto his shoulder, rolls over onto his back and stays there, breathing hard.

I pull down my skirt and wipe my hand on the fabric before relaxing against the side of the nest. Seconds later, though, a terrifying, deafening earthquake of thunder makes the whole mountain tremble. I don't even know how I get to Kyreagan—suddenly I'm just *there*, crushed against him, clawing him closer in a sheer mad panic.

"Sshhh." He strokes my hair. "I won't let it hurt you."

I know he might not be able to keep that promise, but I also know he's utterly sincere about it. And for now, that's enough.

I'm not sure how long we lie there, with his arms around me and my face against his warm chest. The storm roars so loudly we don't bother trying to talk. The wind drives the rain at a nearly horizontal angle, soaking the floor, but thankfully the nest is deep enough in the cave that the pelting drops don't reach us.

After a while, the thunder abates somewhat, which eases my fear, even though I know it will likely get much worse before it gets better.

I fetch Kyreagan a pair of black pants, and after he puts them on I have him move the glowing stones closer together, out of reach of the rain but far enough from the nest so I don't have to worry about setting it alight. I move some of the food supplies from one dish to another so I can free up a stone bowl, which Kyreagan helps me position atop the hot, cube-shaped rocks.

"There. A stove." I smile, pleased with myself.

"You plan to cook?" Kyreagan sits down awkwardly nearby, rearranging his legs several times before he gets comfortable.

"I'm going to make you a stew." I collect the tin of salt and a couple handfuls of starchy roots and wild onions. Then I retrieve the knife-like claw Jessiva gave me and slice a chunk of venison from one of the carcasses at the back of the cave.

"Don't vomit," Kyreagan says dryly.

"I only vomited because I was starving and then you stuck a bloody hunk of meat in my face and told me to eat it *raw*," I retort. "I'm fine with raw meat if it's in the context of cooking. Fetch me that flat sliver of stone, dragon."

After untangling himself from his cross-legged position, he brings it to me. "Why do you need this?"

"Hush, and watch." I plop the hunk of meat onto one end of the flat stone. It serves well as a cutting surface while I slice the meat into smaller pieces and drop them into the stone bowl, along with some juicy bits of fat.

Kyreagan eyes the knife-claw, his shoulders tense. "Where did you get that? It smells like Tenebrix."

"Tenebrix?"

"One of the dragons who died during the plague, right around the same time as my father's death."

"Jessiva gave it to me," I say calmly, continuing to chop the venison.

"She shouldn't have taken it. Bone-relics are precious to our people. That includes claws and teeth. She gave this to you for food preparation?"

"No."

"Then why?"

Instead of replying immediately, I scoop up the rest of the meat and tumble it into the hot stone bowl where it starts to sizzle. In the rivulet of clear water, I wash both my hands and the claw-knife with the orange-scented soap before walking over to Kyreagan. His eyes widen as I swing astride his lap, facing him, chest to chest. Holding his gaze, I set the sharp tip of the claw against the side of his neck, where the blood pumps close to the skin.

"Why do you think she gave it to me?" I ask quietly.

"To protect yourself from me," he replies.

"Not only that. She asked me to kill you if I could. She wants you dead. She thinks the rest of us can go home if you're out of the way."

Firelight glimmers in his dark eyes. "And what do you think?"

I purse my lips, dragging the point of the claw along his strong tanned throat, then tracing the sharp corner of his jaw with it. "I'm not sure yet."

His hand curls around my wrist. "If you're going to kill me, I have one condition."

"And what's that?"

"Kiss me first."

I laugh a little and lean in, pressing my mouth softly to his. He gives a deep sigh of satisfaction, as if he could die happy.

I deepen the kiss, letting my tongue dance with his cloven one. Only when he gasps do I realize that I forgot the knife in my hand. When I rear back, he has a shallow cut under his ear. Blood trickles from it in a thin line.

"Shit, I'm sorry," I gasp.

"Never mind." He reaches for me, tries to pull me back into the kiss, but I move off his lap.

"I have to cook," I tell him. "I'm starving, and if there's anything I've learned since being your prisoner, it's that if I want to eat well, I must feed myself."

"So you're going to postpone slitting my throat until later, then?"

"Obviously. It would be cruel to kill you before you've had a chance to taste the delicious stew I'm going to make."

After washing the knife again, I continue preparing the food, chopping wild onions and adding them in with the sizzling meat.

Kyreagan seems restless now. He rises and begins to pace back and forth, growing steadier in stride with each passing moment.

"What's wrong with you?" I ask.

"What you said before, when you asked how the plague could have traveled between islands—I realized that you were right, and that some creature must have spread it. Blood-beetles are pests who drink from the necks of animals. They are hardy creatures with sturdy wings, able to fly long distances. Large numbers of them would be the ideal solution if someone wanted to spread a plague swiftly."

"You think someone wiped out most of your prey on purpose?"

"To force us to join the war. Yes. The other day, while everyone else was distracted, I noticed Fortunix flying off alone, and I followed him. I discovered a secret cave where he keeps blood-beetles in glass jars that could only have been crafted and provided to him by humans."

My mind races, putting together the clues. "So he might have been working with Vohrain to ensure that your clan would be forced to ally with them against Elekstan. But why would he do that? And why would he keep the beetles around if their job is done?"

"Fortunix hates Elekstan. My father once told me that Fortunix had two life-mates when he was young, which is rare among our kind. Both of them were killed back when Elekstan hunted dragons. I suppose Fortunix must have been waiting for the right time to gain his vengeance. As for the remaining blood-beetles—I'm not sure why he kept them. Perhaps he is saving them in case he needs to manipulate our food sources again."

"Tell me you destroyed them."

"When I discovered them, I didn't yet understand what he'd used them for. I only realized that later, after speaking with you."

"As I recall, you said 'blood-beetles' in a terrible tone and then raced off. I thought perhaps you'd gone mad."

"I went looking for Fortunix. I couldn't find him, and then I saw the Mordvorren approaching, so I had to postpone confronting him. Nor did I see him during our preparations, or during the mating dance."

"Where do you think he went?"

Kyreagan shakes his head. "Perhaps he smelled my scent in his secret cave and realized I knew something of his schemes. Such a betrayal warrants either a battle to the death between him and me, or his immediate exile, whichever the clan decides. Perhaps he fled to avoid both."

"In which case, you won't see him again. Will you tell the clan what he did?"

"Not until I hear the words from his mouth. I won't accuse him based on theory and guesswork."

"Well done. A wise leader waits to be sure." I smile up at him.

Kyreagan's gaze softens with a pleased kind of wonder, like he didn't expect my approval and it meant something to him. My cheeks, already warm from the heat of the dyre-stones, grow hotter beneath his gaze. He's looking at me like he did by the stream, out there in the forest, when we first kissed.

"Stop looking at me that way." The words sound more irritable than I intended, and I flush deeper. "Fetch me some water, dragon."

The prince fills a clay pot with water. At my direction, he pours a little into the stone bowl where I'm making the stew.

"Who formed the clay pots?" I ask.

"My Grimmaw was skilled in that craft," he replies. "As a hatchling, she spent time among humans and learned some of their ways. She wouldn't talk about it, though. Perhaps if she had, I would have known how to take better care of you."

"At least I'm alive." I give him a wink.

"Would you believe the other dragons came to *me* to find out how they should care for their women?"

"I remember many of them stopping by this cave on the first day. What did they ask you, exactly?"

He clears his throat and leans awkwardly against the cave wall. "This and that."

"You probably gave them dreadful advice. You should have asked me. But of course your pride wouldn't let you, would it?"

"I think I did well enough on my own. Though I have been curious about one thing. Does your kind ever bleed from the— the genital area?"

"Of course. Many women bleed monthly as part of their fertility cycle."

"So it's nothing serious? Not a wound that needs to be staunched or treated?"

"Not in most cases."

"Oh." He gives a faint, embarrassed chuckle, and immediately afterward his stomach growls loudly.

"The stew should be ready soon," I assure him. "It won't be *quite* right, since I don't have all the spices and ingredients I need to make it perfect. But it will be a decent meal."

Kyreagan paces again, occasionally pausing to look out at the storm. The stew is simmering nicely, so I throw in the tubers, which, judging by their potato-like consistency, should take less than half an hour to cook. I add a handful of plump gray mushrooms as well.

The lightning keeps hitting a tall, thin mountain opposite us, across the valley, and the searing flashes and cracks of thunder make me jump every time. More than once a chunk of rock is struck clean off the cliffside and goes thundering down to the earth far below.

While the stew simmers, I rinse the tuber starch off my fingers. The rivulet of spring water in the cave has intensified to a stream, and I'm glad of Kyreagan's foresight in widening and deepening its bed. He must have done the job hastily, without much care for appearance, because slash marks from his claws score the rocks on either side of the narrow stream. It's a contrast to the methodical artistry of the cave's engraved walls.

Wiping my fingers on my skirt, I join Kyreagan, who is staring out of the cave mouth at the violent storm.

"Did you decorate this place?" I wave a hand to the engravings.

"No." His face holds a tender sadness. "Grimmaw's life-mate did. His name was Lorgrin. This is Dragonish writing. Poetry, history. Records of my family's bloodline."

"It's beautiful."

"I never met Lorgrin. The elders say he was no good as a warrior or a hunter, that he preferred long hours of quiet carving. Sometimes he would etch designs on the bowls and pots Grimmaw made, or he would decorate another dragon's cave in exchange for game or foraged goods."

"Was he also a king?"

"His brother was. But that Bone-King had no heir, and Lorgrin did not wish to rule, so the leadership passed to my father, by the will of the clan."

"The will of the clan," I murmur. "So everyone agrees upon the next ruler?"

"Yes. When my father died, the clan had already decided that I should rule next. But I did not feel able to do so alone. My siblings and I swore to rule together."

"In Elekstan, the people have no choice in the matter. They are governed by the heir of the reigning bloodline." I hold out my hand, letting the vicious rain beat against my fingertips. It stings so badly I have to draw them back.

With our backs to the glowing dyre-stones, the world seems darker, more dangerous. I can feel Kyreagan's eyes on me in the gloom.

"You would have been a great queen," he says. "Wise and kind, yet forceful."

Never in my life have I been told I would make a good queen, much less a great one. "I think you're full of shit." I give him a half-smile. "But thank you."

A raucous gust of wind whips through the cave mouth, tearing at our clothes and hair, nearly yanking me with it as it roars back out into the void of night. Kyreagan catches me and pulls me farther back into the cave. In that one instant, the wind-driven rain soaked us both to the skin.

"We should take off these wet clothes." Kyreagan's eyes glint as he notices how my white dress is sticking to my form.

"It's fine. The clothes will dry quickly enough. We should eat."

"If I recall correctly, you don't like to be wet... at least not in this way." His voice is a caress, low and coaxing. "As your captor, I must care for you properly, and that means making sure you are dry and warm."

"I'm really fine—" My protest turns into a squeal as he picks me up—hoists me bodily and lays me across his shoulders. I'm not even sure how he conceived of the idea, or how he managed it so fluidly. His control of this body is certainly improving. Still, he can't be allowed to tote me around like a sack of flour. "Put me down this *instant*, dragon!"

He ignores me and marches over to the area where I laid out my supplies from Thelise: undergarments, clothing, the packet of contraceptive herbs, and a few other items. There's even a tiny flask, which I'm sure must hold some kind of powerful liquor.

After putting me down, he seizes the hem of my shift dress in his clawed fingers and drags it up, over my head, in one fluid motion. As he picks up the blanket, I squeal, "I just folded that!" but he pays no attention and uses it to clumsily blot the water from my body.

"Lift your arms," he orders, and when I do, he studiously dries my sides, then my breasts.

I'm already warm, already heated to incandescence by the commanding way he picked me up, then by the careful intentionality of his movements. If he keeps drying me off with that earnest expression on his face, I'm going to end up fucking him right here, right now. And we can't do that, because I've prepared an excellent meal and I'll be damned if I let it burn.

He starts to move the blanket down to my lower belly, but I seize it from him and step back. "I'll do that. You change your pants and then take the stew off the stove. Carefully. Don't spill a drop."

Moments later we're sitting on opposite sides of the big stone bowl, me in the pink dress and him in a simple ivory shirt and black pants. He looks so fucking handsome I can hardly stay focused on the food.

We don't have spoons, of course, but I fetch a couple of clamshells from Kyreagan's collection. I demonstrate how to scoop the stew into the half-shell, how to blow on it to cool the broth, and how to tip the contents into my mouth. The prince copies everything I do, carefully. He's fucking adorable.

"Well?" I watch him, eager for his reaction. "What do you think?"

He blinks, chews a bit more, then swallows. "How did you work this magic?"

"It's not magic. It's science. Different compounds and substances reacting together because of an outside force—in this case, the energy from heat."

"So... magic."

I giggle and scoop more stew with my shell. "Fine. Magic."

We eat in companionable silence, and I only have to remind him *once* to chew with his lips closed. By the time our shells are scraping the bottom of the bowl, I'm pleasantly full and feeling drowsy.

"That may have been the best stew I ever made." I sigh with satisfaction. "I'm glad Jessiva gave me that claw. Without it I couldn't have chopped everything so efficiently. I suppose I could have found a bit of rock to use as a knife, but it wouldn't have worked as well. I wonder if she kept one for herself, too, or if she has something else—"

"Something else?" Kyreagan frowns. "What do you mean?"

"She must have some other kind of weapon for herself, if she—" Oh fuck… I should not have said that.

"If she, what?" Kyreagan holds my gaze, unrelenting. "Why would she need a weapon?"

I squirm. "You know why."

He's too smart not to understand. "She gave you *that* to kill me, and you think she has another weapon ready at hand, so she can kill my brother."

A clap of thunder echoes his words and reverberates through the mountain, shaking the very walls of the cave. Wind screams past the opening with a hollow wail, like a desolate soul being flayed in the night.

"I think she might be planning to try it, yes." My voice is barely audible, even to me, yet somehow he hears it.

"And you didn't think to mention that my brother, the last living member of my family, is in danger?" He's growling now, pure ravenous fury in his voice. Never have I seen such murderous intent in his eyes until this moment.

"I warned Varex," I falter. "I told him to watch his back around her."

"Like me, he will shift into human form," Kyreagan snarls, getting to his feet. "He will be vulnerable, defenseless, without his spikes and scales. He will be alone with a woman who wants to kill him. He could be lying dead at this very moment. If he is, it's your fault."

"I'm sorry," I gasp. "There was so much going on, and I had to think about myself, too. You rejected me, and I didn't know which dragon to choose, where to go…"

"Is this why you chose me, after all?" he cuts in. "Perhaps you weren't simply teasing me earlier. Perhaps you *do* want to kill me. How do you plan to leave this cave after the storm, if I'm dead? You'll have no wings to carry you to the ground. Maybe you and the other women have allies among the clan. Are there more traitors, plotting death and the ruin of our species right under my nose?"

"I can't speak for the other women." I scramble to my feet and back away from him. "But I have no such allies. When I was in the enclosure with the other prisoners, there was some talk of getting a few dragons on our side—"

"And this is the first I'm hearing of it," he snarls. "Just as you failed to warn me about the danger to Varex."

Oddly, his human anger frightens me more than his fury in dragon form. And yet I'm angry, too. Incensed, actually.

"How dare you?" I say through trembling lips. "How dare you act as if I'm your loyal informant, your partner, an ally whose duty it is to report suspicious or treacherous activity? I'm not your mate. I'm your fucking prisoner, as you reminded me just this morning."

He advances, tall and menacing, his black hair flowing like a cloak behind him and his eyes sparking with fury. When I retreat against the side of the cave, he lunges forward, slams a palm against the rock wall near my head. His claws scrape the stone next to my ear, a grating rasp. His bulk dominates me, and his heat floods my skin.

"I thought we were something else, you and I," he grits out. "I was beginning to trust you. It seems I was misled."

"Don't do that." I put both hands against his chest and shove him. It's like trying to shove a mountain. "Don't blame me for the position we're both in. It's not ideal for anyone, and we could go around and around all night, shifting the blame from me to you, from my mother to your father, from the King of Vohrain to Fortunix, from Jessiva to me again. None of that would do any good. I thought that warning your brother would be enough. Even doing that made me feel like a traitor to *my* people. But I'm sorry I didn't tell you, Kyreagan. I am. I don't want your brother dead, nor do I want you dead, especially not now that you have human form."

"So that's it," he sneers. "Now that I look more like *you*, you have pity on me. You're willing to spare me. But me as a dragon—that is too unfamiliar for you. My true form, my language, my culture, my way of life, are unacceptable to you. In this body, I am *palatable*. As I recall, you did not appreciate me using that word about you. Consider, then, how I feel, knowing that if I were still a dragon with no alternate form, you would utterly despise me."

"No." The word escapes me as a breathless gasp. "I touched you in dragon form. I let you—pleasure me."

"Selfishness. You accepted my tongue because you craved physical comfort, and you touched me because you wanted to ride, not be carried. Neither of those acts were for me… only for you."

"What do you want me to say? Of *course* I like you better in this form," I cry out. "We are an entirely different *species*, Ky. I thought you were beautiful, funny, and dangerously seductive *before* Thelise's spell. Can you blame me for being glad that your body is now more compatible with mine? It has nothing to do with our other differences, and everything to do with the fact that you can fit inside me now. It's that simple. Do you understand?"

His chest heaves, and he grabs my lower face in his hand, glaring into my eyes with a lustful rage so fierce and wicked I can hardly breathe. I tuck my thumbs into the waistband of his black pants and pull him nearer with a sharp jerk.

He grinds his thick erection against me as he speaks, his voice low and rough. "You want me inside you?"

I can't turn my head because he's gripping my face, but I angle my eyes away from his.

"Serylla." He gives me a little shake. "Look at me. Do you want me to fuck you?"

A sharp whining gasp escapes me, but I still can't make myself say it, despite the slippery state of my pussy.

"I can smell the change when your body reacts to me. Did you know that?" Kyreagan arches his spine, rubbing his bulge against me like a beast in heat. And perhaps he is. His magical transformation changed things; I wouldn't be surprised if the heat began early.

My hands still clutch his waist, holding him pinned against me, and it's all I can do not to writhe against him, hitch my legs around him, tuck his cock into my warmth... *please, please...*

His cheek grazes mine. "I want to breed you, Princess," he rumbles. "I want to come inside you until you can't hold any more, until your stomach swells with my seed. I want my eggs growing in your belly."

"Oh god," I breathe. Why did every sentence he just spoke send a delicious tingle through my body? There is something deeply wrong with me, because I'm thinking of letting him do exactly what he said. I would have carried the children of some pompous southern prince after all—why not carry the eggs of this dragon who truly needs me? It's dangerous, of course—but in my experience, the best sex involves some risk.

"I don't know about the egg thing," I gasp. But even as I say it, I remember the herbs Thelise gave me. If we fuck, I could take a dose in the morning to prevent pregnancy.

I should give in to him now, and make up my mind about the eggs later. Fuck him just once, and hope the urge leaves my system afterward.

"If you're going to deny me, do it quickly," he rasps. "Before I am beyond the limits of my own strength."

"It's beginning, then? The mating heat?"

"I'm not sure. All I know is that I am a heartbeat away from throwing you down and rutting you on the floor until I can breathe again."

I'm practically dripping beneath my dress, frantically aroused at the bare thought of such compulsive need. Some primitive, shadowed part of me wants to be pursued like that, to be seized and thrown down and fucked so hard I can't form logical thoughts. I ache to be wanted so ferociously, so madly, that a man can't think of anything except losing himself inside me. Not just any man... *this* man. I want him to breed me with that kind of urgency—frenzied, reckless, monstrous. I want to give him all the control and feel him come violently, helplessly inside me.

If I'm being honest with myself, I think I've been craving this dragon since I saw him flying toward my city at the head of his army. Underneath every gush of my hatred for him was a subtle current of fascination, of attraction.

And that mighty dragon is a man now—a man with horns and claws and a gorgeous body that's shuddering against mine. He drags his burning mouth along my cheekbone, lowers his hand from my jaw to my throat.

"I am stronger than you, even in this form." His breath heats my lips, and his eyes are black coals. "Part of me wants to consume you, crush you, force you to submit."

"You won't, though," I whisper. "You're better than that. You're kind."

His lip hitches in a pained grimace. "I'm not. I have killed so many—I would not let myself think on it too hard, or regret it, but now I can hardly bear—"

"Hush." I sway forward, tilting my pelvis, arching against him. "Sit with your guilt later. For now, think only of the game I want to play."

"A game?"

Now it's my turn to murmur in his ear, while lightning blazes and thunder rolls outside. "This is the game. I will run away, fight you, pretend to deny you. And in spite of that denial, you'll take me, hard, whenever you want, any way you like, all night long. If I truly need you to stop, I'll say 'end it now.' You must promise to respect those three words."

"I will, even if I must throw myself into the Mordvorren to do so," he replies.

I arch an eyebrow. "I doubt things will become so drastic."

"You've never seen a dragon in heat. My father told me stories—"

I cup my fingers over his mouth. "Stories I don't need to hear right now."

"Very well." He moves back, creating separation between our bodies. I feel colder without him—empty and hungry. In a world darkened by the dismantling of everything I once knew, he is the one thing that can dispel the shadows.

It means more than I can say that he didn't reject the game I suggested. In this, at least, our goals are aligned. Mine—to be taken out of myself, dominated by someone powerful, transported beyond any need to plan, escape, or even think. And his—to claim me completely and sate his primal need to reproduce. He doesn't have to know that I've made the choice to neutralize his seed. It's my body, and I will give him as much of it as I please, and no more.

With distance between us, Kyreagan still looks ravenous, but there's a hint of uncertainty in his face. "I haven't done this before."

"I've only done it a couple of times," I admit. "Don't overthink it. Just like with walking and speaking, let your body take over. It knows what to do."

He closes his eyes, tilts back his horned head, and draws in a long, slow breath. Something about the twitch of his claws and the tension of his shoulders lets me know that when he finishes exhaling, I'll be done for. There will be no stopping him.

I suspect this is going to get rough, and since clothes are in such short supply, I'd rather he didn't shred the pink dress I'm wearing. I pull it off hastily and toss it over with the rest of my belongings. I throw my shredded slippers in that direction as well. On quiet bare feet, I circle the huge nest and retreat deeper into the gloom at the back of the cave.

I won't drag the game out too long. He has been in human form for a few hours now, and in another four or five hours he'll have to switch back to his dragon shape. I'd like to be thoroughly sated by then. But I want him to work for it.

Kyreagan stands where I left him, eyes closed, but I see his nostrils widen a fraction. The corner of his mouth lifts. Even if I'm standing in the shadows, he can smell me. And the cave, though deep, offers no hiding places.

When he doesn't make a move, I dip my hand between my thighs. Then I hold up my wet fingers.

I don't have to wait long before a cold, damp breeze whirls through the cave, over the nest and back out again, skimming past Kyreagan and carrying the scent of my arousal right under his nose.

He leaps like a snarling panther, like liquid lightning. There's no trace of awkwardness with his human limbs now—he is every bit a predator, caught in the frenzy of the hunt. He barrels around the nest and charges toward me faster than I expected, and the squeal of fright I emit is genuine as I dart away, barely avoiding his fingertips.

I circle the nest and pause on the other side, my eyes on him, breathless with anticipation. He pauses to remove his shirt—easy enough, since he didn't bother to button it. The pants take longer, but he gets them undone and kicks them aside. I've seen him naked, but watching him approach, with that long, sinewy body of his, highlighted in the amber light, is more temptation than I was prepared to handle. I nearly give up on my plan to have him "force" me—my body is begging to submit. But then he hops lightly onto the nest and stalks across it toward me, and my instinct kicks in, warning me that I am *prey*, and that he is a *hunter*.

Slowly I back up, matching his measured pace, until I feel the mist of wind-driven rain against my bare back. I'm still well within the cave, nowhere near the dangerous edge, but Kyreagan checks his stride and says, "Careful, Princess."

He's right. At any moment, another gust of wind could circle through the cave—and not just a breeze this time, but a full-on gale, the arm of a hurricane reaching in to snatch me and carry me out to my death.

I give Kyreagan a devilish smile, and I take one more step back.

Alarm flares in his eyes. "Stop it, Serylla."

Another step back.

"You little fool." He bares his teeth and springs from the nest. "Obey me. Come away from there."

"Make me."

"You endangering yourself was never part of this game, you beautiful fucking trickster," he says.

Another bracing burst of wind, and I gasp, thinking maybe I took this too far, after all. But the gust twirls around my bare body, peaking my nipples with its chill, then skims out of the cave again—no sucking force this time.

Kyreagan doesn't wait to see how intense the gust will be. He's on me in a half-second, whirling me around, shoving me farther back into the safety of the cave.

I dart away from him, but he catches my wrist, jerks me back against his body. A hollow groan rolls through him at the silken flow of my skin against his. He pins me with my spine to his chest, my ass against his upper thighs. His clawed hand squeezes my breast, while his other arm bands my waist.

"You're fucking *mine*," he growls, and I inhale a sharp breath because it's his dragon-voice, deep and guttural, roaring up from the darkest crevices of his wild heart.

"No." I twist my torso in his grip, and the points of his nails draw dots of blood from my flesh, in a half circle around my breast. The moment he senses the blood, he lets me go, and I scramble away.

But he's on me again in a moment, seizing my arm and my thigh, slinging me bodily into the nest. The grass is soft, but a little scratchy, and I crawl forward on my belly as fast as I can, heading for the edge.

Kyreagan grabs my ankle and my hair. He drags me back to him while I thrash and curse. I'm not much of a fighter at the best of times, and it's laughably easy for him to haul me across the grass. He flips me over and pounces on me, his knees on either side of my hips and one hand planted beside my neck. His other hand drags lightly down my chest, over my breasts, and then along my stomach. My belly concaves with shallow breaths as those sharp nails graze my flesh, and I lie still, conscious that this dragon could slice me to ribbons if he wanted to.

My pussy quivers with anticipation as he moves lower. When he crooks his first finger and rubs the knuckle over my clit, I squeal faintly, desperately.

He settles down between my thighs. I fake an effort to pin them together, but he forces me wide open and brushes his lips lightly over my pussy. The delicate touch sends me writhing.

But I don't want him gentle, not now. I want him vicious. I want to be ravaged.

So I slap him, full in the face, and while he snarls in response, I crawl away on hands and knees.

He throws himself on top of me, and I know immediately that this is what I've been craving. My entire world is blotted out, except for the tickle of the grass beneath my stomach and his massive weight crushing me into the nest. His heat and power roll against my skin; his chest swells with the heavy, bestial harshness of his breath. He's panting against my hair. He lifts his hips, straddling me, squeezing my thighs together. Hunched over me like a wolf in rut. One big hand slides under my belly, lifts my pelvis, forces my ass up. What he's doing is instinctive, some combination of human desire and dragon urgency.

The blunt, burning head of his cock nudges against my pussy, and I whimper. Can't form words. Can't think about anything except the fact that I'm on my face, ass in the air, crushed and walled in by the powerful arms and legs of the dragon shifter who desperately wants to breed me.

He arches his body. Bucks his hips forward. Enters me in a violent rush.

My eyes roll back and my lips slacken. I'm stretched taut, on the cusp of pain. He's so big, fuck…

Panting thickly, he draws back, slow and slick, his giant length easing out of my body, almost all the way but not quite. The next second he slams in, surprising a short scream out of me. He growls in response, a feral sound that kicks a vivid thrill through my veins. I want to hear him make more of those wild, masculine sounds, so I moan softly. The hoarse, groaning growl that ripples from his body melts my brain entirely, and I yield.

His mouth finds my shoulder and he licks me with his cloven tongue before venting a breathless moan at the taste of my skin. Either my scent or my flavor seems to drive him mad, and he starts fucking me wildly, brutally. At first he stays hunched over, wolf-like, humping me, pummeling my pussy with his cock, but then he straightens, plants one hand on my head, and pushes the side of my face into the nest while he keeps up the merciless pounding.

My body submits to him completely. Every thought blurs, and the only thing I want, the only thing I need, is the orgasm that keeps winding tighter and tighter at my core. I'm terrified that he'll come, that he'll stop too soon before I get where I need to be.

"Make me come," I whimper through a sob. "Please, please, dragon, make me come, make me come."

With a cruel snarl, he barrels in so deep I think he's going to break me, but it fuels the orgasm, gives me another burst of pleasure, shoves me closer to the peak. I scream out "yes," and he snarls a laugh and thrusts with redoubled force.

"I have the Princess of Elekstan in my nest," he says raggedly, triumphantly. "With her pretty ass in the air, begging to cum on my cock. Say it again, Princess."

I'm beyond pride, beyond grief, beyond everything—entirely compliant. I can barely get the words out because he's fucking me so hard, shaking my entire body, but I manage to mumble, through lust-swollen lips, "Make me come, please. Don't stop, don't ever stop… oh god…" My voice rises to a thin shriek as his fingers twist viciously into my hair, as the claws of his other hand scrape down my back. The ferocity of the act hits me like a blast of dragon fire, lashes my clit into a thrilling frenzy, sends the orgasm searing through my body like liquid flame.

Harsh, short screams shatter from my lips, over and over. I'm not in control of my limbs—my fingers claw deep into the nest, my thighs shudder, and still he fucks me, grunting loud and heavy, faster, faster—he yells out, a cry that sounds like agony, and his body bows over mine. I feel him pulsing thickly inside me, pumping the cum into my womb.

"You will carry my offspring," he whispers, stroking my hair, his length still sunk to the hilt in my pussy. "The essence of my species and yours will join, and we will create a race that is altogether new."

There's something deliciously primal in those words, in the way he rears his hips back and shoves in again, firmly. His cock flexes one more time, draining every bit of cum from his balls into my body.

"Shit," I choke out. I'm a mess—hair tangled, tears on my cheeks, my pale skin flushed red. I've never been so broken down, so yielded to anyone. I feel as if he stripped me raw, past my clothes and skin and flesh, right to my beating heart, and he fucked it until it burst into a fountain of bloody, devoted love.

That's what it feels like to admit the truth, the real reason I let him do this. I can barely whisper it in my own mind. But as he pulls out of me, I allow myself to think the words, just once.

I love you.

No... fuck.

No. I must not indulge those three words. They will trap me here, in this cave, in this life.

Closing my eyes, I speak another three words to myself, a firm order in my mind.

End this now.

23

KYREAGAN

When I pull out of her, glossy white cum spills from between the pink lips of her sex. Never have I seen anything so enticing. I scoop the cum with the side of my first finger, nudging it back inside her while being careful not to damage the delicate tissue with my claws. Then I press my palm firmly over her sex to hold my cum inside her body.

She was right. When the moment came, I knew what to do. And the pleasure I felt when I came inside her was far more intense than the two orgasms I had before.

Serylla was the right choice for this mating season. Whether she and I continue in each other's company or not, whether she lays eggs for me or not, I know I made the right decision, weathering the storm with her.

When she makes a move to get up, I hold her in place. "Wait a moment. I don't want everything I put inside you to spill out."

"You'll get to deposit more," she replies. "Let me up. I have to piss."

She asks me not to watch while she takes care of her physical needs, so I stand at the cave mouth and look out at the storm until she tells me she's done.

When I turn around, she's standing there naked, trying to straighten out her tangled yellow hair with her fingers.

"How does your hair always look perfectly sleek and silky?" she grumbles.

I lift a lock of it, frowning. "Is that not normal?"

"No, it's not. I think it's something Thelise did, a little perk she added to the spell. Maybe I can get her to work something similar on me, so I can have perpetually clean, perfect hair. Speaking of hair—I'm going to use that claw-knife to shave my legs and other parts. I used to do that at the palace, but I haven't had a chance since you took me. I'm all hairy and gross."

"I like you exactly as you are," I tell her.

"Thanks, but this is something I do for *me*." As she collects the knife, she looks up at me, notes the expression on my face. "What is it?"

"The claw-knife, as you call it, belonged to one of our dead. Such relics are revered, not generally used as tools. I said nothing when you used it for cooking, but this seems... disrespectful."

Serylla surveys the claw and nods. "I see what you're saying. I won't use it if you don't want me to."

She's being kind, thoughtful, and respectful, though I can tell she desperately wants to shave herself. I mull it over, considering that Tenebrix found his place in the sky months ago, and that, since he is one with the universe again, he won't know or care what is done with his claw. Perhaps, in such times of upheaval and change, a small transgression might be allowed. Besides, the claw she has is not bone-tribute—there is no name carved into it. So it's a spare that Jessiva found somewhere, which makes it more acceptable for it to be put to use.

"Go on," I tell the Princess. "Tenebrix was a dragon with a ready laugh, always eager to hear a joke or try something new. I don't believe he would mind."

"Thank you." She collects the bar of soap and sits down near the outlet of the stream. I watch, fascinated, as she soaps up her legs and armpits and shaves off the flecks of blond hair.

"You have a few new bruises," I comment. "And I scratched your back. I'm sorry for that."

"Don't apologize! When you clawed me like that, it was exactly what I needed. As long as you keep it light and don't go too deep, it's fine. Now hush—I have to concentrate." She parts her legs and coats her genitals with a film of soap before carefully shaving them as well. I hold my breath, terrified that she'll hurt herself, but she appears fairly confident in the process.

"You've done this many times," I comment.

"I could have had my maids do it," she says. "But I always preferred to do such things myself."

It's strange—I was unbothered by the idea of her walking around naked on that first day, but now, the idea of anyone but me seeing her pussy sends a flare of hot jealousy through my chest. I don't like the idea of her maids touching her there, and I hate picturing her with the two men she fucked before me. It's a foolish, illogical kind of jealousy, one I must strive to curb.

"All done." She rinses herself, parting the folds of her pussy and moving them casually aside as she washes away the soap and the bits of blond hair.

I swallow as my body tightens with sudden need. My heart thuds heavily, a compelling beat through my blood. My cock rises, thick and stiff. A hectic urgency constricts every muscle, roars in my brain, thunders in my chest.

Outside, lightning sears the night, turning everything in the cave blinding white for a moment. A boom of thunder cracks rock somewhere nearby, and Serylla cringes as stones go thundering down the mountain. At the same moment the rain picks up again, and the screaming wind flings sheets of it into the cave. The rain hisses against the dyre-stones, but it doesn't quite reach the nest.

Serylla rises, picks up her white shift dress, and pulls it on over her head. I watch it curtain her lovely body, and I despise it for hiding her shape from me.

She walks over to the nest and hitches one leg up to climb in, presumably planning to sleep. The movement pulls the white fabric taut against the two round cheeks of her bottom.

And I lose my mind.

With a strangled cry of need, I pounce on her. My claws frantically gather the dress, shoving the fabric out of my way. Trembling with aching need, I push my cock into her slit.

The Princess yelps with the shock of my abrupt entry, but she doesn't speak her three escape words, thank fuck. Even if she did, I'm not sure I could stop myself.

A thick groan escapes my throat as I plunge deep into her body. The way her luscious, wet insides tremble and clench around me—it's the best sensation I've ever experienced. I can't imagine that sex in dragon form feels this good.

I hold her by the hips and watch my cock glide in and out beneath the globes of her rear. Experimentally I tease the tiny puckered hole of her ass with the tip of my thumbnail while I fuck her, earning a breathy sigh of surprised delight as my reward. The tiny hole is for elimination, not breeding, but I'm fascinated with it, as I am with every part of her.

Tingling pleasure races along my cock with every fresh surge into my captive's pussy. I'm shuddering, huffing desperate moans into the rain-washed air of the cave because I have never felt anything so perfectly, delicately exquisite—nothing this intensely delicious…

"I love those pretty sounds you're making," Serylla says softly. "Do you want my cunt so badly, dragon?"

I remember hearing the King of Vohrain use that word. It must mean the same thing as pussy. It's harsher somehow, more vulgar and possessive. I didn't like it from his mouth, but I think I love it from hers.

"I crave your cunt, Princess." I draw in a shuddering breath. "You feel like flying through a sunset. Like diving down a waterfall. Like tearing into the fresh, rich, delicious meat of—"

"That's enough dragon poetry." She laughs, but it's smoky and thick with desire. "Shit, Kyreagan—how do you make me feel like this? God, I need you deeper… fucking deeper… moan for me again."

I drag her hips tight against me and thrust balls-deep, and I come with a fractured, helpless moan that makes her whimper with delight. Glorious satisfaction bathes my soul as my balls tighten, spilling another helping of cum into my little mate's womb.

Mate? I must not allow myself to hope for such things. She would never agree to be my life-mate.

She seems willing to carry my young, to help me save my species. But after that—I draw out of her, shivering as the final traces of delight thrill along my cock—after *that,* after the hatching, I must let her go. If I truly care about her, I must give her back her freedom and all her choices. I must ensure that she is happy and well cared for, and then I must leave her alone.

I will take her back to the mainland and set her free somewhere safe, far from Vohrain's reach. She'll be able to live out her days as she wishes to, with her own kind. I'll raise our hatchlings, and at the next mating season, during my fiftieth year, I'll mate with a fellow clan member's daughter—one of the new female dragons who have reached their twenty-fifth year. Those new dragons will be shifters as well, able to transition between forms, which should make the mating heat even more interesting.

My plan sickens me to the core. But I can't see another future for us. Serylla could never be happy here, in this cave, with me. She would never pledge herself as a life-mate to a dragon, not even one who can change his shape.

She lies on her belly, draped over the edge of the nest, panting. After a moment she crawls forward farther into the nest.

She didn't come yet, which is inexcusable on my part. I am determined she will have as many climaxes as I do.

I climb into the nest with her, pull her into a sitting position, and remove her dress. Once she is bared to me, I lay her down on her back, lift her lower body, and hook her legs over my shoulders. I bend forward until my face is between her thighs and I can trace my tongue over her cum-glazed pussy. She throws both arms above her head and yields to me with a sweet gasp of submission.

With each gentle lick, with each tantalizing flicker of my tongue, I gain a deeper understanding of what she enjoys. I'm learning that she prefers to be surprised—something a little different every time.

When I whip my cloven tongue rapidly across her clit in an untiring rhythm, she starts to whine frantically. I ease off, moving to lower areas, soothing her opening, and by the time she's crying for release, I know exactly what to do. I return to that quick rhythm, at exactly the same angle, lashing her tiny clit until I hear the sharp sound I've been waiting for, at the precise moment she crests the peak of her pleasure and soars down it, gliding in freefall. I keep going until she locks both legs around my head and bucks frantically, ramming her pussy against my face. She needs comfort, firmness, so I let her use me to gain that pressure. I'm bathed in her liquid and mine, her scent and mine.

After her legs loosen, I fetch the blankets, and we doze together in the nest, naked, for a long time. I wake slowly, muddled by dreams of fucking her, and I find my cock hard again. Her blanket has slipped off and she's on her side, facing away from me, tempting me with her beautiful bottom. I lift one of her legs and adjust her until I can see her pretty cunt. Lightly I pet it, careful not to let my claws slip inside her. As I stroke her, wetness begins to seep from her body.

Serylla whimpers sleepily and reaches around for my cock, clumsily trying to put it inside herself. With a pleased grin I take myself in hand and slowly slide the head of my cock through her slit, watching the shining wet lips of her sex part around it. The sensation is divine, but more satisfying still are the cute little moans she makes as I drag my cock through her pussy again and again. Her hips shift back, like she's trying to impale herself on me, but I'm taking my time, enjoying every sensation, every tactile wonder that *skin* is capable of. I make her wait. I stroke her gently with my cock, while it swells harder and hotter in my hand.

I have *hands*. Legs. Smooth skin that can rub against hers without being too abrasive. This is not a curse—it's a miracle. A million new sensations to enjoy.

Experimentally I wipe the head of my cock on the smooth cheek of the Princess's ass, just to watch the streak of arousal glisten on her skin. So many textures, so much sensory delight.

"Please." A soft whine from Serylla.

"That's my good fucking Princess," I whisper, patting her pussy with my cock before sliding in. She's slippery, silken—my mind might explode from the sheer glory of entering her. Her body swallows me, tugs at my cock each time I pull back for another thrust, as if she's hugging me and doesn't want to let me go.

She hums with pleasure, wriggles her ass with a contented mew as I keep thrusting. The gliding suction sends stars bursting in my brain, drives me to the brink of blissful insanity. I'm coming inside her, I'm coming, and fuck, it's beautiful, it's everything.

I stay buried in her for a long time—so long, in fact, that my cock hardens again. She's asleep, so I move gently inside her, thrusting slow and steady. After a few moments she rouses with a pretty moan and puts her fingers between her legs while I fuck her. We come at the same moment this time, and the sensation of her body clenching and fluttering around my throbbing cock is my new favorite thing, better than a flight through sunset skies, better than any of my limited experiences. Before her, I had no idea what real pleasure was.

But as the orgasm fades, I feel a buzzing vibration through my bones.

My time in this form is over, and my dragon self is returning.

Hastily I disentangle myself from Serylla, leap out of the nest, and head toward the mouth of the cave. There, on the rain-soaked stone, I transform once again.

Strength and security accompanies my dragon form. It is the body I was born to occupy, the shape of my ancestors. But I can't help feeling a sense of loss as well. I stand uncertainly on all fours, my wings lax against the stone, thunder and lightning crashing through the darkness behind me.

Serylla rises, naked and lovely, and swings her legs over the edge of the nest. She wobbles a little on pleasure-weakened limbs, but she rights herself, walks over to me, and places both arms around my scaly neck.

"Come back to the nest," she says. "It's time to sleep."

I'm not sure how long I sleep with my Princess nestled against the broad, warm scales of my belly. But when I wake, she isn't there. I can hear her moving quietly near the supplies. There's a rustling sound, a strong herbal scent, then the sound of chewing.

The dyre-stones are nearly out—they're barely glowing. If she wants to get up and cook something, I'll need to heat them again.

Lifting my head, I turn to see what she is eating. "Are you hungry?"

She half-chokes, but manages to swallow whatever is in her mouth. "Um... no."

"But you were eating."

"Medicinal herbs."

"Are you ill? Was I too rough with you?" I rise, my wings flaring with anxiety.

"No, no! It's nothing like that. It's..." She winces, averting her eyes. Then words spill out in a rush. "It's just that I'm not ready to carry dragon eggs. The herbs I took are to prevent your cum from making me pregnant."

Disappointment washes through me like a sweep of cold rain. "They will make you permanently infertile?"

"No! They will be in effect for a few hours, and they'll end anything that may have started. But I'll be fertile again after that."

"I see." I flatten my wings against my back and rest my muzzle on my forepaws. "I understand why you took them. It is your right to protect yourself from a future you don't want."

"Kyreagan." Her tone is gentle, sympathetic. "I know how much this means to you. I just need a little more time to consider it. That's all."

I close my eyes, wishing I could return to the dream I was having, in which I bred her successfully and we were raising a family of small dragons together...

"You're sad now," she says, her voice soft with pity. "I'm sorry... I shouldn't have taken the herbs. We can try again once you're in human form—"

"Don't feel regret on my account." I rise abruptly, gazing at her with all the fierce adoration in my heart. "What I was planning to do, forcing you to take dragon form—I was wrong about all of it. You shouldn't agree to anything you do not wholeheartedly desire. Your happiness means more to me than any offspring—and so does your freedom. When this storm is over, I will return you to the mainland. We'll go south, far from Vohrain, and I will give you treasure from my hoard so you can purchase anything you need. Perhaps you can have a small farm of your own, marry a kind human, have his children. You can do everything you wish for. *That* will please me, Serylla, and nothing else. I will live out my days in peace on Ouroskelle, knowing that you are safe and happy. It is enough—" I hesitate, because she's climbing into the nest, her eyes fiercely aflame, and she looks so beautiful that I rasp out the truth— "It will have to be enough."

"You would do that?" She seizes my muzzle between her hands. "You'd let me go? Even if I don't give you a single hatchling?"

"Yes."

"Why?"

Fire roils inside me, churning, swelling, threatening to unleash itself. I swallow it down.

"Speak, Kyreagan," she urges. "Tell me. You refused to release me before. Why would you agree to it now?"

"I have become... attached," I growl, bristling.

"How attached?"

"Deeply attached."

"If you were just *attached* to me, like a possession, you'd want to keep me here. You wouldn't be talking about setting me free. There's more to it."

My growl intensifies.

She nods, with a little half-smile. "Yes, and?"

I wrench my head from her grasp and spew a focused line of fire out into the storm. The rain sizzles into clouds of steam which billow into the cave, shrouding us both in wisps of fog.

Serylla steps through the mist, small and strong and determined. Her true self, not the person she pretended to be when I first brought her here.

"What else, Kyreagan?" She looks up at me, sweet and fearless, and I am enthralled. I am undone. I have been, ever since Vohrain's king told me he wanted her.

"It grows worse with every passing day," I confess. "I did not ask for it. I do not deserve it."

"Name it," she says.

Through a snarl, I mutter, "Love."

A smile spreads over her face, lighting up her eyes, lighting up the whole fucking cave. "You say that word like it tastes bad."

"It fucking hurts."

"Of course it does. Haven't you heard any love songs?"

"Precious few."

"Maybe I'll write you one."

My heart pulses, aching, hopeful. "You're toying with me."

"Only a little. Who knew such a big, terrible, spiky dragon could be so sensitive." She pats my foreleg. "Lie down. We should rest more."

I can't sense whether it's morning or not, thanks to the pitch darkness of the Mordvorren whirling outside, dashing its torrents against the mountain. As she said, we may as well rest, so I settle down on my side in the nest, and she leans against my belly.

Serylla did not reciprocate my grudging confession of love, though she seemed pleased by it. I suppose it is only fair that I experience a taste of what Mordessa endured when she vowed her love for me, and I failed to respond. The uncertainty I'm suffering now is a kind of justice.

"Do you think the others are alright?" Serylla murmurs after a while.

"They have supplies."

"That's not exactly what I meant."

"If any have been sealed in their caves due to rockfalls, we can't help them until the Mordvorren is over. Winds like these would dash a dragon to pieces against the mountain."

"That's... not quite what I meant, either."

"You're talking about the mating heat."

"I know you warned the males not to force anything, but I can't help being a little afraid for the other women."

"Are you not afraid for yourself?"

She chuckles and pats my shoulder. "No."

"And why not?"

"Because I know you now. Not all of you, yet, but enough. And I—" She stops abruptly, and my skin tightens with the agony of wondering what word might have come next.

But she says nothing else.

There's less thunder now, which means we're in a band between the cells of the great multi-storm. We both doze again, lulled by the pounding rain.

A horrific explosion sends me to my feet, and I nearly step on Serylla. I don't think she would have been hurt, since the nest is springy, but the terror of damaging her is enough that I leap straight out of the nest.

I blow on one of the dyre-stones so Serylla can have some light if she wakes, but she seems to have fallen back asleep instantly.

I, on the other hand, cannot relax again. My body crackles with unexpected energy, and for a moment I think I'm reverting to human form. When nothing happens, I attempt the change, mentally leaning into the impulse like I did last time. But my shape remains the same. I'm more conscious of it than ever—my own hulking size, my massive shoulders, the lethal spikes along my spine and tail, the tough, thin webbing of my wings. I feel powerful. Glorious. Godlike.

I prowl to the back of the cave and tear down one of the carcasses there—a fat sheep. I carry it to the cave mouth and slice it open, deftly carving out the meat with my claws and swallowing chunks of it. Tendons and viscera stretch as I seize another hunk of meat in my jaws and pull it free. I swallow down some of the organs, too—heart, brain, liver, kidneys. When nothing but the skeleton and scraps remain, I shove them out into the dark, off the lip of the cliff.

Slanted rain shatters into the entrance of my cave, creating clear rivulets that snake through the blood. Dimly I know that I would not usually be so messy with my kill. But I am a predator. Predators kill, and predators eat.

Prince and predator. That is what I am. This powerful form, these great wings, my razor-sharp teeth and fine claws—all of them are traits that should outlast me, that must be passed down to my offspring.

Since I woke, my thoughts have simplified, condensed into basic urges. First hunger, and now, at the thought of offspring, a new desire surfaces.

Mate.

My blood pounds hotter, snaking through my veins, roaring into my cock. A heated haze fills my mind, obliterating complex thoughts, fixated on one need.

Mate now.

I can smell *female* in my cave.

Serylla is female. Serylla is mine.

With heavy steps I prowl to the nest. There she is, where she's meant to be. My female, in my nest. Her body is limp, warm, and rosy.

A doubt pierces the blazing fog in my brain. *Too small.*

Every scale on my body feels as though insects are crawling beneath it, their raspy legs scratching at my skin. Deep in my body, my balls are swollen almost to bursting. My cock is thick and rock-hard, weighing against its concealing slit, threatening to emerge. Agony and craving twist along my spine as I crawl slowly into the nest, toward Serylla. My head is low, my shoulders tense, wings pinned tight.

Fuck her, mate her.

She's on her side with her legs curled up, so I nudge her over onto her back so I can put my nose at the apex of her thighs and inhale the sweet fragrance from her womb.

Mine. Mate her.

No... too small.

I snort and swing my head from side to side. The urge to mount her shudders through me from head to tail. The slit between my back legs, at the root of my tail, widens, allowing my cock to push its way out. It hangs there, huge and throbbing.

Mate her. Fuck her. Fuck fuck FUCK...

My cock is sore, raw, aching to be plunged into a welcoming hole. Pain twitches through my insides as the seed inside me strains to be released inside the warm slick of a female.

This is agony. This is a mortal need, and without relief I swear I'm going to fucking die.

24

SERYLLA

A roar of anguish wakes me.

Kyreagan is clawing his way out of the nest, snarling and groaning. He throws himself against the cave wall, scrapes his side along it like he's trying to peel off his own scales.

"Ky!" I leap up. "What's wrong?"

"No," he groans. "No… fuck…" He dashes his head against the wall, and I scream.

"Stop it, Ky! Stop hurting yourself!"

Through clenched fangs he slurs, "Better… me… than you."

That's when I see it. The giant dragon cock between his legs. It's enormous and purple, with a bulging violet head. Fortunately it's not spiked or serrated. That part was a myth. But it's far too big for any human to take. A string of clear precum hangs from the tip, swinging with his movements.

"Don't fucking look at me," he snarls. "Hide somewhere, go away…" His words dissolve into a groan of wretched need.

This is the mating heat, then. It looks incredibly painful and difficult to resist. If all the dragons are in the same shape as Kyreagan, there's not much hope for the other women.

"Can you shift?" I ask, trying not to let my voice tremble.

"I tried."

"Try again."

His whole body quakes with the effort, and more precum leaks from his cock. He tosses his horned head and screams his frustration at the cave ceiling, heating the rocks to amber.

"Your cock is the size of my whole leg, so you definitely can't fuck me," I tell him firmly. "But you can't stay like this, either. Come here."

"No." His head swings back and forth, and his yellow eyes hold a glittering madness. "If I get too close I'll fuck you right down the middle. Split you open. Kill you."

"If you can manage a *little* self-control, I have an idea that might help. Remember what I taught you, about the pleasure that can be had without actually entering someone else?"

He hesitates, heaving rough breaths.

"I'm going to lie on my back," I tell him. "You'll rub your cock along my front, and I'll circle it with my arms and legs. We'll stroke together until you come."

"But… mating…" he says thickly. "Breeding."

"I'll put some of your cum inside me afterward. Will that help? If not, just think about what you can do to me once you're back in human form. Once you're human again, you can slip all the way inside, and—"

Mistake, oh that was a mistake—

He's on top of me, pushing me down against the nest. His cock prods viciously between my arched knees, forcing them apart, and he vents a hoarse groan tinged with fire. Then his massive cock head bumps against my pussy, and for one blinding, terror-filled second, I think he's going to forge inside me and tear me apart.

All the blood drains from my face. "Kyreagan." I keep my voice as steady as I can. "Wait."

He manages to hold himself still. But he stares at me as if he has been starving for centuries and I'm the one meal that will make him blissful and satisfied forever.

I lift the dragon cock up and settle myself into position beneath it, so its underside rests along the front of my body. It feels very similar to a human cock, but much hotter, with thicker skin. I wrap my arms and legs around it to provide Kyreagan with more friction.

"This is your hole," I tell him. "This is the tunnel you can rut until you feel better."

He doesn't wait for any further direction, just starts fucking himself against me. At the first full contact with my body, he groans in abject relief.

"Good dragon," I say. "Rub that poor aching cock against my soft skin. Run it between my breasts, just like that. That feels better, doesn't it?"

The rubbing chafes a bit until I get the idea to slather myself in his precum. After that, things proceed much more smoothly. He thrusts along my belly and chest, and I rub my slippery arms and legs along his length to stimulate him.

"Close your eyes," I order. "Pretend I'm a dragon—a beautiful female dragon with black scales just like yours, and you're fucking me deep."

He hums low in his chest, which I take as encouragement to continue.

"Your huge dragon cock feels so good inside me." Fuck, I'm making myself wet by speaking to him like this.

With my legs wrapped around him, my pussy is splayed open, fully exposed to the friction of his thick shaft. Every time he surges forward, tingling pleasure throbs through my clit. I can't resist the urge to lift my hips a little, to increase the pressure.

"You're going to spill everything inside me, all that rich cum from those painful swollen balls of yours," I murmur. "It will gush into me and fill me so full it drips out when you're done. You're going to breed me, make babies with me—"

God, what am I saying—I need to stop thinking about making baby dragons with him. Although the idea seems to be doing the trick. His breathing grows rougher, and his cock thickens.

"Oh, fuck," I gasp, arching against the surging length. The friction is more than I can bear—just a little more—a little more—I moan as the pleasure bursts through me. It's not as intense as the other orgasms he has given me, but it's good, so good.

By the depth of the dragon's groans and the increased frenzy of his thrusts, I can tell he's about to come—on my face.

"You don't spew lava or boiling hot cum in this form, do you?" I ask.

He doesn't answer. He's too far gone.

"Shit," I whisper, and I shut my eyes. "Do it, Kyreagan. Come for me."

With a guttural roar, he comes. It's a hot fountain all over my face and my hair—I'm drenched with it, completely coated, but thankfully not burned. The temperature is about the same as the hot spring, I'd guess. His scent thickens the air; it's rich and earthy, but not unpleasant. It reminds me of the way a rock smells in the sunshine, with a hint of woodsmoke.

He pumps twice more, and then I sense him moving away, giving me space. With my eyes still closed, I sit up and wipe the cum off my face with both hands.

The dragon looks unsettled as he stares down at my body. A low, displeased growl ripples from his throat.

"The breeding part." I nod. "I'll take care of that. Look."

I spread my legs and swipe my cum-covered fingers into my pussy. Then I scoop up some more of his cum and put that into my opening as well. I don't think it's deep enough in me to cause a pregnancy, but the dragon seems satisfied, for now. He collapses in the nest, with his neck stretched out long and his tail draped limply over the edge. His cock is once more tucked away where it belongs, and I can't help feeling a little relieved about that.

By the time I've finished washing myself in the stream and pulling on my dress, he's breathing slowly, sound asleep. I suppose he exhausted himself.

I lie down beside his long neck, near his head. The slow hum of his breath relaxes me, and I stroke my hand along the flat scales shielding the underside of his throat.

"You did it," I whisper. "You made it through without hurting me. Which means you can do it again. We'll work through this together, as many times as we need to."

25

KYREAGAN

I awaken in human form, my cock already hard. But I don't mention it or touch the Princess. I wash myself with soap as I've seen her do, and I get dressed before she wakes up.

Serylla cooks us food again, while I dispose of the cum-stained grass from the nest. Then I worry over the swollen stream, which is beginning to overflow its bed slightly and trickle along the cave floor. Next time I'm in dragon form, I must carve the groove even deeper, to keep our resting place from being flooded. That is, if I can control myself next time I shift.

I remember everything I was thinking, what I felt, and what I almost did to Serylla. I came far too close to hurting her, and I can't bear the knowledge that she saw me in that feral state, dripping with need, mad with the urge to mate.

"The food is ready," she says. "Come and eat."

"I'm not hungry." I keep my back to her, my eyes on the stream.

For several moments she's quiet, and then I hear the patter of her bare feet on the stone.

"Fuck this." She steps across the stream and faces me. "You're embarrassed. I understand. But we're both alright. I'm not angry, and I'm not scared of you."

"You must be disgusted."

She tilts her head aside and gives me one of her adorable half-smiles. "No. The mating heat is not something you chose. It's part of your nature, and if you were allowed to experience it normally, with another dragon, it would be a beautiful, passionate thing, not a frightening one. You didn't want to hurt me, so you struggled against it, and you won. I admire that strength."

Her acceptance stuns me. I can't seem to form words in response.

"Come eat." She takes my hand, laces her slender fingers between my clawed ones, and leads me over to the food—chopped vegetables and fried, salted meat. It is delicious. While we eat, she keeps humming snatches of melody, then frowning intently, her gaze distant.

"Are you composing a song?" I ask.

"Sshh." She puts a finger to her lips, frowning deeper. "Ah, you made me lose the phrase I was thinking of. I wish I had paper and pens, and ink."

"I could carve the words for you."

"In the stone? No, no, they're not ready to be committed to existence so permanently. I have to play with it more first."

And I would like to play with you more. Once again, I'm having difficulty controlling myself—her mouth looks too damn luscious as it forms silent words. Then she pops a berry between her lips, and *fuck*... I nearly come in my pants. Hastily I rise and walk straight to the cave entrance. A vicious wind drives the cold rain over my body, soaking my clothes.

"Kyreagan."

"You have to stop saying my name," I snarl without turning around. "And stop talking. And eating. And sitting like that."

"So... I need to stop existing. Is that what you're saying?"

"No, but—why do you have to look so beautiful all the damn time? By the bones, it's enough to drive anyone mad."

I bow my head to the wind and rain, letting it slick my horns and hair. The wet clothes cling to my body like a soggy skin.

And then I feel a small hand squeeze my ass.

That one spark ignites my entire being.

I whirl around, seize her shoulders, and claim her mouth with mine. She is fire and sweetness, honey and rain. My tongue twists around hers as I walk her backward to the nest. I push her onto it and unfasten my pants with shaking fingers.

She already has her skirts hiked up to her waist, her legs spread wide, her pussy gleaming wet. She smirks at me, and I grin back, delicious warmth spreading through my chest.

"Get inside me, dragon," she hisses, and I climb over her, lifting her legs over my shoulders and sliding my cock into her glistening heat. I haven't fucked her like this yet—face to face. I've been missing out. Watching her head tip back, watching her eyes close as she moans—it's a gift straight from the Bone-Builder.

I lean down to nibble at her parted lips, to taste the soft moans slipping from her mouth. I hunger for every shifting expression, every flutter of her lashes, every gasp of light breath. My hips rock, pumping my cock through her in a slow, heavy rhythm.

"Faster," she whispers. I kiss her and comply, speeding up my thrusts. After a moment I pull out and bury my face between her legs, coaxing her sweet little clit with my tongue, lapping around her entrance until she gasps out, "Dragon, if you don't breed me right now, I'm going to fucking kill you."

With a low growl, I thrust inside her again. The sensation along my cock is unbearably thrilling, and I nearly come just from entering her.

"Don't play with me, Serylla," I tell her hoarsely. "Not about this."

She weaves her fingers into my hair, pulls me closer so she can kiss me. "I'm not tormenting you this time. I've decided. I'll have your baby dragons."

I want to burst into song, except I don't know any songs that could express the heights of my joy. I press deeper inside her, just to watch her eyes glaze over with bliss.

"God, you feel so good," she whimpers. "Oh shit, I'm going to come…"

Grinning, I brace myself and fuck her as fast as I can, tipping her over the edge.

Watching her come is like watching a sunrise. It's all the colors of passion, beauty, and delight, blending into exquisite peace. I groan as I join her, my cum flowing deep into her body.

I stay inside until I've softened completely. When I slide out, a trickle of cum leaks from her pink slit, and I push it back in with my thumb. She shivers and sighs at the brush of my hand over her clit, so I massage it lightly and swiftly with my fingertips until she comes again, only a little flutter this time.

"I've never wanted sex so badly," she whispers, blushing. "I feel so weak and full and perfect, all at the same time."

I settle in beside her and stroke my palm over her flat stomach. Soon it will swell with our little ones… if she truly meant what she said.

"So you will not take the herbs this time?" I ask.

"No."

"What changed your mind?"

"Two things." She holds up two fingers. "First, when you said you'd let me go. Second, when you battled yourself during the mating heat, and managed to stay in control. There's kindness in you, and mercy. You just need to learn how to show it, and to share it more widely, not just with your own species."

"I know." The admission grates on me, but she's right.

I don't press the matter of offspring, nor does she push me to explore my motives further. After a few minutes she climbs out of the nest and surveys the remaining deer hanging in the back of the cave. "We should cook this before it spoils. It's chilly back here, but not cold enough. Cooking the meat will help it last a bit longer."

We spent the next several hours preparing the meat and cooking it. She tries to teach me, explaining many rules that I don't understand, describing all the different pots, pans, and implements she would typically use, listing her favorite seasonings and spices. I listen until my brain feels like it will shatter if I cram anything else into it. To make her stop talking, I lift her onto my shoulders, facing me, with her back to the cave wall and her pussy in front of my face, and I devour her until she comes with a shrill scream. Then I push her down to her hands and knees and fuck her, while the slapping sounds of our flesh echo through the cave.

Those sounds occur often over the next few days. I'm addicted to the softness of her body, the beauty of her breasts, the snug comfort of her pussy, and the shining joy in her eyes when she looks at me.

When I'm in dragon form, the heat is less urgent than it was the first time. Her scent has changed slightly, and somehow I know she's already carrying my young, so the urge to breed her isn't as powerful. The desire to fuck, though, is a compulsion all its own.

By the fourth day, her belly is noticeably larger. She's quiet about it, and sometimes I catch her running her hand over the bump, uncertainty furrowing her brow.

I try to help. "You'll be alright. Thelise said the eggs will be small enough for you to lay them easily."

"I know that." She shoots me an irritated look. "And I'm happy to do this for you, but it's unsettling, all the same. I love babies, and I always planned to have them, but I never imagined it being like this. It's happening so fast."

I fold my wings back and prowl closer to her, curious. "How long does pregnancy last for humans?"

"Nine months."

"Nine fucking months? Females carry their offspring in their bodies for almost a year? That seems cruel."

Serylla laughs, which pleases me, though I wasn't trying to be funny.

"It *is* cruel," she says. "Some women enjoy it, while others hate it, but either way it's a long time. Birth isn't easy, either. It's agonizing, and usually involves the tearing of skin and tissues. Sometimes there are dangerous complications, and either the baby or the mother die."

"Laying eggs is harmless for the females of my kind. The eggs slip out easily. But sometimes they never hatch."

"Humans don't have eggs. The babies are born from a sac inside the mother. It's a slimy, bloody process."

"It sounds disgusting."

She laughs again and pats my nose. "It is, rather. Tell me, how large are a dragon's eggs, typically?"

"It's been a long time since I saw my brother's and sister's eggs, but I would say—perhaps about this size." I draw an oval shape with my claw on the floor of the cave.

"Oh." She sighs with relief. "That's about the size of an infant's head. And Thelise said these eggs should be even smaller. The hatchlings must be tiny when they're born."

"Miniscule. But they grow astonishingly fast. And they can speak Dragonish very soon after birth. They learn by hearing it through the egg, you see."

"Clever little things," murmurs Serylla. "I wonder what ours will look like, and what they'll think of me if I—" She stops speaking and chews her lip.

"If you what?"

She looks up at me, her blue eyes clouded with guilt. "I was thinking it might be better for me to return to the mainland before they hatch. It would be cruel to let them see me and bond with me if I plan to leave."

Liquid fire churns in my gut, a visceral reaction to the thought of her departure. I shouldn't be surprised she would bring it up—after all, I offered to let her go. But over these past few days, I've allowed myself to indulge the foolish hope that she might stay, after all—that a princess might live willingly in a cave with a dragon who devours bloody carcasses and takes his shits off the edge of a cliff and vomits streams of fire when he's angry or anxious…

Fuck, it sounds ridiculous when I think of it that way. I've been a fool.

My human form doesn't have much more to offer her than my dragon self does. I'm gaining more control over the timing of each shift, but I have no other skills as a human. The only useful thing I can do in that form is fuck my captive properly.

It's no surprise she would rather not stay.

She's watching me, waiting for me to speak, so I say quietly, "Yes, that might be best. Hatchlings imprint on their parents at first sight. It will be easier if they never see you."

Pain flickers across her face, but she crushes it down resolutely. Ever since the mating heat began, I've had a stronger sense of her emotions, a heightened awareness of where she is in the room, even when I'm sleeping. My father told me that after their first mating season, male dragons can sense the location and well-being of all the females in the clan, and they in turn can sense the males. It's a vague awareness at first, one that becomes stronger with age. Since Serylla isn't a dragon, I wasn't sure if I would have such a feeling about her, and I'm pleased that I do. I don't sense anything related to the other captives, though, so my connection to her must be a result of our frequent mating.

I want to ask her why she is so determined to leave. But I can guess the answer. Hearing it out aloud would only hurt more.

"What about the other women?" she asks. "Will they be free to leave as well?"

"Why not?" I stalk morosely over to the stream and drink deeply.

And we don't discuss the topic again for three days.

We cook, we fuck, and we sleep. I teach Serylla some rudimentary Dragonish phrases and simple poetry, and she teaches me a game played with chips of rock on a grid that I carve into the cave floor at her direction. Her belly swells larger, and still the Mordvorren rages on. Sometimes I think it's tapering off, and then another storm cell hits, piercing rock with its lightning, threatening to shake the island apart with the force of its thunder. It's as if the entire ocean has been poured out upon us, and I worry that when we finally emerge, we'll find the whole island underwater, with just a few rocky peaks jutting out of the sea.

As our food supply dwindles, I grow increasingly concerned for the fate of the island's few remaining animals. The sheep and goats can climb, and the wild boars are resourceful, but I'm concerned that every last one will have perished by now. And what of the flocks and herds residing in the Middenwold Isles? Are they safe? If many of them have been lost to the storm, we may find ourselves in no better position than before the war. Which would mean I have done all of this for nothing.

The longer the storm continues, the lower my mood sinks. What if there's no food left once we emerge from shelter? What if some of my dragons have harmed their women during the mating heat? I will have to destroy those males myself, according to the law I declared before the storm began. What if many women and dragons have been killed by flooding, lightning, or rockfalls? What if this season yields only a few hatchlings, and they all starve?

I should have spoken to Thelise before the storm hit and asked if her magic might be of any use against the Mordvorren. But I'm fairly sure there's nothing she could have done. This storm is older and more powerful than any of us.

The meat is gone. The vegetables are nearly gone. All that remain are seeds, nuts, and a handful of bruised berries. If the Mordvorren does not move on soon, we will starve. I've already been eating much less than I would like, trying to ensure that Serylla has enough. She's much hungrier than usual, which is to be expected. The little ones inside her are growing rapidly.

I'm lying across the mouth of the cave, frowning at the rain, wondering if it's truly slackening or if it's simply my imagination, when Serylla approaches me and touches the edge of my wing.

When I look around, she's holding her swollen belly, her eyes wide with mingled terror and excitement.

"Ky, I think something is happening," she whispers.

26

SERYLLA

Kyreagan startles up, all traces of his dark mood gone. "What do you mean, something is happening?"

"My stomach aches. It's like the cramps I get when it's my monthly bleeding time, but worse. And there's pressure." I cup my hands under my stomach to support it. It's not nearly as large as women get when they're carrying human babies, but it's still unnerving—more so because I've barely had time to get used to it, and now— "I think the eggs are coming out."

Not in my wildest dreams did I imagine having to say those words.

"It's too early," Kyreagan says. "You should have another day or two before it happens."

My stomach contracts painfully, and I double over, groaning. "Tell that to my fucking body! It's time to get these things out of me. And you're going to help."

He gapes at me, his lower jaw so slack it's comical. "I—I don't know what to do. Egg laying should be a painless process, done in private—"

"Fuck that!" I yell. "You put them inside me, so by god, you're going to get me through this, do you hear?"

"Yes, yes," he exclaims, looking terrified. "Come to the nest."

He leaps toward it himself, his wingtip brushing my shoulder. I toddle over, already feeling the pressure of *something* emerging between my legs. Kyreagan helps me into the nest by nudging my rear awkwardly with his muzzle.

I witnessed two births at the palace. One was a chambermaid of mine whose labor came on unexpectedly, and she had to take my bed for the birth. The other birth I witnessed was that of Taren, my little protégé, the son of Huli, the second cook in the palace kitchens. When Huli was put on bed rest for the last two months of her pregnancy, I interceded for her with my mother and ensured that she would continue to be paid during that time. Huli asked me if I wanted to witness the birth and be the baby's patroness, and I said *yes* wholeheartedly.

My mother never knew about either instance; she would have thought both were inappropriate. But I loved watching the tiny, slimy, red creatures emerge into the world—loved cleaning them up, hearing their first cries, watching them nuzzle against their mother. I loved the expression on each woman's face as she held her baby for the first time.

I wonder where those children and their mothers are now—Huli and Taren, especially. I hope they're well and safe. Though "well and safe" no longer means the same thing it used to, for me. Right now I'm crouching in a giant nest with my skirts hiked up, while a male dragon watches anxiously, smoke sifting from his nostrils. And yet, in spite of the strangeness of it all, I am well, and I am safe.

During one of the births I witnessed, a midwife recommended the crouching position, but after trying it for a few moments, I realize it isn't working for me. My thighs are starting to ache, and I have enough aches right now. So I scoot back against the edge of the nest and sit there with my legs bent and spread, sweating and panting through another contraction.

Kyreagan dips his head forward, inspecting between my thighs.

"I hate you for this," I snarl at him, and he pulls back, chuffing a fiery breath.

"You agreed to it," he mutters.

"Shut up. Shut the fuck up... oh god, this shit *hurts!*"

He approaches again, nuzzling apologetically along my inner thigh. His tongue slips out, and he licks my vagina gently.

For a moment, the pain eases.

"Do that again," I gasp. "It helps."

Encouraged, he licks all around my opening. Perhaps there's something in the saliva of male dragons that eases pain, or perhaps I'm just relaxing more because of his caresses, but the difference in my pain level is startling. Within seconds, the egg stretches me wide, then pops out, tumbling onto the grass.

It's slightly smaller than Kyreagan's drawing. The smooth shell is iridescent violet, gleaming wet.

"Thank the Bone-Builder," Kyreagan chokes out.

"Thank *me*," I tell him. "And keep licking. I think there's another one."

Obediently he bathes the sore edges of my vagina. It's nothing sexual—the act is pure gentleness, pure love.

I reach out and grip one of his horns as my stomach tenses again.

"I see the egg," he rumbles wonderingly, in that deep dragon voice of his, and I think of the moment I first saw him soaring across the fields, leading his army to doom my city.

"You're doing so well, beautiful." His yellow eyes meet mine. "You're so strong."

Tears gather in my eyes. "You used to call me weak," I whisper.

"That was before I knew better."

My breath hisses sharply through my teeth as I grip his horn tighter. With all my might I push, and my hole stretches tight again, strained by the shell of the egg.

Kyreagan strokes me with his tongue, lapping all around the circumference of the egg. I relax a little, and then I push one more time, wrenching on his horn.

With a soft plop, the egg falls out of me, into the nest. This one is a deep, vivid blue, marbled with white swirls.

"They're so beautiful, both of them," I whisper.

Kyreagan keeps licking me, soothing the sore flesh. "Such a good fucking girl," he murmurs. "You were wonderful. Rest now."

The cramps still roll through my belly occasionally, but they don't feel as urgent or powerful as before. These cramps are my stomach muscles tightening themselves again, working to return my belly to its normal shape. I'm fairly sure that will take days, if not longer. And I'll have a dozen silvery marks where my skin stretched, to remind me of all this.

I'm still planning to leave my dragon and the babies we created together. During these past few days I've become more and more anxious about everyone I left behind in Elekstan. I can't help thinking that I've failed them. I was their princess, and if I don't try to raise an army and return to set them free, what sort of princess am I?

It doesn't matter that I would rather do anything but rule. That's not the point. The point is, my name might still carry some weight with a few of the southern kingdoms. If I promised myself in marriage to one of those princes, he might help me take back my country and save my people from the King of Vohrain. The dragons wouldn't attack us again—Kyreagan wouldn't allow it. I could protect everyone I love, everyone who made me feel worthy and wanted when my mother despised me. Don't I owe them that? Shouldn't I at least try to help them?

Pleasure swells between my legs as the dragon prince worships me with his tongue. I can sense his gratitude, his devotion. He would do anything for me.

"Kyreagan, stop," I whisper. "You're making me feel so good, but I can't. Not right now. Please."

The dragon lifts his head, licking his lips. "As you wish."

As soon as the words leave his mouth, a ray of pale yellow light shines into the cave. I lift my eyes, astonished. The rain has slackened to a sparkling veil of drops, casting rainbow shadows across the Dragonish symbols on the cave walls.

"It's over," I breathe.

Kyreagan whirls and charges out of the nest so fast I can't help laughing. He hasn't been able to fly in days, and I know he's aching to check on everyone. But he hesitates, glancing back at me.

"You should have fresh meat and fruit," he says. "It may be difficult to find, but I will do my best. And I must visit the other dragons, and the women."

"Go," I tell him. "I'm fine. There's no blood, no damage— I'll be alright."

But he comes back, fetches the blankets, and drapes both of them over me awkwardly with his claws. "I'll return as quickly as I can, after I have assessed the damage and found you something fresh to eat."

"When you get back, we need to talk," I tell him.

His lips twitch over his fangs, and he glances away. He's not looking forward to that conversation any more than I am.

"We'll talk," he agrees.

"Do I need to warm the eggs? You know—sit on them or something?"

He snorts. "No. We're not birds. The eggs are fine on their own, until they hatch."

"Oh, good. Go on, then."

With a joyful bound that reminds me more of a puppy than anything else, he springs from the ledge and soars out through the twinkling rain, into the sunshine.

I settle down in the nest and snuggle under the blankets. I'm sore, but not really in pain. All in all, that "birth" was far easier than the human ones I've witnessed.

After gazing at the two eggs for a moment, I scoot closer to them. It's hard to imagine that, if we're lucky, they'll hatch in a week or so, and two little dragons will emerge.

What if Thelise's magic went wrong and they're some kind of awkward mutation of dragon and human, with blended bodies? A dragon wing here, a human arm there, scales on scalps instead of hair—

Enough, Serylla, I tell myself sternly.

"Whatever you look like, he will love you just the same," I say aloud. Then I clap my hand over my mouth, because if I'm planning to leave the eggs, I probably shouldn't talk to them.

Or maybe I really should.

"It might be hard for you to understand why I have to leave you," I tell the eggs quietly. "You see, I have to help all the people who cared for me, respected me, and loved me. I have to take care of my kingdom first, which means giving up my... my babies... shit. That's not right, is it? Because that would make me *my mother*. She always put the kingdom first over family. Well, that's not exactly true, either—she put *herself* first. Still, if I do this, will I be making one of many mistakes that could lead me down the same path?"

The eggs sit there, glowing with rich color in the sunlight.

"Fuck all of this," I whisper. "Oh, and don't you dare say that word until you're older, you understand me? It's only appropriate for adults—for primes."

A dark shadow obliterates the sun for a moment, and a large winged shape lands in the mouth of the cave.

I sit up, squinting. "You're back already?"

But the shape moving toward the nest isn't Kyreagan. It's a great stone-colored dragon whose huge wings bear countless scars.

"Greetings, Princess." There's menace in the low rumble of his voice. "I am Fortunix."

Fortunix. The dragon who used plague-ridden blood-beetles to wipe out prey and force his clan to ally with Vohrain. If that's true, he's as merciless and vengeful as they come. And I'm the Crown Princess of the kingdom he hated.

He spots the two eggs, but at the same moment, I move forward in the nest, putting my body between him and them. It's instinctive—I don't even realize I'm doing it until I'm there, facing him. Protecting them.

Fortunix snorts. "Abominations. Our whole clan has been polluted. Congratulations, Princess—your family is responsible for the extinction of dragonkind. You must be so proud."

"I'm not," I reply. "And dragons aren't extinct, they're just going to be different from now on."

"Ruined," he snarls through his spiked muzzle, pacing forward on giant, ponderous claws. "Ruined because of *you*, your mother, her sorcerer, and your whole fucking kingdom."

He's coarsely, ruggedly built, a fearsome monster that I could never hope to outrun or outmatch. I shouldn't argue with him, but I can't help saying, "You played a role in this, too. You spread the plague and forced your clan so close to starvation that they had to involve themselves in a mainland war. That's what started all this."

The ridges of the dragon's craggy brow sink lower, giving his eyes a cruel look. "So Kyreagan knows, then. I smelled him in my cave—I thought he might have figured it out, so I made myself scarce. I hid in a cavern Kyreagan doesn't know about, connected to an underground river. Not a bad place to weather a storm. Lots of eels, good eating. It's one of my little secrets—like my arrangement with the King of Vohrain."

Dread crawls up my spine and sticks in my throat, choking me. "What kind of arrangement?"

"One that gets you out of Kyreagan's way and ends the evil of your human influence over him. I love these two princes like they're my own hatchlings, but sometimes you have to guide the ones you love. They take the wrong wind-path, and you have to push them into the right one. Sometimes you might have to give them a good swat to correct their behavior. Look what a mess they've made so far! Little wormy humans in our nests, shitting out half-breed, undersized eggs?" He lowers his boulderlike muzzle toward me. "I can't believe Kyreagan lowered himself to fucking you. I suppose he couldn't help it, with the mating heat and all. But you're done here, little girl. I'm taking you to your new home."

My voice trembles. "The King of Vohrain will do terrible things to me."

"Exactly." Fortunix bares his teeth in a dragonesque grin. "I look forward to hearing tales of how he debases you."

I glance around, desperate for anything that might help me fight him. But all I have is my simple white dress, and there's nothing within arm's reach besides the two eggs and the blankets.

"Keep quiet, and maybe I won't knock you out for the flight," Fortunix says. "Before we go, I'll be sticking a claw into each of these eggs."

"No!" I gasp out. "Please—you say you love Kyreagan. If you destroy these eggs, it will break his heart. Listen, they might not even hatch… please, please leave them alone. I'll go with you quietly. I won't scream, I won't call for help, and I won't struggle."

Fortunix considers me for a moment. "It would be a pity if I accidentally killed you while trying to quiet you. I've been promised a significant reward for delivering you safely. Very well, worm. You stay quiet, and I'll leave the abominations alone."

"Agreed." I crawl forward, out of the nest.

Fortunix grasps me with a big, scaly front claw, and without giving me time to prepare myself for flight, he heaves his bulk out of the cave and into the air. Once we're off the ledge, he closes the other front claw around my body.

The pounding of his great wings nearly deafens me, and after so many days in the dark, the sun is painfully bright. I shut my eyes, holding back a scream as Fortunix rises higher and higher with labored wingbeats. The breeze whips my hair against my face.

I could break my word and shriek with all my might. A friendly dragon might hear me. But before he could come to my aid, Fortunix would dive back down to the cave and crush the two eggs. He looks as if he's made of granite—I doubt one dragon alone could stop him.

It's not worth the risk. So I stay quiet, and I force my eyes open a crack.

Blue sky. No sign of the storm anywhere, which is odd—I should be able to spot it moving back out to sea, but it's just… gone. Strange.

I spot a few dragons, tiny and far away, wheeling among the mountain peaks of Ouroskelle. Is one of them Kyreagan, or is he in some cave, checking on the others? What will he do when he finds me gone? Will he assume I left of my own free will? I was planning to leave, and he knows it. Maybe he'll think I got a ride to the mainland from one of the other dragons. Maybe he won't come after me. After all, he has what he needs—the two beautiful eggs we made together.

He can't follow me, even if he wants to. He has to remain on Ouroskelle and deal with the aftermath of the storm. He has to look after our eggs, survey the new islands, and feed the hatchlings. There will be no time for chasing after an annoying princess.

Part of me knows I'm not giving him enough credit, that I'm being overly dramatic—but I'm exhausted, in body and mind, weary from my whirlwind pregnancy, sore from the birth and from the claws roughly clutching my body. I'm being kidnapped, *again*. I deserve to be as dramatic as I fucking please.

I survived my first kidnapping—the terror, the uncertainty, the deprivation. Granted, I'm now being delivered to someone far worse than Kyreagan—but I'll be damned if I let the King of Vohrain break me. I'll watch, and I'll scheme, and I'll survive until I can manage to escape.

This is not the end.

I'm far too stubborn for that.

The next book in the "Merciless Dragons" series is *Warriors of Wind and Ash*, the continuation of Kyreagan and Serylla's story. Future books will follow the adventures of the other dragons and their partners, some of whom you met in this book. I can't wait to share their love stories with you!

Sign up for my newsletter through my website and get a freebie!

More Books by Rebecca F. Kenney

The WICKED DARLINGS Fae retellings series
A Court of Sugar and Spice
A Court of Hearts and Hunger
A City of Emeralds and Envy
A Prison of Ink and Ice

A Hunt So Wild and Cruel

The DARK RULERS adult fantasy romance series
Bride to the Fiend Prince
Captive of the Pirate King
Prize of the Warlord
The Warlord's Treasure
Healer to the Ash King
Pawn of the Cruel Princess
Jailer to the Death God
Slayer of the Pirate Lord

The BELOVED VILLAINS series
The Sea Witch (Little Mermaid retelling with male Sea Witch)
The Maleficent Faerie (Sleeping Beauty retelling with male Maleficent)
The Nameless Trickster (Rumpelstiltskin retelling)

The PANDEMIC MONSTERS trilogy
The Vampires Will Save You
The Chimera Will Claim You
The Monster Will Rescue You

The GILDED MONSTERS classic retellings series
Beautiful Villain (retelling of "The Great Gatsby")
Charming Devil (retelling of "The Picture of Dorian Gray")
Ruthless Devotion

The IMMORTAL WARRIORS adult fantasy romance series
Jack Frost
The Gargoyle Prince
Wendy, Darling (Neverland Fae Book 1)
Captain Pan (Neverland Fae Book 2)
Hades: God of the Dead
Apollo: God of the Sun

Related Content: *The Horseman of Sleepy Hollow*

The INFERNAL CONTESTS adult fantasy romance series
Interior Design for Demons
Infernal Trials for Humans

The SAVAGE SEAS books
The Teeth in the Tide
The Demons in the Deep

MORE BOOKS
Lair of Thieves and Foxes (medieval French folklore retelling)
Of Beasts and Bruises (A Beauty & two Beasts retelling)

Made in the USA
Columbia, SC
29 September 2024